52
REAON
TO HATE MY
FATHER

JESSICA BRODY

52 REAON TO HATE MY FATHER

SQUARE
FISH

FARRAR STRAUS GIROUX
NEW YORK

SQUARE
FISH

An Imprint of Macmillan

Square Fish and the Square Fish logo are trademarks of Macmillan and
are used by Farrar Straus Giroux under license from Macmillan.

Library of Congress Cataloging-in-Publication Data

Brody, Jessica.
    52 reasons to hate my father / Jessica Brody.
        p.   cm.
    Summary: On her eighteenth birthday, spoiled party girl Lexington Larrabee learns
that her days of making tabloid headlines may be at an end when her ever-absent father
decides she must learn some values by working a different, low-wage job every week for
a year or forfeit her multimillion-dollar trust fund.
    ISBN 978-1-250-02459-6
    ISBN 978-1-4299-5523-2 (e-book)
    [1. Fathers and daughters—Fiction.   2. Conduct of life—Fiction.   3. Work—
Fiction.   4. Wealth—Fiction.   5. Inheritance and succession—Fiction.   6. Social
classes—Fiction.   7. Bel Air (Los Angeles, Calif.)—Fiction.]   I. Title.   II. Title:
Fifty-two reasons to hate my father.

PZ7.B786157Aaj 2012
[Fic]—dc22

                                                                            2011012931

Originally published in the United States by Farrar Straus Giroux
First Square Fish Edition: February 2013
Square Fish logo designed by Filomena Tuosto
Book designed by Andrew Arnold
macteenbooks.com

2   4   6   8   10   9   7   5   3   1

LEXILE: 790L

To Janine O'Malley—
for putting up with all of my alls

Fathers, be good to your daughters
Daughters will love like you do.
—John Mayer

CONTENTS

THE CRASH WITHOUT THE BURN

My FATHER IS GOING TO KILL ME.

Actually, on second thought, he probably doesn't have time to kill me. But he *is* going to send someone to do it for him. He's really good at that. Sending people. He's done it for every major event in my life. First day of school, first date, sweet sixteen party, birthdays, dance recitals, even my high school graduation last week. All of them faithfully attended and video documented by one of my father's minions. He's got loads of them. So many I can hardly remember any of their names anymore. But without fail, anytime something significant happens, one of them always manages to show up in my father's place to perform the requisite parental duty. In fact, I wouldn't be surprised if he sent someone to walk me down the aisle on my wedding day. Although I'm sure his publicity team would never allow him to miss out on such a great opportunity for positive media exposure.

This, on the other hand, falls into that *other* category of media exposure. The kind that makes my father, his company, and everyone associated with our family look bad. The kind that is quickly hushed up and excused by cleverly concocted scapegoats and promises of rehab. Not that I'll ever go. Not that I've *ever* gone. But it's the *thought* that makes people feel better—or more important—that makes the tabloids shift their focus. Because once you're shipped off to rehab the story is over. In the media's eyes, you're as good as cured.

Well, until you screw up again.

Until you do something like this.

I'm convinced my father has spies working all over the world. They've infiltrated national and foreign governments, they've weaseled their way into law enforcement offices, they've set up shop in the streets. They're like elves. Santa's helpers. Magically stealing through the night, doing his bidding, protecting the company name. The *family* name. Because really, there's no other explanation for how fast things happen. How quickly they're able to get to the site of the "disturbance." Like tonight, for instance. My father has "people" on the scene even before all the emergency vehicles have arrived. Dressed smartly in their dark suits and designer shoes, even though it's three o'clock in the morning. As if they simply go to bed that way.

Magic elves, I tell you.

Although following that analogy would mean my father would have to be Santa Claus. And trust me, besides the part about being elusive, never seen, and only staying in your living room for a total of two minutes before disappearing into the night, he's definitely *no* Santa Claus.

The first thing they do when they arrive is tell me not to speak. Then I'm ushered away from the limelight and flashes of paparazzi bulbs and hastily stowed inside a black limousine with windows tinted so darkly I can barely see out. There's a woman seated across from me. She speaks with a diluted French accent, expertly fielding a flutter of phone calls and e-mails with a cell phone in each hand. She pauses her current conversation long enough to assure me that everything is being taken care of.

But I don't need to be assured. Everything is *always* taken care of. When my father's name is involved, charges are mysteriously dropped, lawsuits are inexplicably settled out of court, and angry business owners threatening revenge are suddenly sending Christmas cards with photos of their family on a two-week cruise in the Greek Isles.

I'm never quite sure *how* it's done but you can be sure money changes hands. Lots and lots of money. Probably in the form of large, unmarked bills. Contracts are most likely signed, threats are almost certainly made, and secrets are most definitely leveraged.

It's the mafia without the strip clubs and the cheap New York accents. And instead of guns and cement shoes, all the members have BlackBerrys and Harvard MBAs.

It's no wonder that my father has entire law offices working exclusively for him.

Through the tinted glass I can just make out the arrival of two more news vans. The woman sitting across from me notices them too and hurriedly presses a single button on one of her phones before bringing it to her ear.

"Are we clear?" There's a moment of silence as she waits for a response. "Tell them she has no comment." And then into the other phone, "Good, we're leaving."

With a chilling sharpness, she clicks off both phones, taps on the glass behind her with the back side of her knuckles, and, like a fluid, well-oiled machine that has performed the same routine thousands of times, for hundreds of years, the message is communicated and the car is off.

The woman is already on another call before we've even pulled away from the curb. "What's the situation at the Nest?"

I can make out a hint of a grimace on her tightly pulled face, and without saying another word, she turns on the flat screen and flips to CNN. My vision is cloudy and my memory is still a bit fuzzy from the accident but I eventually recognize the street corner that the breaking news reporter is standing on. It's the same one we just left. And the demolished convenience store behind her still has my car parked smack-dab in the center aisle, next to the aspirin.

Should have grabbed one of those before I left, I think to myself. *My head feels like it's being pounded by a jackhammer.*

I collapse back against the seat with my hand covering my eyes.

"Change of plans," I hear the French woman tell the driver after lowering the glass half an inch. "We're going to the Landing Pad."

The driver nods and I feel the long black car yank into an abrupt U-turn that almost makes me lose the contents of my stomach. Not that there's much in there to lose. Except vodka. Lots and lots of vodka. With maybe a few drops of water from the ice.

"No!" I protest, struggling to sit upright. "Why are we going there? None of my stuff is there. I want to go home!"

But then I catch sight of the TV again and the answer is suddenly very clear to me. The breaking news story has moved locations and now a second reporter is standing outside of my house along with every other news outlet on earth.

Great.

"Don't worry," the woman says to me, getting back on the phone again. "We have people on their way to your house to pick up some of your belongings."

"Fine." I surrender with an exaggerated sigh, falling over onto my side and curling into a ball on the bench seat. "But make sure they get Holly. She can't sleep by herself."

The woman nods and switches to the second phone. "Bring the dog."

Although the volume is turned down low, I can still hear the reporter's pretentious voice emanating from the TV, spelling out my tragic life story as if she were reciting her fifth-grade book report.

"For those of you just tuning in, we're live in Bel Air, California, at the famed estate of Larrabee Media CEO, Richard Larrabee, only minutes after his seventeen-year-old daughter, Lexington Larrabee, crashed her Mercedes-Benz SLR McLaren convertible, valued at over $500,000, into a convenience store on Sunset Boulevard. The well-known socialite was returning from an exclusive Hollywood nightclub where several eyewitnesses claim they saw her drinking heavily with friends before getting behind the wheel. Although spokespeople for the Larrabee family have denied early allegations that Lexington was under the influence of alcohol, the police are still investigating the matter closely. This devastation to the Larrabee family comes only a few days after reports started circulating that Lexington's rocky two-year relationship with wealthy European heir Mendi Milos was once again on the verge of a split.

"The famous on-again-off-again couple broke up at the end of last year after which Lexington spent two weeks at a mental health facility in Palm Springs where she was admitted for 'depression and anxiety.' The decision to send his daughter for help was made by Richard Larrabee himself after Lexington was found passed out in a Beverly Hills gas station bathroom and was rushed to Cedars-Sinai Medical Center where she was treated for minor alcohol poisoning. Richard Larrabee expressed his genuine concern for his only daughter—"

"Oh, God, shut it off!" I growl, groaning and pulling my hair over my face.

Silence fills the limo in a matter of seconds and I close my eyes.

Freaking Mendi. This is *all* his fault. If he had just gone back to Europe like he promised, none of this would have happened. We could have continued with our plan to take a short break away from each other, reunited in Europe in a couple of weeks, and everything would have been fine. But *nooo*. He had to show up at the club and start dancing with some floozy wannabe tramp right in front of me. Now it's *definitely* over. After the things we said to each other tonight, there's no way we can get back together.

God, my head hurts.

I can make out flashes of light on the backs of my eyelids and I pry them open to see that the TV is still on but the volume has been muted. CNN is back at the intersection as a tow truck pulls my car from the wreckage. It looks like crap. The whole front end is smashed in and there's nothing but a few shards of glass where the windshield used to be.

Damn. I really liked that car.

I just got it too. And it was custom made at the plant in

Germany. Now I'll have to wait for them to make a brand-new one to replace it. And who knows how long that will take.

The whole thing is really starting to bum me out and I don't want to watch it anymore. "I said. Shut. It. Off," I repeat. "I don't need to see it. I freaking *lived* it, all right?"

The woman is already on another call. This one, apparently, in French. *"Oui, oui, je comprends,"* she says, pointing the remote at the television and zapping the screen to black. Her eyes dart toward me for a second and then she mumbles into the phone, *"Je te le dis, elle est un enfant gâtée."*

I can feel my face grow hot with rage. Did she really call me a spoiled brat?

"Excuse me," I demand.

"Un moment," she says to the caller, then takes a deep breath, pulls the phone away from her mouth, and plasters on an artificial smile. "Yes?"

"What exactly do you do for my father?"

She is clearly annoyed by my interruption but fights to hide it. "I am his new head publicist."

"Well," I begin, before smoothly transitioning into flawless French to say, "Maybe if you had done all your research, you would have known that this 'spoiled brat' spent half of her childhood in France."

Then I shut my eyes to her stunned expression, pull my hair back over my face, and grumble, "Just wake me up when we get there, okay?"

ALL IN THE FAMILY

MY FATHER HAS A PERMANENT SUITE AT THE Beverly Wilshire hotel. Supposedly it's so he has a place to entertain business associates when they come to LA. But I know that's total crap. The suite is so he doesn't have to sleep at the house. Everyone knows sleeping over somewhere requires a certain level of intimacy. I don't care whether you're in a romantic relationship or a family relationship, sleeping is an intimate act. Waking up in the morning is personal. Sharing breakfast is for families. And regardless of what the newspapers might call us, the Larrabees are certainly *not* a family.

In my father's mind, making brief, fleeting appearances at our primary home in Bel Air is just enough to call himself a resident. But, of course, it's never long enough to actually get involved in any aspect of my life. Back when I was a kid, I was still naïve enough to try to get the most out of his rare visits, racing to the front door with drawings I had made in art class or dressed in my latest ballet ensemble ready to bust out whatever new dance move I had learned. I was always desperate for his approval. Starving for those empty, one-word appraisals that I would hungrily gobble up and store in my cheeks like a chipmunk who didn't know when it would be able to eat again.

Now I know better. I don't waste my time. And when my dad is "scheduled" for a visit (yes, they're almost *always* scheduled), I try to make myself as scarce as possible.

"Your father is on his way from New York," I'm informed by a familiar male voice as soon as I walk into the suite and collapse onto the silk-wrapped chaise longue in the living room.

Like I said, *almost* always scheduled.

"Thanks for the warning," I reply snidely.

"Don't take that tone with me," Bruce snarls, stalking over from the table in the dining room and looking down at me with a menacing stare. "You really screwed up this time, Lexi. Do you realize you could have *killed* someone? Including yourself."

I roll onto my side so I don't have to look at him. "Oh, come off it, *Bruce*. I've been through hell tonight. Can't you let up for one second?"

Bruce is my father's personal lawyer. As opposed to one of his corporate goons. He handles all of my father's estates, income, wills, trust funds, and, most important, family business (that would be me right now). The truth is, ever since my mother died when I was five, I've spent more time with Bruce than with my own father. The unfortunate result being that he often tries to treat me like a daughter. Meaning, he seems to get some kind of perverse pleasure out of reprimanding me. As though it's not really in his job description but he's inwardly congratulating himself for going above and beyond the call of duty.

"You *crashed* your *car* into a convenience store, Lexi!" he bellows. "Need I remind you of the significance of such an event?"

"You mean, do you need to remind me of how my mother died?" I ask disdainfully. "No, I think I've got that covered, thanks."

He lowers his voice to an angry hiss. "You put this family in serious jeopardy tonight."

I groan and roll my eyes. "You say that like you're *part* of this family."

"I am!" he shoots back indignantly. "I look out for the family's best interests. At all times. Your father, your brothers, and you. I am *personally* vested in this family's well-being. And *that,* Lexington Larrabee, is more than I can say for *you.*"

I spin back around to face him so fast that the room doesn't stop rotating right away. But I'm too busy screaming to even notice. "You have absolutely *no* idea what it's like to be part of this family!" The boiling anger inside me is exacerbating my headache at an alarming rate but I don't care. The emotion has taken over now and once that happens, there's nothing I can do to stop it. "You have no idea what it's like to be tucked into bed and kissed goodnight *every* night by someone who's being *paid* to do it. You can't even imagine what it feels like to receive your high school diploma, look out into the crowd, and see Larrabee Media's latest Harvard recruit in the front row fumbling to get a brand-new camcorder out of the box so that he can record a video that your father will never even watch. And until you pass out in a gas station bathroom and wake up in a hospital room with a stranger *hired* to hold your hand and tell you that everything is going to be fine, I don't want to *ever* hear you claim to be part of *this* family."

I can see in his eyes that he's lost the battle. Or at least he's decided to hoist up the white flag and leave it be for now. I turn back around and press my face into the fabric of the chaise, finding minor relief in the feel of its cool, satiny surface against my skin.

The doorbell of the suite hasn't stopped ringing since I got here. There's a flurry of activity, mostly relating to the cover-up that's in the works for tonight's "incident." That's how the minions have started referring to it. And as much as I hate all the noise and commotion, I don't complain, in fear that they might pack up and move their base camp to a conference room downstairs and then I'll be left alone in this giant suite.

At half past three in the morning, the door opens and a bellhop enters pushing a cart stacked with suitcases and boxes of my stuff from home. Holly, my brown and white papillon, is perched contentedly on top of my Louis Vuitton train case, enjoying her chauffeured ride through the lavish, gold-trimmed hallways of the hotel. Upon seeing me, her little tail starts wagging and she lets out a cheerful bark and leaps from the cart directly into my lap.

I hold her tightly and coo into her tall, butterfly-shaped ears, rubbing my nose in the soft fur of her neck. I rescued Holly from a busted puppy mill three years ago. She was a mess when I first got her, refusing to come anywhere near me for almost six months. But now we're inseparable. And despite what you might see or read in the tabloids, she's not just another fashion accessory for me. She's my world. My lifeline.

In fact, simply having her here with me now instantly shifts my mood. It's amazing how she's able to do that. People can be so annoying sometimes. With all their stupid opinions and hidden agendas. But dogs? Dogs don't have any agendas. They're as honest and open and devoted as you can get. And that's why they'll always cheer you up. They'll always love you. No matter how badly you screw up. No matter where you happen to crash your Mercedes convertible.

Thankfully, I manage to find a bottle of ibuprofen in my train case. I shake a handful into my palm and down them with a swig of the Italian mineral water that's sitting on the coffee table, grimacing at the aftertaste.

"Oh, gross!" I gag. "I can't believe my father drinks this crap." Without even turning around, I yell out to no one in particular, "Can someone bring me some Voss, please?"

The water arrives less than a minute later, as if there's a Voss vending machine stashed in the shower stall or something. I gulp it down eagerly and then pour some into the bottle's oversize cylindrical cap and offer it to Holly.

Bruce exits the master bedroom where he was making a call and announces to everyone that the Captain has landed and is boarding the chopper now. He'll be here in twenty minutes.

In case you haven't figured it out yet, the Captain is my father. He insists everyone use these stupid code names for everything. The Nest is our main house, the Landing Pad is this place, the Apple Core is our Park Avenue town house in Manhattan, and Bruce, my father's go-to man for practically everything, is known simply as the Lieutenant. There's a whole list somewhere. It's updated monthly and sent out by e-mail. I haven't seen one for years though. Ever since I discovered how to use my spam filter.

As people start buzzing around the room in preparation for the Captain's grand entrance, I execute some prep work of my own. After downing the remainder of the water, I fire off a text message to Jia and T, my two best friends in the whole world, and implore them to get here ASAP for moral support. Then I head into the bathroom to check my face.

My reflection actually frightens me to the point where I swear I'm having one of those body-swapping experiences that you see in the movies. I don't even look like myself. My mascara is smudged to oblivion, my hair is flattened against one side of my head, and my eyes are the color of pinot noir, with more bags under them than the bellhop wheeled in on his cart ten minutes ago.

I turn on the faucet, dip my hand under the tap, and carefully rub my fingertip from my eyelashes to my cheekbone, smearing my mascara even more so that it now runs down my face in long tear-like streaks.

I smile at my handiwork.

Perfect.

Then I switch off the light, shuffle back into the living room, and sink into my chaise longue to await my father's arrival.

COME AND GONE

JIA AND T ARE THE FIRST TO ARRIVE. THEY MUST have been close by when they received my text. Bruce watches reproachfully as they sashay through the door, gasp dramatically upon seeing my disheveled state, and dash over to me, spewing rapid words of sympathy and disbelief like two overeager fountains. He catches my eye and gives me a look of disdain but I promptly ignore it, turning my attention back to my *real* support team.

"Oh my God, Lex," Jia exclaims, kneeling on the floor next to the chaise. "We heard the news on Twitter on the way home from the club. We couldn't believe it!"

"We told Klein to turn the car around straightaway!" T explains breathlessly in her flawless Queen's English accent.

Jia's dark brown eyes glisten with tears before her head collapses against my stomach. "We thought you were dead!"

With a laugh, I reach out and touch a spirally lock of her short caramel-colored hair. "I'm fine, you guys. Thanks for coming."

Jia, T, and I have been best friends since the first year of prep school. "The troublesome trio," as the teachers quickly came to call us. Jia is the daughter of basketball legend Devin Jones, who used to play for the Lakers and now owns like a hundred car dealerships, movie theaters, and T.G.I. Friday's restaurants. Not that she'd ever be caught eating at one.

T's mom used to be a member of this really famous British girl band that had a bunch of platinum albums in the early nineties. Her dad was a guitar player who toured with them but T hardly sees him anymore because when the band broke up and T's mom quickly blew through all her album royalties, she ended up moving from London to LA to marry the president of this huge software corporation and she brought T with her. Now T lives in Malibu in this crazy, environmentally conscious Smart Home with a refrigerator that talks to you when you run out of milk and a thermostat that automatically adjusts to your body temperature.

"Oh my God," Jia says, lifting her head back up. The bronzer on her smooth mocha skin shimmers under the track lighting of the hotel suite. "You'll never guess what Mendi did after you left."

"*Never* guess." T confirms with a nod of her head.

"Wait," I say, biting my lip in anticipation. "Let me try. Give me a hint."

But before they can answer, Bruce clears his throat so loudly and obnoxiously you would think he had an entire chicken wing wedged in there. The girls look up at him expectantly while I just roll my eyes and groan. "What is it, Bruce?"

I can see his left cheek twitching. It means he's gnawing on the inside of his mouth again. He does that when he's attempting to hold something back. My guess is it's probably another outburst.

He takes a deep breath and then in an even, yet tense voice says, "While we're all grateful for Jia and Tessa's—"

"T." She's quick to correct him.

The twitching begins again but after a few seconds, it's dispelled by a tight-lipped smile in her direction. "Jia and *T*'s support," he amends. "Given the imminence of your father's arrival, I suggest they wait downstairs in the lobby."

The girls start to rise, but I grab hold of Jia's arm and yank her back down. "No!" I cry, narrowing my eyes at Bruce. "These are my friends—my *family*," I add, knowing how much it'll piss him off. "They stay."

"It's all right, love," T soothes, grabbing my hand and squeezing it. "You should have some alone time with your dad."

"Ha!" I let out an indignant snort and gesture to the roomful of people. "Yeah. Me, my father, and all of our closest friends. We're one big happy family."

But T just offers me a meager smile in response as she lets my hand drop with a thud against the side of the chaise. "We'll be right downstairs," she says.

I watch helplessly as my friends—my life rafts—sail out the door, before turning my angry glare back on Bruce. I'm ready to really let him have it this time but unfortunately I'm not given the opportunity. The entire room is suddenly silenced by the sound of the door opening again.

I don't need to pull myself up to know that it's my father who has just walked into the room. I can see it on the faces of his doting employees. I can hear it in the unmistakable sound of his imposing footsteps. In the way the door clicks obediently closed behind him. In the reverent silence that follows. After seventeen years of living with Richard Larrabee as a father, you learn to recognize the sound of his entrance. And of his exit.

All activity flutters to a halt. Phone conversations are put on hold. Pens stop scratching against paper. Deft fingers immobilize atop keyboards. Every pair of eyes is on the man who walked through the door. Who now stands tall and ominous behind my chaise longue. I can hear him breathing. Feel his shadow fall across my face. I quietly suck in a breath and wait.

"What's the situation?" he asks Bruce, stepping past my make-shift bed and stalking through the living room of the suite.

Bruce moves in step with him as if to loyally accompany him the ten lousy steps it takes to get to the dining room. "It's being handled," he assures him. "The store owner will not press charges. I have a judge on call who is willing to be lenient in the DUI sentencing. No jail time. Just a fine."

"Good. And the press?"

"Caroline is handling the press." Bruce nods to the French-woman who escorted me here in the limo, and she dutifully rises from her chair at the table, brandishing a phone in either hand as if to provide visual proof as to exactly how busy she's been.

"I've issued an official statement but I think a press conference with you in the morning would be a prudent move at this point."

"Fine." My father agrees with a slight wave of his hand, indicating that Caroline's part in this conversation is over. She returns to her seat.

Bruce continues to ramble as my father paces back and forth along the length of the dining room table, every so often supplying succinct one- or two-word decrees when Bruce comes to the end of a sentence that warrants instruction.

Holly wedges herself between my inclined body and the back of the chaise and starts to tremble, her ears pinned back in fear. In the three years I've had her, she's never taken a particular liking to my father and I don't blame her. Holly has always been an excellent judge of character.

I scratch the back of her neck and whisper soothing words.

"What's the total?" I hear my father demand after Bruce has finished his laundry list of damages.

Bruce takes a pen out of his suit jacket pocket, scribbles something on a hotel notepad, then rips off the top sheet and hands it to my father.

I watch his face carefully for a reaction but of course there's none. It's foolish of me to expect otherwise. To expect to see something magically appear where there's never been anything.

That's how my father got to be who he is. How Larrabee Media got to be the most successful media corporation in the world. Because of his uncanny ability to remain completely impassive. Completely detached.

Even in the face of disaster.

"Fine," he says, allowing one authoritative nod. "Make it happen."

He turns to the remaining eager faces that hover around the table awaiting their next directive like soldiers in a war zone.

"Good work, everyone," he declares in a solid, unwavering tone. "Thanks for your diligence in this . . . unfortunate matter. I'll make sure you're well compensated for your extra efforts."

Then he turns to me, acknowledging my existence for the first time since he entered the room. Without even bothering to sit up, I let my gaze drift toward him. Our eyes connect but nothing is exchanged. No information communicated. No emotions bartered. At least when Bruce shoots me one of his looks, I know what he's thinking. My father's eyes are empty. Void of all feeling.

Indifferent.

Once again, I'm not really sure why I expected anything else.

In one swift motion, his gaze breaks from mine, leaving me with the distinct sensation of falling. Like the inevitable snap of a single piece of fishing line that's been holding me suspended two hundred feet above the ground.

"I'll be at the Lighthouse if anyone needs me," he announces as he stalks back through the living room. His large frame disappears behind the chaise longue and I hear the all-too-familiar sound of a door opening and closing.

Then the flurry of activity resumes as everyone goes back to work.

COST ANALYSIS

I DON'T TEXT JIA AND T RIGHT AWAY TO TELL THEM that the coast is clear. They'll see my father marching through the hotel lobby soon enough. Instead, I shuffle over to the dining room table and, amid the commotion of phone calls, e-mails, and frenetic conversations, I manage to discreetly slip the small hotel notepad off the table and carry it, concealed against my thigh, into the bedroom.

"I'm going to sleep," I say in a voice soft enough that no one will hear, and then close the double doors behind me.

I lift Holly onto the fluffy, white king-size bed and she quickly goes to work pawing at the duvet, arranging it to her liking, before plopping down and curling into a perfect little doughnut of fur. She's relaxed now that he's gone.

I wish I was that resilient.

I perch on the edge of the bed and remove a pencil from the nightstand drawer. Then I lightly brush the tip back and forth over the blank pad, watching the indentation left behind from the last note magically reveal itself through the zigzag of graphite scribbles.

I squint my eyes and hold the pad up to the dim light of the bedside lamp until I can make out Bruce's messy handwriting.

The only thing that's written is a number.

1.7

The cost of my most recent mistake. The financial burden my father will have to bear to make it all go away. To keep the family name from being marred by the muddy footprints that I manage to leave behind wherever I go.

There's no doubt the estimate is in millions. When you deal in the kind of numbers my father does, the scale is implied. Writing it out would only mean superfluous zeros. My father doesn't deal in hundreds or thousands. It's simply not worth his time.

I toss the notepad aside and fall back against the pillows. This night has become a total disaster. First Mendi, then the crash and the press, and now *this*.

I allow myself thirty seconds of tears—no more—before quickly pulling myself together in preparation for my friends' return. Fortunately, my makeup is already smeared so they can't tell I've been crying when they burst into the room and collapse on the bed next to me.

As I listen to them go back and forth, taking turns asking questions and offering condolences, I can feel my eyelids start to get heavy. The events of the evening are starting to take their toll and the adrenaline is wearing off. Suddenly the only thing I can think about is sleep.

T must notice me dozing because she cuts herself off mid-sentence and says, "Oh, Lex, I'm so sorry. You must be totally knackered. We'll be sure to stay so you don't have to be alone."

I smile through my haze. "You don' haf to do that," I garble. "I'm jus' fine. Go home . . . call you when I wake up."

"And we'll go shopping," Jia adds.

I nod dazedly. "Yes. Shopping. Equals good."

I can hear them both giggle as T helps me under the covers and pulls them up to my chin, kissing me lightly on the forehead. "Four more days," she reminds me as she gently touches my cheek. "Four more days and this will all be over, right?"

"Righ'," I say in a ragged voice.

The door closes softly behind them and I roll onto my side and pull Holly into the crook of my arm, burying my face in her silky fur. She doesn't protest.

I can still hear the din of voices outside the bedroom door but they're drowned out by the sound of T's words echoing in my ears.

Four more days.

Four more days and I can escape this place.

With that thought running through my mind, I manage to drift off to sleep with a smile on my face.

KEEPING UP WITH THE LARRABEES

I WAKE TO THE SOUND OF MY FATHER'S VOICE. AT first I'm far too groggy to fully comprehend the situation and for a moment I think that he's actually here. In the bedroom of the suite. Talking directly *to* me. The thought jolts me awake and I sit upright in bed, frightening Holly, who darts up from beneath the covers where she's buried herself somewhere during the abbreviated night.

Then I see my father on TV, addressing a roomful of cameras and inquiring members of the press, and I sink back down and relax.

I glance at the clock on the nightstand. It's eleven in the morning. It certainly didn't take Caroline long to organize that press conference she suggested last night. Not that I'm surprised. Things tend to move at a "right now" pace whenever my father is concerned.

I'm not sure who turned on the TV, but the remote is nowhere to be seen and I'm far too lazy to get out of bed to shut it off so I simply close my eyes and try to zone out the sound. This proves difficult as my father has a presence that's nearly impossible to ignore.

"I am deeply saddened and distressed about last night's incident involving my beloved daughter, Lexington," he is saying. "It was a very scary moment for me and all the members of the Larrabee family and we are extremely grateful that she has survived it unharmed. Please be assured that Lexington is fine, albeit a bit shaken up and incredibly remorseful about her actions. I flew in from New York last night to spend time with her and comfort her through this difficult time. She is currently recuperating and was therefore unable to join me this morning but she asked me to communicate her deepest and most sincere apologies to the kind owners of the convenience store that was damaged during the accident. As you know, Lexington is my only daughter. She is extremely important to me and I love her very much. I assure you that her well-being is my number-one priority at this point and I am taking it upon myself, personally, to make sure she gets the help and guidance she needs to make a full recovery and to come out of this experience a healthier and more grounded person. Thank you."

My hand grapples for something—anything!—on the nightstand. I clutch my fingers around the first thing I come in contact with—my cell phone—and chuck it as hard as I can at the screen. It manages to make contact with the mute button before falling to the floor with a horrible cracking sound.

The silence is beautiful but, unfortunately, short-lived. The door creaks open a few seconds later and a head pops in. It's not someone I recognize, which means the night shift has been replaced by a new crew of lackeys.

"Is everything okay?" the woman asks, looking uneasily from me to the busted cell phone on the floor.

"No!" I bark. "My phone is broken. I need a new one."

She nods. "No problem." And backs out the door, closing it softly behind her.

The screen fills with the faces of eager reporters, jumping up and down like monkeys, vying for the chance to ask some stupid, pointless question and get an even stupider, more pointless answer. I don't need to hear what's being said to know that any response my father gives will be just as full of crap as his speech was.

We'll make sure she gets all the help she needs . . .

My one and only beloved daughter whom I love so much . . .

Blah blah blah. I suddenly feel like throwing up. And it's definitely *not* from the monstrous hangover that's setting up camp in my temples.

In my seventeen years of life I can remember four times that my father has said he loved me . . . and every single one of them occurred on national television.

But that's simply how the Larrabee family works. That's how it's *always* worked. For as long as I can remember. It's all for show. For entertainment. For the benefit of the press. We're about as genuine as a reality TV show.

And like any good reality show, everyone has a role to play. A character to embody. First and foremost there's my father, Richard Larrabee, the founder and CEO of Larrabee Media. The world adores him because he's self-made. Started out with nothing and now he has everything. It's the classic rags-to-riches, American-dream story—lower class, below-the-poverty-line teen runs away from home, starts a business, and becomes a billionaire—and the press just gobbles it up and begs for more.

My mother was killed in a car crash when I was five. An eighteen-wheeler lost control and hit her head-on. She didn't stand a chance. I don't remember much about her, except for a few fleeting and hazy memories. And since nearly every photograph of her disappeared from our house after she died, those fuzzy memories are all I have to go by. But everyone who knew her tells me she was wonderful. Loving, maternal, supportive. Everything a mother should be.

Since her death there's been a constant revolving door of "Mrs. Larrabees," each younger and more unbearable than the last. The job requirements for "Mrs. Larrabee" are fairly simple and straightforward: show up for charity events, governors' balls, society weddings, and openings; stay glued to my father's arm the entire night, in an evening gown that's just risqué enough to get people's attention but not enough to cause a scandal; and act interested and engaged in the conversation around you, even if you don't understand a word of what's being said. Do all that and the rest of the time is yours to do with what you want—e.g., spa hopping or traipsing around my father's private island in the Caribbean.

The women who hold this role traditionally don't last very long. On average it takes about two to three years for my father to tire of them. Then they take their more-than-generous divorce settlements, complete with European villas, and move on.

Currently the position of stepmother to the Larrabee children is vacant. But for the past few months my father's been courting a new recruit. Rêve is her name, according to Page Six of the *New York Post*. Although I'd be willing to bet anything that her birth certificate says something like "Gertrude" or "Ursula." I haven't met her yet but I'm sure she's just as horrendous as the rest of them.

Before my mother died, she had five children. The famous Larrabee siblings. Thank God my dad underwent his little "anti-baby-making procedure" after I was born, otherwise who knows how many half breeds there'd be running around, trying to lay claim to a share of the Larrabee fortune. Four wives in twelve years? You do the math.

I'm the youngest and the only girl. Richard Junior (RJ) is the EVP of business development at Larrabee Media, dutifully fulfilling his obligations as next in line for the throne. He's all right, I guess, but I hardly know him. He left for college when I was nine and I haven't seen much of him since then. After him, there are the twins, Hudson and Harrison, who are both finishing up their law degrees at Yale and are expected to graduate first and second in their class, respectively. Then there's Cooper, the child prodigy who graduated from college when he was only sixteen. He's been playing Mozart's Concerto no. 15 for Piano since he was three. Now he plays it backward with his eyes closed just for fun. Coop and I are only two years apart so we were close growing up but ever since he decided to join the Peace Corps and go on some hunger-relief tour around the world, we hardly ever talk anymore. Especially when most of the places he visits don't even have running water, let alone cell reception. I usually don't know where he is until I get a postcard in the mail.

And finally there's me. And I think we all know what my role is in this family.

If you don't, just tune in to the press conference that's being aired on Channel 4 right now.

I can't stand to watch it anymore—even on mute—so I grab a

pillow and hold it over my face, pulling it down tight around my ears until I can barely breathe. But somehow it's not enough. I can still *feel* his face on the screen. Like he's watching me. As he carefully fields the reporters' questions, his grayish-blue eyes seem to be staring *through* the cameras, through the TV screen, right into this room. Those eyes are famous, you know. World-renowned. They've graced the cover of every magazine from *Time* to *Fortune* to *GQ*. And although the press have been known to call my father's eyes "enchanting," "alluring," and sometimes even "sexy," the only thing I see in them is disappointment.

Not for long though.

Four more days and I'm free. From all of them. Especially him.

Because despite our obvious differences, there is *one* thing we five Larrabee children have in common.

And that's the trust fund.

There's one set up in each of our names in the amount of twenty-five million dollars. But it's completely untouchable until the day we turn eighteen. Which, for me, is in four days.

I remember when Cooper got his two years ago. He was so blasé about the whole thing. Talking about donating it all to charity or some such nonsense. I, on the other hand, have been dreaming about this day for nearly eighteen years.

Jia, T, and I already have plans to cruise the Mediterranean for the summer. We rented an enormous three-hundred-foot yacht with nine other friends from school to celebrate our graduation. It sets sail in three weeks from Marseilles and I can't *wait* to be on it. Three whole months of doing nothing but lounging around during the day, partying at night, and shopping from port to port. Pure heaven. It's *exactly* what I need to unwind and decompress from my stressful life. Away from Mendi and my father and everyone. And after that? Who knows? London, Rio, Paris, Fiji . . . the possibilities are endless. It's exhilarating to think that soon I'll be able to pick up and go anywhere. Do *anything*. I'll no longer be tied to my father or the empire he controls. My life will finally be *mine*.

This is the thought that finally gets me out of bed. I head into the bathroom to take a long, extra-hot shower. It feels incredible.

By the time I get out, there's a new cell phone waiting for me on the nightstand, with all my phone numbers and settings already programmed. I check for any missed calls, silently hoping that after having heard about the accident, Mendi might have felt bad about the things he said in the club last night and called to apologize. But the screen is blank.

I guess it's really over this time.

I glance at the TV. It looks like my father is wrapping up his press conference. He bids goodbye to the cameras and is ushered offstage by Caroline. His fake smile has already been wiped clean and he's muttering something that is evidently so unpleasant it makes his lips droop into a scowl. I'll give you *one* guess who he's talking about.

I grip my new phone tightly in my hand and call Jia.

"Hey," I say brusquely the moment she picks up, "are you still down for shopping today? Because I could really use a new outfit for my birthday."

MISS INDEPENDENT

THE PRESS PACKED UP AND LEFT THE MAIN HOUSE a few days ago so, fortunately, when the morning of my long-awaited eighteenth birthday finally arrives, I'm able to get ready in my own bedroom. Which is a huge relief because I have some major prep work to do before I'm scheduled to meet Bruce at one o'clock at his office in Century City.

I bound out of bed at seven-thirty. And for a girl who's only seen the sunrise on the way home from partying all night at a club that's saying a lot.

Jia and T helped me pick up the most perfect outfit for today. One that they assured me screams *independently wealthy!* I'm wearing a pair of high-waisted navy trousers and a cream-colored silk sleeveless blouse with a ruffled trim underneath a tweed cropped Chanel suit jacket. I clasp a pearl choker around my neck, swoop my hair back with a silk headband, and top the whole thing off with a men's vintage gold Rolex watch that I swiped from my father's closet.

I figure since he has like twenty of them, it's not as though he'll even notice it's gone.

Jia and T flew to Vegas this morning to finish up the preparations for the birthday party they're throwing me at the Bellagio tonight so I promised to send pictures once the whole "look" was assembled. I give my cell phone to Horatio, our middle-aged Argentinean butler who's worked for us since before I was born, and make him take zillions of photos.

"What do you think, Horatio?" I ask, posing in front of the grand marble staircase that spirals through the entry hall. "Do I look like a million bucks?"

"*Sí, señorita,*" he responds faithfully in his silky Spanish, bowing his head slightly the way he always does when he answers a question.

"What about *twenty-five* million bucks?"

To this he only smiles. But I take it as another yes.

He hands my cell phone back to me and walks over to a table at the far end of the foyer. "You will be needing a car?" he asks, picking up the house phone and preparing to dial Kingston, our chauffeur.

"No!" I practically scream, diving for the table and pushing down on his hand until the receiver is back in the cradle. "Duh, Horatio. Today I'm an independent woman. I don't need people my father *pays* to drive me around." I glance in the antique gilded mirror hanging on the wall and flash a satisfied smile at my reflection. "I'll drive myself."

Horatio hesitates for a moment before saying, "I am to remind you, Miss Larrabee, that your car is currently in an impound lot in Torrance."

I watch my mouth fall into a sullen frown. "Oh, yeah."

But then I quickly pep myself back up and refresh my smile. "That's okay," I tell him. "I'll just take the Bentley."

"Your *father's* Bentley?" Horatio asks, raising his eyebrows.

I shoot him an irritated look. "What? It's not like he ever drives it."

Thirty minutes later I pull into the parking garage of Bruce's building, place Holly in my oversize Birkin bag, toss the keys to the awaiting valet, and prance into the elevator.

People are looking at me—quite strangely actually—but it doesn't faze me. Being the daughter of Richard Larrabee, you get accustomed to the stares pretty quickly. It used to be only the older, business-y people who would recognize me. You know, subscribers to those *serious* magazines that always have downer stories on the covers about oil spills and the decline of health care. But ever since I started making the cover of more important magazines like *Us Weekly* (the first in the Larrabee family to do so, might I add!) I get recognized by *everyone*.

"Lexi!" Bruce greets me cheerfully the moment I walk through the door of his office. "Happy birthday, kiddo!"

Actually, on second thought, it's a tad *too* cheerful. And terribly out of character for Bummer Bruce. What's he so excited about? That he's finally getting rid of me? That after today, I'm officially an adult and therefore no longer his responsibility?

Well, to be fair, the feeling is mutual. So I decide to play along. "Hi, Brucey," I chorus.

He beams and reaches out to scratch Holly's head. "And hello to you," he coos in an obnoxious baby voice before returning his attention to me. "You look great, Lex. New outfit?"

Okay, *now* I'm getting a little weirded out. I mean, I understand his excitement about getting me off his daily watch list, but this is a bit much. His grin literally goes from ear to ear. I don't think I've ever seen such an expression on his face before. In fact, I've seen him do so much scowling lately, I forgot he was even capable of smiling. And since when does Bruce *ever* notice my outfit, let alone comment on it?

I warily glance down at my blouse and smooth out the hem. "Yes," I reply guardedly.

"Well, it's adorable."

Adorable?

"Thanks," I mumble, placing my bag with Holly in it on the floor and sliding into the seat across from the desk. I'm careful to keep my eyes locked on Bruce. Just in case the alien inhabiting his body suddenly decides to break free and attack. "Someone's in a good mood," I point out.

His grin broadens (if that's even possible) and he sinks down into his chair and clasps his hands in his lap. "Today's a good day," he replies smugly.

I nod, feeling the anticipation rise up inside me again. "It is."

For a moment, he doesn't speak. He simply stares at me with that stupid grin on his face while he lightly twirls his desk chair from side to side.

"So," I prompt, eager to move this thing along and finish packing for Vegas. I can almost *feel* the check in my hand. *See* all those beautiful liberating zeros lined up across the page.

"So," he echoes back unassumingly. As if he doesn't already know why I'm here. As if this isn't the single most important day of my entire life.

I fight back a groan. "So, what do I have to do? Just sign a piece of paper to say that I received it or something?"

He raises his eyebrows inquisitively.

"The *check*," I remind him, growing impatient.

"Oh right," he replies, his amused expression never fading. "The check."

It takes every ounce of strength for me not to roll my eyes and say "Duh!" Instead I offer him a tight-lipped smile.

"Actually, it's a bit more complicated than that."

"Okay," I reply slowly. I don't really remember Cooper saying anything about the process being complicated. But then again, he was so nonchalant about it. Infuriatingly so. I remember drilling him for hours the moment he got home, demanding to see the check and insisting he divulge every detail of the encounter. But he just kept shrugging and telling me it was no big deal. So I pretty much assumed that I would take a seat, sign a few documents, and that would be it. But then again, Cooper downplays everything. And I suppose when you're dealing with a check that size, there's bound to be a few legalities involved.

I glance at my watch. "Well, do you know about how long it's going to take? I booked a plane to Vegas tonight. Jia and T are throwing me a birthday party."

Bruce flashes me another smile, although this one is suddenly different. It's almost condescending. As though he knows something I don't and it's going to bring him great pleasure to share it with me. "It might take a while," is all he says.

I'm not sure why, but there's something in his tone that sends a shiver down my spine. And when I look into his eyes again, an unexpected feeling of dread suddenly settles into the pit of my stomach.

Something is not right. Something is off. I can't put my finger on what, exactly, but I can just *feel* it.

"Bruce." I pronounce his name vehemently. "What's going on?"

He leans back in his chair, like he's getting comfortable for a long movie or something. "Well," he begins in a light and friendly tone, "your father has made some *adjustments* to the arrangement."

"Adjustments," I hear myself repeat, although my lips are growing numb so I can barely even feel the words form on them. "What *kind* of adjustments?"

When he doesn't answer me, my heart starts to thud in my chest and the dread in my stomach has now brewed into some kind of lumpy soup. "I'm still getting my check today though," I press him. "Right?"

Bruce's mouth twists into a contorted, almost sadistic half smile. "Actually," he says calmly, his fearless gaze never leaving mine, "there's been a change of plans."

BRUCE ALMIGHTY

I FEEL MY BODY LIFT FROM MY SEAT AND SUDDENLY I'm on my feet. There's a burning sensation behind my eyes as they bore down on Bruce, skewering him with my vicious glare. But he seems completely unaffected, looking as content as can be in his little twirling desk chair, with his hands clasped casually on his lap. It makes the fire inside my chest glow with heat.

"What do you mean there's been a change of plans?" I'm honestly surprised at the sound that's coming out of my mouth right now. It's like a low, guttural growl. Similar to something you'd expect to hear from a teen werewolf right before he phases.

Holly must be surprised to hear it too because her head pops out of my bag and she glances around the room with her ears at full alert.

"Sit down, Lexington," Bruce commands in an authoritative tone, seamlessly transitioning into that father-figure role he loves to play so much.

I cross my arms defiantly over my chest. "No," I assert without a single waver in my voice. "Not until you tell me *exactly* what's going on here."

Bruce picks his battles, evidently electing out of this one. "Fine." He surrenders with a shrug. "Your father has had some . . ."—he pauses, wheeling his hand in a circle, as though trying to reel the right word out of his brain—". . . well, *concerns*, about your behavior lately."

The heat inside me intensifies but I remain silent.

"And he feels that, given recent events, it would behoove you and the family to delay the distribution of your trust fund."

"No." I shake my head adamantly from side to side, refusing to believe that this is real. That this is actually happening to me right now. "He can't do that."

"I'm afraid he can."

"For how long?" I demand through gritted teeth.

"A year."

"A year!" I spit out. "You can't make me wait a YEAR! I've been waiting for this day for *eighteen* years! What am I supposed to do for an entire year?"

"Actually," Bruce begins steadily, opening a manila folder on his desk and placing a pair of square-framed reading glasses onto the bridge of his nose, "your father has a very specific plan for how he intends you to spend this year."

I snort loudly. "Well, it better include a yacht in the Mediterranean."

"It doesn't," he counters with a deadpan expression, glaring down the tip of his nose at me. "Your father would like you to spend the next year working."

"Working?" I repeat incredulously, as though the word is completely foreign to me. Originating from some far-off country in the

South Pacific. Written in a language that looks more like pictures than letters.

"Yes," Bruce replies matter-of-factly.

"If my father thinks I'm gonna follow him around the office like some little lapdog for a year, pretending to care about stupid spreadsheets and prophet-and-lost statements, then he is *surely* mistaken. I am *not* RJ."

"No," Bruce says, removing his glasses and placing them down across the open folder. "Your father has no intention of you working for Larrabee Media."

I feel some sense of relief, but it's extremely short-lived. "Where does he *intend* for me to work, then?"

"Your father feels that you would benefit most by experiencing several *different* jobs. A buffet, if you will, of occupations. He believes this is the key to helping you appreciate the daily struggles that most people in this world have to endure to obtain even a fraction of what you have been so graciously given."

I roll my eyes. "Quit with the Mother Teresa crap, Bruce, and just get on with it."

He smiles indulgently. "Your father has selected precisely fifty-two occupations for you to undertake."

"Fifty-two," I repeat in shock. "He wants me to do fifty-two different jobs!?"

"Yes. One for every week of the year."

"But that has to be like . . . extortion or something. This can't be legal."

"I assure you, it's perfectly legal," Bruce defends, his tone slipping momentarily into that pompous, courtroom-lawyer voice he assumes whenever anyone brings up the subject of legality.

"What *kinds* of jobs are we talking about here? Acting? Modeling?"

Bruce looks like he's stifling a chuckle, which manages to piss me off even more. "No," he replies with a firm shake of his head. "These jobs are . . . well, slightly less glamorous. Minimum-wage-type stuff. Intended to teach you something about life. To show you how the other half lives."

"What *other* half?" I snarl.

"The half that doesn't receive a five-hundred-thousand-dollar Mercedes convertible and then crash it into a convenience store the very next day."

I bite my tongue so hard I can taste metal.

Bruce hands me a piece of paper. "Here's a complete listing of the jobs you'll be undertaking over the next year. You're scheduled to start tomorrow."

I gruffly snatch the paper from his hand and glance over the list. It seems to go on forever. My eyes graze over words like *janitor, waitress, dishwasher, fast-food restaurant employee,* and *gas station attendant,* and I can't bear to read any further. I chuck the paper back in his direction. "No frickin' way I'm doing any of those things!"

"I'm afraid you're going to have to, Lex," he says, picking up the page from where it landed on the floor and placing it neatly back in the folder. "Unless, of course, you want to forfeit your trust fund."

I start to pace the length of the office, mumbling to myself.

"This is ludicrous! He can't make me do this." I stop and turn back to Bruce, throwing my arms in the air. "Is he *crazy*?"

"Actually," Bruce answers my rhetorical question, "I happen to think it's the sanest decision he's made in a long time."

"I'm a *Larrabee* for God's sake!" I shout. "That's *supposed* to mean something. Larrabees don't work at gas stations."

"Do I have to remind you of where your father came from?" Bruce interjects calmly. "Of his humble roots?"

No, he doesn't have to remind me. I'm reminded every day. By every magazine article about my father or me. About how he started with nothing—a lowly copy-room employee at some small-town, local newspaper—and now he has everything and why didn't he opt to instill some of those hard-working values in his spoiled brat of a daughter?

But I don't say this to Bruce. I'm not about to give him *any* ammunition. So instead, I bypass his question altogether and scream, "That trust fund is mine! It has *my* name on it. It was promised to *me*! Just like all the others. RJ, Harrison, Hudson, *and* Cooper. They got what was promised to them. None of them were subjected to this insanity. None of them had to wait tables or wash dishes or whatever else is on that stupid list. They all got their twenty-five million free and clear. He can't go back on his word like that. He can't just change his mind without notice. I *earned* that money."

Bruce apparently can't stifle his amusement any longer because he suddenly breaks out into boisterous cackles of laughter. "Earned it? Doing what, may I ask?"

I'm so angry right now, my nostrils are flaring and my breath is coming out in ragged wheezes. I pace faster, hoping it will calm my nerves, but mostly so my feet have something to do besides karate chop Bruce's mahogany desk in half. "This is not fair," I hiss.

"Well," Bruce says, plucking a tissue from the box next to his computer and proceeding to clean the lenses of his spectacles, "*fair* is a very relative term, isn't it?"

I stop pacing. My feet freeze in their tracks as a sudden realization hits me like a truck. I narrow my eyes across the desk. "This was *your* idea, wasn't it?" I take a menacing step toward him. "You've had a vendetta against me from the moment I was born. This was *your* doing, wasn't it, *Bruce*?" I spit out his name.

He throws his hands in the air in surrender. "I swear I had nothing to do with it."

"Oh come on. This has Bruce Spiegelmann written all over it."

But Bruce simply shakes his head. "I'm afraid I can't take the credit. It was entirely your father's idea. He only asked me to help execute it. But I have to admit, I think it's nothing short of genius."

I can feel my fists ball up at my sides. The thought of my father and Bruce conspiring against me is making my insides boil with rage. The flames are lashing at the walls of my chest now, devouring my heart and lungs, the smoke stinging my throat. I look around for something to hit, something to throw, something to demonstrate just how livid I really am. My eyes land on a dozen gold-plated plaques lining the office wall. Some kind of stupid lawyer-of-the-year awards, no doubt. I take one purposeful step toward them but Bruce, obviously having read my thoughts in that freakish way that only he can, is out of his seat in a flash, stepping in my path. "I wouldn't if I were you," he warns.

I struggle to get past him but his arms wrap around me, holding me back. I immediately start thrashing. Holly jumps out of my bag and runs circles around us, barking her yippy little bark.

"Let me go!" I scream.

"Not if you're going to trash the place."

I continue to struggle against him, like an animal ensnared in a hunter's trap. But I make no progress. Bruce is stronger than he looks.

"You can't tell me what to do!" I screech into his ear.

He flinches but his grasp never falters. And when he speaks again, his tone is infuriatingly calm. "This two-year-old temper tantrum might work on Horatio or Kingston or whoever else you've managed to lure into your web, but it won't work on me, Lexington."

With that I stop thrashing, my arms falling to my sides. But still, he doesn't release me. As though he doesn't trust my surrender. "You don't have a choice," he whispers earnestly. "For once in your life, Lex, can't you just trust that someone else might know what's good for you? That your father might have your best interests at heart?"

In one fast, fluid motion, I raise my arms and slam them down hard, taking Bruce by surprise and breaking his tight clutch around me. But I don't continue for the wall of plaques like I originally intended. I'm over my petty, violent quest for revenge now. I'm suddenly on a new mission. I scoop up Holly and my bag and head straight for the door, determined to get out of here as fast as I can.

This time, Bruce doesn't try to stop me. Instead, he collapses against the edge of his desk, the struggle having left him slightly winded. "Lex," he mutters feebly, "your father has made up his mind. You can't fight this."

"Oh, yeah?" I say, raising my eyebrows. "Watch me."

LEXINGTON'S LAST STAND

AFTER A QUICK CALL TO KINGSTON, OUR DRIVER, I confirm that my father is still in LA and currently in his downtown offices. I drive straight there and, with Holly tucked under one arm, march through the doors of the lobby like I own the place . . . and, well, technically I do. Or I *will*, anyway. When my father dies and I inherit one-fifth of his empire.

Not one person tries to stop me. Not the security guards, not the receptionists, not even the parking garage attendants who guard my father's reserved parking spots like Knights Templar guarding the Holy Grail. I think everyone is just so surprised to see me—because, let's face it, it's not like I'm a regular visitor around here—that they can barely even utter a "Hello, Miss Larrabee," let alone inquire about the nature of my visit.

When I finally get to the fifty-sixth floor, I've managed to totally pump myself up. I'm like a soldier prepared to fight and die for my cause. My blood is boiling, my teeth—or my veneers, rather—are bared, and I'm ready for battle.

I don't say hello to anyone. I don't stop to make meaningless chitchat with the assistants or the mail-room staff or anyone. I have zeroed in on my target—the closed door of my father's corner office—and nothing will get in my way.

Except that.

Or I guess I should say . . . *him.*

A body in a dark gray suit suddenly appears out of nowhere, obstructing my path a mere three paces from my goal. I glance up at the unfamiliar face and sigh. "Excuse me," I say, not even bothering to cover up my annoyance with a fake smile. "You're in my way."

"I'm afraid I can't let you in there," he replies unsympathetically, his large hazel eyes not even flickering for a second. "Mr. Larrabee is in the middle of an important phone call."

I frown impatiently. "Don't you *know* who I am?"

His expression doesn't change. "I know *exactly* who you are. And you still can't go in."

I give a light laugh. "You must be new here."

"I am, in fact," he replies, with distinct pride in his voice. "I'm interning. Just started last week."

"Well, newbie," I sneer, "let me clue you in. I'm Lexington Larrabee and in case no one told you, you *have* to let me in. My father owns this place."

"Your father," he's quick to correct in a snide tone, "is the chairman of the board. Larrabee Media is a public company. Technically the shareholders own it."

My eyes widen in disbelief as I give the young man in front of me a spiteful once-over. He's tall and fit. His honey-brown hair is cut short and gelled into submission in that traditional corporate-droid style. If we had met under any other circumstances—like in a club—I probably would have thought he was cute, maybe slightly too generic for my long-term taste, but cute enough to have shamelessly flirted with. But right now, under *these* circumstances, he's pretty much the most obnoxious person I've ever met.

Plus, he looks *way* too young to be bossing people around. I don't care what kind of stuffy corporate suit he's wearing.

"What are you, like, seventeen?"

"I'm twenty," he says defensively. "Not that it matters."

"Look," I say, infusing my voice with an artificial gentleness, "you're new here. I'm sure you haven't had a chance to be properly . . . trained or whatever, but if you don't let me pass, I'm going to have you fired."

He doesn't move. In fact, he doesn't even blink. He just continues to stand there, blocking the door to my father's office like a marble statue. "I told you," he says steadfastly, "your father is on a call and has insisted he not be bothered . . . by *anyone*."

Jeez, what is *with* people today? Has everyone forgotten who I am? Who my father is? How much power I hold? It's like the whole world has gotten temporary amnesia and suddenly I'm this nobody that everyone steps on.

"If you don't let me in," I insist through clenched teeth, "I swear I will knock you over."

"And if you don't turn around and wait in the lobby like everyone else, I'll call security."

I have to chuckle at this because it's so completely absurd. "Oh my God, you really *are* dense." I set Holly down at my feet and place my hands on my hips. "Security can't do anything to me. I'm Lexington Larrabee!" I scream the last part loud enough for everyone within a two-mile radius to hear. I'm half hoping that *someone* will come to my rescue. That some receptionist or accountant or whoever will pop out of his or her office and tell this moron that he's treading on thin ice right now. But the only door that opens is the one behind him and suddenly my father is standing in front of me.

"What is going on out here?" he barks.

"Daddy!" I cry, pushing roughly past the annoying gatekeeper and throwing my arms around my father's neck. I hastily transition into a soft, tuneful voice. "Thank God you came out. I simply *have* to talk to you and this idiot wouldn't let me come in."

My father's body stiffens under my embrace and eventually he reaches up to disengage my grasp. "Luke is my new intern. I told him I wasn't to be bothered." He gives the young man behind me a grateful nod and then looks at me with that familiar vacant expression. "At least someone can follow simple directions."

I turn my head around long enough to catch sight of Luke's nauseatingly smug expression.

I'm going to kill that guy.

Well, just as soon as I'm finished here.

"What do you want?" my dad asks pointedly.

I take a deep breath and lower my voice. "I *really* need to talk to you. Can we go in your office?"

He shakes his head. "I'm running late to a meeting."

"But—"

"I'm not changing my mind, Lexington," my father replies, obviously having already guessed the reason behind my unexpected visit. "You'll do the fifty-two jobs I've selected for you and you'll complete each one of them to my satisfaction or the trust fund will be reassigned."

He starts walking. I jog to catch up with him. Holly follows closely at my heels.

"But Daddy," I try again.

"I'm sorry, Lexington. This is the way it's going to be."

"But it's not fair!" I cry out, not caring that a dozen or so people have poked their heads out of their offices to see what is going on. "Cooper never had to do anything for his money. Or RJ! Or Hudson and Harrison! This is totally sexist!"

My father comes to a sudden halt and turns to face me, the most unpleasant expression plastered across his face.

Okay, maybe the sexist remark was going a bit too far.

"You think this is about *gender*?" he growls in that low, malicious tone that used to give me nightmares as a child. "You think I'm doing this because you're a *girl*? If anything, I have given you more leeway, more advantages, more *leniency* than any of your brothers. And I can see now what a colossal mistake that was because you have done nothing with any of it except lead a life of gluttony and ingratitude. And up until a few days ago, I was at a complete loss as to how to turn that around. This is my last hope for you, Lexington. My last effort to instill some sense into you. Some values. Some *humanity*."

I can feel tears stinging my eyes but I fight them back with a few quick blinks. Just as I've always done. I haven't let my father see me cry since I was eight years old and he told me he was going to be in Hong Kong for Christmas and I couldn't come. And I'm not about to start again now. "I won't do it," I vow, but my voice breaks.

"This isn't a choice, Lexington."

"You can't make me do it!" I assert, feeling slightly more confident. "I'll leave. I'll run away. My friends and I have plans, you know? I have places to go. I don't have to stay around here and play poverty camp with a bunch of low-rent, high school dropouts."

My father's face remains a blank page but he leans in closer to me—close enough that I can feel his breath on my forehead. The proximity is making my stomach flip so I take an instinctive step back. "You'll do it," he promises ominously. "Or you'll lose everything."

And with that, my father turns around and continues down the hall, disappearing into a conference room and closing the door behind him.

GROUNDED

I NEED TO GET OUT OF HERE. I NEED TO ESCAPE.
I can't handle all this pressure! My flight to Vegas is scheduled for
six p.m. but I can't wait that long. I have to leave now. I need a distraction. I need to be surrounded by friends and noise and commotion. And I can't think of a better place to do that than Las Vegas.

Plus, I'm absolutely positive that given enough time to think
and digest everything that's happened, my father will inevitably
change his mind and this will all be over. It's obvious he's just being
rash. A total overreaction to last week's event. All he needs is a little
time and space for the reality of his decision to sink in and then
he'll realize how ridiculous and unreasonable he's being. I know
my father. No one can talk him out of a decision except himself. So
I need to give him a chance to do that. It'll probably take him a few
hours—maybe even a day—to see the error of his ways. Then I'll
get a phone call from Bruce, who will most likely be wallowing in
defeat, grumbling about how the whole thing is called off, how
sorry he is for being so rude in his office, not to mention physically
violent (which was *totally* out of line, by the way) and *how about a*

lovely send-off party for your cruise as a token of my remorse? And, of course, I'll accept. Because I'm forgiving like that.

I take a deep breath and steer my father's Bentley onto the 10 Freeway. See, I already feel better. How silly it was for me to get riled up like that. Everything will be just fine. It'll all work out. There's no need to do anything drastic . . . like run my father's car into a cement wall.

I choose not to return home first. Instead, I proceed straight to the Santa Monica airport, where the Larrabee jets are kept. I can't deal with the house right now. Or Horatio and anyone else who's there. I'll just head to Vegas early, pick up some new clothes when I get there, and try to relax until this blows over.

I turn to Holly, who has been staring anxiously at me from the passenger seat, and give her head a quick, reassuring scratch. "Don't worry, baby," I tell her in the lullaby voice I reserve only for her. "I'm okay. Thanks for your concern though. It's nice to know *someone* is looking out for me."

She seems to be satisfied with this and her body finally relaxes. She curls into a ball on the seat and closes her eyes.

Twenty minutes later, I pull up in front of the Larrabee hangar, scoop Holly from the front seat, and toss my bag over my shoulder. A man in a blue uniform comes running out of the hangar, looking extremely nervous as his eyes dart back and forth up the tarmac.

"Miss Larrabee," he says apprehensively, as though he has no idea what on earth I'm doing here.

Great, another annoying newbie I'm going to have to hand-hold.

"Hi," I say, trying to sound bright and friendly. I paint on a wide smile. "I'm here for my flight to Vegas."

He wrings his hands together and glances behind me at the Bentley, which I've left running.

"The keys are in the ignition," I inform him stiffly. "Can you fill up the tank before I get back?"

"But—" he begins, his face twisted in some kind of painful-looking grimace.

"Yes, I know I'm not supposed to take off until six but there's been a change of plans and I want to go now."

He shakes his head quickly. To be honest, it looks more like a nervous tic than a negation. "B-b-b-ut . . . you can't," he stammers. "I'm . . . It's . . ."

I roll my eyes and tap my fingers impatiently against the shoulder strap of my bag. What is with this guy? Why is he so jittery? It's only a stupid schedule change. It happens all the time. It's not like I'm asking him to call off a war or something.

He's still bumbling like an idiot so I decide to take control of the situation. "Look," I say shortly, "is the plane here?"

He nods hurriedly.

"Good. Is there fuel in the tank?"

"Y-y-y-es."

"Is there a pilot here?"

"Yes, but . . ."

I flash him an insincere smile and pat him brusquely on the shoulder. "Well, then there you go. Problem solved."

I step past him and strut toward the hangar. A moment later, I hear the patter of hassled footsteps behind me and suddenly the man is at my side again. I stifle a groan. "Oh, God. What *now?*"

"It's just that . . ." He starts to fumble for words again and it takes every ounce of strength in me not to slap him on the back of the head to try to get him to speak fluidly. "Y-y-your father," he barely manages to choke out.

My heart starts to pound in my chest as I narrow my eyes at the squirrelly man in front of me. "What about my father?" I hiss.

He swallows hard. I can actually see the lump of anxiety move its way down his throat. "He told us you weren't authorized to fly anywhere."

HEDGED IN

I'M SO ANGRY I COULD SCREAM. ACTUALLY I HAVE been screaming. For about the last three hours. I screamed at the brainless worker at the Larrabee airport hangar who wouldn't let me get on the plane and actually had the nerve to restrain me when I tried to make a run for the jet. I screamed at the ticket agent at the American Airlines counter at LAX who wouldn't sell me a seat on the next flight to Vegas because she *claimed* that all my credit cards had been declined. This is after I had swallowed my pride and *deigned* to fly commercial, something I haven't done since . . . well, *ever*. Then I screamed at the ATM when it spit out a piece of paper declaring that my account had been frozen. I even screamed at some lawyer whose picture was on the back of a bus that happened to stop in front of me at a red light. The ad *swore* he could help me with my legal problems, but after I phoned him and he'd talked to me for a whole five minutes he said there was no way on earth he was going up against Richard Larrabee, especially in a case I didn't have the slightest chance of winning. Not to mention how was I expecting to *pay* a lawyer when my entire source of income originated from my father's estate? Or did I really expect my father to shell out the very money that would be used to sue him?

Then he laughed and I screamed some more.

I screech into my driveway, throw the Bentley into park with the car halfway on the pavement and halfway on the grass, and storm into the house. I toss the keys haphazardly on the table in the foyer. They make a loud clanking sound against the polished stone surface. Good. The more noise I can make the better.

"Kingston!" I call at the top of my lungs. My voice echoes across the marble floors and up the spiral staircase.

Kingston appears a moment later. "Yes, Miss Larrabee," he says obligingly.

"Oh good, you're here," I say breathlessly as I start trudging up the stairs. Holly follows closely behind. She requires the momentum of her entire body to make it up each step. After about five, I bend down to pick her up and tuck her under my arm. "I'm just throwing a few things into a bag," I tell him. "Then I need you to drive me to Vegas."

There's a silence at the bottom of the stairs and it takes me a moment to realize that Kingston's usual swift response, "Of course, miss, I'll be waiting out front," has not yet been verbalized.

I slow to a stop but don't turn around. I keep my eyes straight ahead as I say, in a measured tone, "Kingston, did you not hear me?"

"I did, miss," comes his response, followed by another sickening lull.

"Then why are you just standing there?" I ask. I still haven't dared look behind me but I *know* that he hasn't moved an inch. I can hear him breathing.

"Well . . ." he begins, his voice wavering. "You see, your father has instructed me not to drive you anywhere."

Now I turn around. My eyes cold and piercing. *"What?"* I growl.

He winces against my stare and drops his head, avoiding my gaze.

"Look," I continue when he doesn't answer me, "I don't *care* what my father told you, Kingston. You work for me too. And *I* am telling you to drive me to Vegas."

"I'm sorry, Miss Larrabee," he replies sheepishly, "but your father told me he'd fire me if I drove you anywhere."

I can't breathe. My lungs feel like they're trapped inside a box. Then I watch wide-eyed as Kingston sidles up to the foyer table and proceeds to slide the keys to the Bentley off the surface and drop them into the pocket of his suit pants.

"What are you doing?" I ask anxiously.

He still refuses to meet my eye. "Your father has also asked me to collect the keys to any vehicle registered to the Larrabee estate." His voice is pained, indicating that he's clearly troubled by the message he's been asked to relay. But I could really care less about *his* agony right now. It can't even *begin* to compare to my own.

"Horatio!" I call out. I'm so furious, my body is actually shaking. Like in convulsions. I have to set Holly back down in fear that I might drop her.

Horatio appears from the kitchen. He saunters calmly toward the foot of the stairs, his pace neither quickened nor slowed by my evident impatience. He, on the other hand, has no problem meeting my eye. He stops in front of the banister and looks directly up at me.

"Can you *please* tell me what is going on here?"

His face registers no emotion. Not a smile. Not a scowl. "Your father called," he pronounces slowly in his silky Argentinean accent. "He regrets to inform you that your credit cards have been canceled, your bank account frozen, and your allowance suspended." Then with a slight nod of his head he adds, "Until further notice."

"Further notice?" I scream back. "What is *that* supposed to mean?"

How he can be so gosh-darn calm in the face of such catastrophe is beyond me. "It means," he replies smoothly, his tone unaffected by my outbursts, "Mr. Larrabee is cutting you off until you agree to his arrangement."

I'm about *this* close to calling my shrink and suggesting he have my father committed because he's *clearly* lost his mind. It must be the old age. He's going to be fifty in a few years and the senility is obviously already starting to settle in. But really, how unfair is it that *I* have to be the one to experience the wrath of his lunacy? Just because I'm the youngest. RJ and Harrison and Hudson never had to deal with this kind of madness. Or even Cooper! The world is a very cruel place.

The sun is starting to set now and I'm physically and mentally exhausted. My voice is hoarse from the screaming, my feet hurt from shuffling around Los Angeles all day, and my spirit is beyond broken. I walk alone in the darkening gardens behind the house. It's a breathtaking five-thousand-square-foot labyrinth of flawlessly groomed hedges and bright and vibrant blankets of flowers. My mother designed the gardens to be smaller replicas of the ones found at the Château de Villandry in France. Before she died, of course. They've been featured at least a dozen times in a variety of home-and-garden magazines. Always pictured with my father posing somewhere in the middle. As though he were personally responsible for the maintenance of such an elaborate landscape, when in reality he's barely around long enough to appreciate the place, let alone trim hedges. There's a staff of about ten gardeners who come twice a week to do that. My father just sits back and takes the credit. Nothing new, I suppose.

When I was little, I used to love to play out here. I made Horatio play countless rounds of hide-and-seek and freeze tag and any other game I could think of. That's when I was short enough to be concealed by the sheer height of the hedges and Horatio would have to squat down and crawl on hands and knees to avoid being spotted. After about five minutes of breathless pursuit, his head would inevitably pop up over a shrub somewhere and I would giggle in delight and run to capture him. He would fall prey to my attack and then convincingly complain that he was simply too tall for this game and that it was unfair because I had the clear advantage. I remember how special that made me feel. How *lucky* I was to be little.

It wasn't until years later that I realized Horatio would reveal himself on purpose. The moment he grew weary or had other business inside the house to attend to, he would stand up and surrender and the game would be over. And ever since that realization, I've always wondered if a real parent—not a paid replacement—would have given up so easily.

The waist-high walls of the garden hedges don't conceal me now. Nor do they do anything to appease me. I've been pacing along them for nearly an hour and I still feel sick to my stomach. Holly got tired and gave up trying to follow me half an hour ago. She's curled up on a lounge chair by the pool, waiting for me to finish whatever it is I'm doing so we can go back inside.

As I walk, navigating the various twists and turns of the complicated network of sculpted shrubs, gurgling fountains, and heart-shaped flower beds, I mentally work through my options. Trying desperately to find one that doesn't result in a dead end.

But even though I've been walking this garden for nearly fifteen years, even though I know this green maze like the back of my hand, I still feel trapped at every turn. There's nowhere to run. No-where to hide. No matter which direction I choose, my father always wins.

I'm not sure why I ever thought I could go up against Richard Larrabee and succeed. No one else ever has. Why should I be any different? In this game, my father is the one who holds the advantage. In *every* game he plays, actually. It's simply the way it is. The way it's always been. And it's pretty clear to me now—with a wallet full of canceled credit cards and a bank account as frozen as the arctic circle—that he isn't going to just change his mind. He isn't going to reconsider.

This time, I'm the one who's going to have to surrender.

So with a hollow feeling in my chest and a bitter taste in my mouth, I pull my cell phone out of my pocket and call Bruce.

THAT'S WHAT FRIENDS ARE FOR

I LIE ON MY BED, STARING OUT THROUGH THE small slit in the curtain canopy that I've drawn closed around me like a cocoon. I wish I could stay in here forever. Hidden away from this cruel world that I inhabit. But my life is like a ticking clock now. Like a bomb waiting to explode. Because in less than twenty-four hours, everything will change. Nothing will be the same.

Bruce said on the phone that he was proud of me for making the decision to go along with my father's plan. I snorted in response. For one, his choice of words annoyed me. He's *proud* of me? Please. How many times do I have to remind this man that he is *not* my father? And second, since when was there *ever* a "decision" to be made here? When was I *ever* given a choice in this matter? The answer is . . . never.

My father doesn't give choices. He doesn't leave options.

Bruce told me to come into his office first thing tomorrow morning so we could get started. I mumbled some kind of agreement and hung up the phone, anxious to end that particular call as quickly as possible.

Now all I can do is wait. And imagine how horrible my life is going to be for the next . . . wait for it . . . *year.* This is by far the worst birthday in the history of the world.

The second phone call I've been dreading comes at eight p.m., an hour after I'm supposed to have arrived at the Bellagio in Las Vegas. I don't really want to answer. I don't want to have to tell my friends about everything I've been through today. It's too humiliating. Too heartbreaking. Too horrific. But I know I have to answer. I can't just not show up to my eighteenth birthday party without an explanation.

"Hey Ji," I say into the phone. My voice sounds far away and defeated.

"Hey sweetness," Jia drawls. "What's taking you so long? Is there traffic? You're going to *die* when you see what we've done with this club. You won't even recognize it! T had this awesome idea to—"

"Jia," I interrupt her before she has a chance to tell me about all the other fabulous things that I'll never be able to see because my idiot father decided to schedule a tornado to strike on my eighteenth birthday. "I'm not coming."

I wait through the stunned silence before she finally replies, "What are you talking about? I thought you scheduled the jet for six?"

"My flight was canceled."

At this she laughs. "That's ridiculous. Private planes don't get canceled unless there's bad weather. And there hasn't been a cloud in the sky."

"Oh, there have been plenty of clouds here. Dark ones."

More silence and then, "Lex, are you screwing with me? Are

you going to like jump out of a closet somewhere and try to get me to scream?" I can hear the shuffle of movement and I assume that's Jia glancing around her, pulling back curtains, and opening doors, looking for evidence of my practical joke.

I sigh gravely. "I wish this was a joke. I really do. All day, the only thing I've been able to do is wish that it's one big, stupid, not-funny joke."

Her voice softens. She knows I'm serious now. "Okay, talk to me. What happened?"

I tell her everything. I talk until my throat is sore and the tears are streaming down my face. She listens quietly and doesn't say anything except for the occasional gasp and sigh when I get to a particularly atrocious part. When I finally finish, I expect her to get all lecture-y on me, ranting about the injustice of the whole thing and how my father should never be able to get away with this. But she doesn't say that. Like a good friend, she bypasses all that unhelpful dribble that is certain to only rile me up again and gets right to the solution. "Stay where you are," she instructs me. "I'm sending someone to pick you up."

I'm a little surprised by her response, which is why it takes me a second to say, "Huh? Ji, what are you talking about?"

She makes a small *pfff* sound. "What do you think I'm talking about, Lex? If there were *ever* a night to party, it's tonight. Before you're forced to do God-knows-what tomorrow. Tonight may be the last chance you have to do anything fun. I don't care what your stupid father says. He can empty your bank account and cancel your credit cards, but he can't cancel mine. It's your eighteenth birthday and I'm bringing you to Vegas."

After I hang up the phone, I start sprinting around my room, throwing items into a bag. Jia told me not to worry about clothes. That she and T will take care of everything I need, but I'm packing a few essentials just in case.

God, I love my friends. I love them more than anything. How amazing are they? Seriously!

Holly gives me a strange look from the bed as she watches me scramble to get ready.

I run over to her and scoop her up under my arm. "I know you hate Vegas, baby," I tell her. "So don't worry. I'll leave you with Horatio. He'll take good care of you."

Then, with Holly in one hand and my hastily packed overnight bag in the other, I scurry out my bedroom door.

I try not to think about where I have to be at nine tomorrow morning or what I'm going to have to endure for the next fifty-two weeks of my life. The only thing on my mind as the hired limo pulls out of my driveway is that Jia is absolutely right. If there were ever a night to party, it's tonight. Tonight has to be *huge*. The *hugest*. I have to make it count. Every other night has to pale in comparison to the festivities that lie ahead. There will be no sleeping. No resting. I am prepared to go *all* night.

This may very well be the last night of fun I'm going to have for a long, long time. My last night of freedom before I'm forced to enter the Richard Larrabee Boot Camp for Ungrateful, Spoiled Daughters.

Tonight is my equivalent of the Last Supper.

As the plane takes off and I watch the ground get smaller and smaller beneath me, I can't help but smile as I imagine the look on

Bruce's face when I walk into his office tomorrow morning, after having partied the entire night away. And then I think about the call he'll make to my father, informing him of my incapacitated state. Complaining about my total lack of respect for the family name and everything it represents.

A blond and bubbly flight attendant arrives with a silver serving tray and offers me a glass of champagne. I bypass the glass and just take the bottle, guzzling it down like an athlete in a Gatorade commercial.

My father might be able to force me to do manual labor. But he definitely can't force me to care.

ADVENTURES IN BABYSITTING

I'M GOING TO KILL THE SUN. I SWEAR TO GOD, IF it doesn't stop shining, I'm going to hire a hit man and have it whacked. Who makes these sunglasses? Tom Ford? Well, they suck. They need to be like five hundred thousand times darker. I can't believe they even have the nerve to call these sunglasses when they don't do *anything* to block out the sun.

My head feels like it's been hit by an asteroid hurtling to earth at seven thousand gazillion miles per hour. I'm not sure I've ever been this hungover in my life. In fact, I don't think *anyone* has ever been this hungover in the history of the universe.

I would tell you about the party last night but I honestly don't remember much of it. I remember arriving at the penthouse suite. I remember the pre-party cocktails we had while we were getting dressed. Then I remember walking into the club and my jaw dropping to the floor upon seeing the amazing 1920s-Hollywood theme that my friends came up with, complete with an actual car from 1925 parked right in the middle of the dance floor. I remember doing a round of shots and then dancing on the hood of that car. And the rest is pretty much a giant black hole.

Just as planned, I haven't slept at all. Unless you count the thirty-minute catnap I took on the flight back to LA that I had to board at seven-thirty this morning in order to be at Bruce's office by nine. Which I don't. Actually, come to think of it, I'm probably still a little bit drunk.

Kingston picks me up at the airport and drives me to Century City. I rest my cheek against the soft, cool leather of the backseat and try to resist puking the entire way there. I'm saving that for the potted plant next to Bruce's desk.

I'm still wearing the 1920s-inspired flapper dress (designed especially for the occasion by Karl Lagerfeld) and hot-pink feather boa that Jia and T surprised me with for my birthday party last night. My black fishnet stockings have about fifteen holes in them, and the chin-length black wig complete with feather headband is sitting crooked on my head, but I'm far too debilitated to bother trying to fix it. And I don't even want to *think* about what my makeup must look like right now. I haven't looked into a mirror since we left the penthouse suite at ten last night and I'm not about to start now. I literally went straight from the dance floor to the airport. But I remember Jia caking it on my face last night as we were getting ready. Layer after layer of dark shadow, black-as-night eyeliner, and bloodred lipstick. By now I probably look like a head-on collision between death and a clown car.

I stumble through the doors of Spiegelmann, Klein & Lipstein Law Offices, bypass the receptionist completely, and zigzag down the hallway to Bruce's office. Then I collapse onto his couch, curling up into a ball.

"Jesus Christ," he breathes.

"I'm ready to work," I slur, shutting my eyes against the harsh light of his office. "Bring it on."

"You reek."

I hug a throw pillow to my chest. "Oh good. I thought it was you."

My eyes remain closed and I still have my sunglasses on for fear of permanent retina damage if I were to remove them, but I can tell he's *not* amused. I can hear it in the way he breathes. Heavy and strenuous. Through his nose. It sounds like he's trying to expel something that's stuck up there.

I have to fight back the smile that's inching its way across my lips. Mostly because it hurts to move my face.

I hear him start to pace. He's muttering something incomprehensible and I don't even bother trying to make sense of it. That would only require energy I don't have.

"You know what," he eventually says after a few more seconds of incomprehensible ranting (although technically it could have been longer—I think I dozed off there for a minute), "I don't care what kind of shape you're in." He suddenly sounds all decisive and boastful, as though he's been having a long, heated debate with himself and is pleased that he's finally won. "Consequences are more effective than concepts and it's about time you started learning some."

"That's the spirit, Brucey," I mutter dazedly, managing to muster a weak fist pump.

He ignores my goading tone and continues with authority. "Your first job starts today. And you're not getting out of it just because you're an overindulged, spoiled brat who refuses to take responsibility for her actions. At least not anymore. Those days are over, Lexington. You're still going to work today. And you'll complete a full five days on the job. We're not postponing."

I blow on a feather from my headband that has fallen limply over my face. "No problem."

I hear Bruce's pacing slow to a stop. I open one eye to see what's going on. He's now seated behind his desk, jabbing at a button on his phone.

"Yes, Mr. Spiegelmann?" His assistant's voice comes through the speaker.

"Is he here?" Bruce asks.

"Yes, he's just arrived."

"Good. Send him in."

I sit up, struggling to hold back the bile that's burbling up from my stomach, and glance suspiciously from Bruce to the phone. "Who?" I demand, praying to God it's not my father. I really don't think I could deal with him right now. "Who are you sending in?"

The answer comes a second later when Bruce's office door swings open and a young man in a stuffy dark gray suit carrying a leather briefcase strides pompously into the room. Despite my foggy head and blurred vision, I recognize his pretty-boy face and conventional preppy haircut immediately.

"Lexington, this is Luke Carver. An intern at Larrabee Media."

"Oh, God," I say with a loud groan, collapsing back onto my side. "Not *you* again."

It's that annoying, arrogant jerk I had the displeasure of meeting at my father's office yesterday. The one who had the *nerve* to restrict me from seeing him.

He gives me a long, disapproving once-over. "Nice to see you again, Lexington."

"Oh, good," Bruce says delightedly. "You two have already met."

"Unfortunately," I mumble, turning my glare on Bruce. "What is he doing here?"

Bruce rises to his feet and gives Luke a light pat on the shoulder. "She's your problem now," he says unsympathetically, and then stalks out the door.

I launch back up to a seated position and watch, wide-eyed, as Bruce disappears down the hallway without even so much as a goodbye. "Bruce!" I call out exasperatedly. "What are you talking about? Where are you going?"

But he doesn't come back and now I'm left alone in his big office with this half-wit. I turn my angry glare on him. "Can someone please tell me what is going on around here?"

Luke stands like a statue, both hands in front of him, clasped tightly around the handle of his briefcase. "Your father," he begins stiffly, "has placed me in charge of this particular . . ."—he struggles for the word—". . . project."

"What does that mean?"

"It means I've been assigned to report back on your progress as you tackle your various jobs."

I push my sunglasses up over my crooked wig, squinting against all sorts of unwanted light. "Excuse me? Are you telling me you've been assigned to *babysit* me?"

Luke does not look especially pleased at my choice of words but he hides his discontent with a tight-lipped smile. "I'd prefer to think of myself as more of a *liaison*. Between you and your father. I'm here to make sure you complete each of your fifty-two occupations to your father's satisfaction."

"You've *got* to be kidding me!" I screech, completely horrified.

Luke doesn't reply. He simply continues to stand at attention next to the door. I leap to my feet, ignoring the thunderbolt of pain that rockets through my head, brush past him, and barrel down the hallway. "Bruce!" I call at the top of my lungs.

I find him standing at the reception desk, sipping on a fresh cup of coffee and perusing a legal brief like it's just another warm, sunny day at the office.

"You can't be serious about this."

"I'm sorry, Lexington," he replies unhelpfully. "Once again, this was your father's call. I had nothing to do with it."

"You mean to tell me I'm stuck with this guy for the next *year*?"

Bruce shrugs as though he doesn't see why I'm getting so bent out of shape. "Well . . . yeah."

I glance back in the direction I came from. Luke is suddenly behind me, looking like a total corporate robot with his hardened jawline and prepackaged haircut.

I can't hold it in any longer. I feel the sickness rising up in my chest, stinging my throat. I turn helplessly toward Bruce and vomit all over his Armani suit.

DANGEROUS LIAISONS

I FALL INTO THE FRONT SEAT OF LUKE'S CAR AND he thrusts a trash can that he evidently stole from Bruce's office into my lap and slams the door closed. I cringe at the sound.

He gets in behind the wheel and fastens his seat belt. Then he proceeds to go through some five-minute procedure of checking and rechecking the mirrors, radio volume, wiper functionality, warning lights, and climate controls, as though he's preparing for a transatlantic flight as opposed to just a stupid car ride.

I stare at him for a few moments and then my eyes simply can't handle being open any longer and I allow them to close as I let out a pained groan.

"*Please* don't puke in my car," he says as he puts the shifter into reverse and backs out of the spot. "It's new."

I open my eyes long enough to glance around at the boring gray cloth interior, cheap plastic paneling, and manual door locks and windows. "Oh, yeah," I mock. "I wouldn't want to mess up your brand new *Kia*."

I notice his knuckles turn white around the steering wheel as he slowly makes his way down the long, windy spiral ramp that leads out of the parking garage. "It's a Honda Civic," he replies through gritted teeth, and then adds, *"Hybrid,"* as if that's supposed to be some kind of improvement.

I roll my eyes. "Well, the color is awful. And it's making me carsick."

"Not all of us are lucky enough to receive a Lexus for our sixteenth birthdays."

I flash him a look of repulsion. "Eww. Like I'd ever be caught *dead* in a Lexus."

Luke takes a long, deep breath. He looks like he's about to close his eyes and start chanting *Om* or something and then suddenly, as if a switch has been flipped, he's all business again. "Here's how this is going to work," he says importantly, as though he's addressing a boardroom. I can see why my father likes this guy so much. He's like a Richard Larrabee mini-me. "Your father has selected fifty-two jobs for you to undertake over the course of the next year. You will *not* be granted access to your trust fund until all fifty-two jobs have been completed. You will be given an allowance to cover your regular expenses as long as you fulfill your weekly obligations to this project. Should you decide to quit at any time or if it is determined that you are not taking the assignments seriously, your father will not hesitate to cut you off completely. Is that clear?"

I'm barely paying attention. I've started to drift off again. My head is sagging forward against my chest. I feel a violent jerk as the car lurches to a stop at a red light and I snap awake. "Huh?"

"I said," Luke repeats impatiently, "is that clear?"

"Yeah, whatever," I mumble in response before twisting to my side, pulling my legs up underneath me, tucking my hands under my cheek, and attempting to doze off again. If I can just get a few minutes of sleep, I'll be fine.

But it soon becomes evident that this is a lost cause because Luke suddenly decides to treat the brake like it's the snare pedal on a Rock Band drum kit. Every time my eyes start to drift closed, the car wrenches forward and back and I'm jolted awake like a crash test dummy hitting a brick wall. Then I look over at him with pure hatred in my eyes and he simply smiles, shrugs, and goes, "Sorry," in this really high-pitched, singsongy voice. And I swear I see him laugh under his breath.

He starts jabbering again. "I'll expect regular status reports from you. This is a job and you'll treat it as such."

"Regular *what*?" I ask, pressing both index fingers against my forehead.

"Status reports. Summarizing what you've done at each job, what you've learned, and any insights that you've had."

"So what do you want me to do?" I say with a sarcastic snort. "Fax them to you?"

"I don't care what format you present them in, as long as the information is there."

I sigh and push my head back into the headrest. "I don't remember that being part of the original arrangement."

"Well," Luke says coldly, "it is now. And if you fail to comply, I'll report back to your father that you're being uncooperative."

I groan. Leave it to my father to *hire* someone to communicate with me on his behalf. Because God forbid he actually has to talk to me himself. Oh no, he has to pay a "liaison." A freaking *liaison*! I mean, sure he's been doing it for years, through hundreds of different people—Horatio, Bruce, Kingston, whatever eager new publicist he's sent to clean up my latest mess—but until now, he's never given it an official title. He's never actually called a duck a duck.

Although calling this Luke person a duck is far too kind. He's more like a bug. A cockroach. And if he didn't hold my financial future in his grubby little hands, I'd just as soon squash him underneath my Christian Louboutin heel.

"Where are you taking me?" I ask, looking out the window at the familiar landscape. Until now I hadn't even noticed where we were going. It appears we've landed in a neighborhood of Brentwood.

"To your first job assignment," Luke replies rigidly. "I'll be driving you to all of your jobs and picking you up at the end of the day."

"Thanks, but I have a car."

"Hmm." Luke pretends to contemplate. "That's not what CNN is reporting."

"I have a *driver*," I amend.

"Well, it looks like you won't be needing him for this. It's my job to make sure you show up on time every morning so I'll be taking you."

Oh, God. Can this day *possibly* get any worse?

And right then, as if the universe is answering my unspoken question with a smug, self-satisfied chuckle, Luke pulls into the driveway of a large Tudor-style mansion and parks the car. I see a short, blond-haired woman standing out front, dressed in a pale-blue-and-white-striped, calf-length uniform with short sleeves and a crisp white collar. In one hand she holds a red compartmentalized bucket filled with various plastic bottles of unidentifiable liquids. In the other she holds a second uniform, identical to her own.

Luke walks around the hood of the car, opens my door, and beckons for me to get out but I don't move. Instead I grip the edge of the seat so hard I think my nails might actually be puncturing the ugly gray fabric.

The harsh-looking woman with the tight blond bun and dark sallow bags under her eyes elongates her neck and briskly approaches the car. She thrusts the red bucket toward me, like she's the chief of some indigenous tribe making a peace offering to the strange newcomer. Like I'm actually supposed to take it and start jumping for joy, throwing my arms around her neck and thanking her for such a thoughtful gift.

I recognize the bucket. We have one exactly like it at the house. But I've never touched it. I've never *dared* touch it. Because it belongs to Carmen.

Our *maid*.

"Here," the woman says in a thick Eastern European accent. The way her tongue rolls harshly across the *r* in *here* makes it sound like she wants to murder the letter in cold blood, as opposed to just pronouncing it. "You take."

"No!" I immediately reply without even thinking, reaching out for the handle and yanking the car door closed. I quickly jab my hand down on the manual lock.

"Lexi," Luke says, knocking on the glass, "c'mon, open the door."

I cross my arms over my chest and lean back in the seat. I'm *not* going out there. I'll sit in here all day if I have to. I don't care. It's better than what I'm expected to do out there.

Clean houses? I *so* don't think so.

There's another knock on the glass. "Lexi," Luke urges, "you're acting like a child."

"Am not!" I shout back.

Luke rolls his eyes and produces the car keys from his pocket. He unlocks the door and opens it with an impatient sigh.

Damn it. I wasn't expecting him to have the keys.

"Lexi," he says gruffly, "this is Katarzyna. She works for Majestic Maids. She'll be training you to clean houses this week. She knows about the project and has agreed to participate. She's been instructed to report everything back to me."

"No," I say again. "This is insane. I'm not doing it."

"If you don't get out of the car," Luke warns, "I'll have to call your father."

"Fine," I tell him stubbornly. "Call him. I don't care."

"Fine," Luke challenges, calmly calling my bluff. I watch him pull his cell phone out of his pocket and start dialing.

"No!" I scream, leaping out of the car to grab his phone. "Don't call him. I'll do it. Whatever." I violently slam the door behind me.

Luke smiles, seemingly satisfied with his mini-victory, and opens the back door of the car. He leans in, riffles through his briefcase until he finds a plain manila folder, and flips it open. I tilt my head to read what's typed in a crisp black font on the tab. All it says is *Job #1.*

"You'll work eight hours a day for the next five days," he informs me in an official tone, reading from the folder.

"Eight hours!" I screech. "That's not humanly possible."

Katarzyna clears her throat and I reluctantly look at her.

"Yes, Katarzyna?" Luke prompts.

"Last week I work double shift EVERY day!" she roars in broken English, like she's taking this whole thing *way* too personally. "I work SIXTEEN hours each day for seven days!"

Perfect, I think. *I'm training with Hitler's maid.*

"Well, I guess that settles the debate on human possibilities," Luke says, sounding *far* too amused for my liking.

"I don't think that counts," I argue. "She's a professional."

"And you will be too." He smiles at me.

Katarzyna pushes the red bucket toward me. This time, however, I'm not given much choice in the matter because she thrusts it against my gut and I manage to grab on to it before it plummets to the ground.

"Thanks," I mutter.

Then she throws the extra uniform over my shoulder and tightly nods. "Okay. We go!"

"Good luck!" Luke calls after me as I reluctantly follow her toward the front door. And just before the door swings shut behind us, I glance longingly at the freedom of the outside world. At Luke's little silver sedan backing out of the driveway. At the white minivan with the Majestic Maids logo emblazoned on the side. The swirly pink letters twist and turn in large ornate loops and bows. As if a frilly logo is supposed to magically turn housecleaning into some kind of merry, whistle-while-you-work job fit for a princess.

When really it's the other way around.

It's Cinderella in reverse.

This fairy tale has officially become a horror story. Happily Ever After on a yacht in the Mediterranean has turned into Crappily Ever After in the dark dungeons of Brentwood. And the princess—who used to be so glamorous and beautiful and on the VIP list of every ball in town—has been handed a bucketful of cleaning supplies and *poofed* into a maid.

HOUSECLEANING FOR DUMMIES

PEOPLE ARE *DISGUSTING*. THIS PLACE IS AN absolute pigsty. Dirty laundry is hanging from every object and piece of furniture that even halfway resembles a hook. There are muddy footprints from some unidentified animal running in dizzying circles across the entire entry hall. Dishes are stacked on the stairs. On. The. *Stairs*. Why would someone put dishes on the stairs? Who even *does* that?

And what is stuck on the bottom of my shoe? It better not be gum.

Oh, God. It's worse. It's underwear.

I am *so* out of here.

I turn and bolt for the door. But Katarzyna is surprisingly strong . . . and fast. Before I can blink, she's got her long bony fingers clutched around my arm.

"Nuh-uh," she says, shaking her head in disapproval and making a *tsk* sound with her tongue. "You stay. And clean!" She snatches the uniform from my shoulder and thrusts it into my hands. Then she points at a door off to the side. "That bathroom," she huffs. "You change inside. Then you clean it."

I can't *believe* this woman. Doesn't she see how hungover I am? How pale and nearly *green* my skin is? I mean I'm practically on the verge of collapsing here!

"I'm sorry," I say woozily as I stumble over to the foot of the stairs and plop myself down. "But I have to rest a little. I don't feel so good."

But the minute my butt hits the floor it's being yanked up again. Her hand is back around my arm and she's now literally *dragging* me to the bathroom.

"Ow!" I whine once she releases me, rubbing my sore biceps. "That's gonna leave a mark."

With a deep, bitter scowl, I stand in the doorway of the bathroom and wait for my apology. It never comes. Instead the door slams in my face, about half an inch from the tip of my nose. Let's just say it's a good thing I got that nose job in the tenth grade, otherwise it would have been a direct hit.

After I've scowled and pouted in there for a good five minutes, there's a bang on the door, followed by a gruff, "Time's up! You change and clean. Or I call Luke!"

With a sigh, I grumpily slide out of my flapper dress, stuff it in my bag, and pull the blue-and-white-striped dress over my head, shoving my arms through the sleeves and yanking the hem down.

I turn and face myself in the mirror and instantly wish that I hadn't.

It's even worse than I thought.

The cut is terrible. The material is totally stiff and uncomfortable. Like it's made out of recycled newspaper or something.

My only salvation is the black, chin-length, 1920s-style wig, which I decide to keep on, although I do make the effort to straighten it so it looks a tad more realistic. If I'm going to have to wear this hideous uniform, the least I can do is disguise the rest of myself. Now when I look in the mirror I can *almost* fool myself into thinking it's not really me.

It's a small consolation prize, but I'll take it.

More pounding on the door. "You are cleaning, yes?"

"Yes!" I call back in annoyance.

I stare at my reflection for a few moments more. My expression is a sad mix of horror and desolation. I'm mourning my former life. Less than twelve hours ago I was dancing in the hottest club in Vegas, being catered to by gorgeous shirtless waiters pouring me champagne that costs more per bottle than most people's monthly rent, surrounded by the most beautiful and important people in the world, and wearing clothes personally designed for me by one of the most sought-after designers in the fashion industry.

And now I'm about to clean someone's toilet.

Fan-freaking-tastic.

I reluctantly turn and face the porcelain beast, reaching out my leg and using the toe of my shoe to hoist the lid from the seat. Without getting too close, I lean over to peer inside. Lining the bowl, there's a disgusting brownish-gray ring of I-don't-even-want-to-know-what.

Well, I guess that answers the question of whether my gag reflexes are working.

I scrounge around in my bucket until I come across a squirt bottle labeled *All-Purpose Cleaner.* Sounds pretty all-encompassing to me. With one arm covering my nose and mouth, I do a quick misting of the entire room—toilet bowl, sink, walls, mirror, and floor—flush the toilet with my foot, and then get the heck out of there.

"Okay!" I call, stepping back into the entry hall and closing the door hastily behind me. "I'm done with the bathroom!"

Katarzyna appears around a corner, holding a mop. She nods toward a red vacuum cleaner sitting in the foyer. "Good. Now you vacuum. Upstairs."

I groan and start for the stairs, lugging the vacuum behind me. It's freakishly heavy and bangs loudly against each wooden step.

"No!" Katarzyna screams from the bottom of the stairs. "Pick up! Pick up!"

I roll my eyes and heave on the giant machine until it's a few inches off the floor, and continue my climb.

The first room I come to looks like the bedroom of a thirteen-year-old girl. A very *messy* thirteen-year-old girl. I glance around at the pinned-up posters of various teen heartthrobs, posing shirtless with sexy, far-off stares. I find it ironic that half of those people were *at* my party in Vegas last night.

With a sigh, I search for an empty electrical socket and plug in the vacuum. Now I just have to figure out how to turn it on. There has to be a switch somewhere.

Switch. Switch. Switch.

Okay, how about a button?

Button. Button. Button.

How on earth are you supposed to work this thing?

I creep out to the hallway and peek over the banister. Katarzyna is on her hands and knees with a bucket of soapy water, scrubbing the unidentified animal footprints from the floor.

I tiptoe back into the room. Okay, definitely not asking her for help. She might make me switch jobs with her. And I'd much rather be in here—I glance again at the posters on the wall—among friends, than down there.

I whip out my cell phone, open the Internet browser, and Google *How to turn on a vacuum cleaner.* After a few minutes, I finally find a schematic of a device that looks similar to the one standing idle next to me. There's a small pedal on the left-hand side, labeled *On.*

I frown down at the live version in front of me, locate an identical pedal, and jam my foot downward on it. The vacuum roars to life, lurching out from under me. I spring forward to catch it.

Okay. That's done. Now. How do you *use* a vacuum cleaner?

A few more clicks through Google leads me to a YouTube video of some woman in heels and a 1950s-style swing dress pushing an old-fashioned vacuum cleaner with a broad smile painted across her fully made-up face.

That doesn't look so complicated. Just a little back-and-forth action and I'm done. I glance down at the floor in front of me and frown. I can barely even *see* the carpet. It's covered in junk. Clothes and knickknacks and papers and hair accessories.

Well, that's not *my* problem. If this stupid girl refuses to pick up her stuff, then too bad for her.

With a grunt and a heave, I start pushing the giant whining machine along the floor. It's not exactly as easy as the woman makes it seem in the video but then again, she had an empty floor to deal with. Mine is covered in crap. It's like trying to drive a Porsche over a bumpy mountain path that's usually reserved for SUVs and off-roading vehicles. But it's doing a pretty impressive job at sucking up everything. The smaller items—like socks, underwear, hair clips, and paper—go up without a fight. The larger stuff—like bras, skirts, DVDs, and jewelry—require a little more coaxing.

I stop and admire my handiwork.

Ahhh . . . now that's better.

I can see the carpet. It's baby pink. With several mysterious stains scattered throughout.

Either way, it's still a *major* improvement over—

Grrruppppppp!

What was that? That horrible retching sound. It was like the noise Holly once made after she accidentally swallowed an oversize bug and then tried to hack it up.

I turn around to see that the noise is coming from the vacuum cleaner. It's actually starting to convulse. And there's smoke emerging from the base. Okay, that could be a problem.

I dig out my phone and replay the YouTube video.

I definitely don't see any smoke there. And no vomiting sounds either. That woman still looks like she's having the time of her life with that vacuum. As if there's nothing in the world she'd rather be doing than pushing a carpet-cleaning machine back and forth all day.

She must be drunk.

Holy crap, that smoke really stinks. Like burned rubber mixed with body odor. I have to do something about that before

Katarzyna smells it and comes up here and starts screaming at me again. I glance around the room until my eyes land on a cup of water on the nightstand next to the princess-pink bed.

I lunge for it and dump it on the vacuum cleaner. The smoke instantly vanishes and I breathe a sigh of relief.

That is, until sparks start flying. And the wall socket begins to make a weird zapping sound. And then the entire house goes dark.

THE ULTIMATE DISGUISE

SO THE VACUUM CLEANER IS TOAST. AND KATAR-
zyna is *really* pissed. She's been cursing me in Polish for the last
fifteen minutes. At least I *assume* those are curse words. The only
thing I've really been able to get, from the bits and pieces of English
she throws in from time to time, is that you're *not* supposed to
vacuum *over* things, but rather pick them up first.

Well, how on earth was I supposed to know that? She just said
vacuum! Am I expected to be *born* with inherent vacuuming
knowledge? The least she could have done is give me a few point-
ers before feeding me to the wolves.

I'm guessing she's already come to a similar conclusion because
after she manages to find the circuit breaker, get the power in
the house turned back on, and salvage the sucked-up items from
the inside of the vacuum bag, she doesn't leave my side for the rest
of the day. She stands above me, barking orders like a drill ser-
geant. Making me scrub floors and sinks and toilets and glass
coffee tables over and over again until there isn't a single micro-
organism alive anywhere.

At about two o'clock, we're nearly finished. Katarzyna is

watching me as I dust the living room when I hear a door slam shut and then the patter of footsteps running through the foyer.

I stare wide-eyed at Katarzyna who gives me a look that says *keep dusting.*

A refrigerator door opens and closes in the distant kitchen and then a small girl with thick wavy hair and braces comes trotting into the living room and jumps onto the couch. She props her dirty tennis shoes on the coffee table that I just spent the better half of an hour cleaning and starts slurping away at her drink.

I look to Katarzyna again, this time with fury in my eyes, but she flashes me the same look.

Then the girl pulls out a magazine, opens it up, and starts reading. I nearly gasp when I see that it's the latest issue of *Tattle,* one of the most popular tabloid magazines in the country. And who do you think is on the freaking cover? Yep, that's right. Yours truly.

It's a shot of me taken right after I pulled myself out of my crashed Mercedes on Sunset. Of course I look like crap.

I stand frozen in place as I watch the oblivious preteen sip on soda and hungrily devour page after page of the periodical.

Then, for the first time since she scampered into the house, she looks up at me. Our eyes meet and the most horrific, terrified panic rockets through my entire body.

This is it. This is the end. Now this stupid little girl is going to whip out her cell phone, call her best friend, and start gabbing: *You won't believe this but* Lexington Larrabee *is cleaning my house right now! No . . . the Lexington Larrabee. I swear it's her! She's got the maid's uniform and everything!* And before you know it, the paparazzi will be swarming the place like a SWAT team at a hostage situation and then *bam!* there's a picture of me wearing *this* god-awful thing on the *next* cover of *Tattle*.

I wonder if I can convince them it was all a joke. That I'm staging some huge prank or something. Or better yet, acting out the wager of a lost bet. There's got to be a believable explanation for this.

"What?" the girl asks snidely, scrunching up her nose. And when I don't reply—or blink—she gets even more annoyed and goes, "What are you looking at?"

"Uh," I say quickly, coming out of my trance and ducking my head down, suddenly very engrossed in dusting a nearby vase, "nothing."

I glance up from under my lashes long enough to see the girl roll her eyes and go back to her magazine as a staggering, mind-blowing revelation sucker punches me in the gut.

She doesn't recognize me.

I'm standing right in front of her and she doesn't even *freaking* recognize me.

My mind is reeling. Caught in an agonizing internal battle between feeling relieved and feeling totally insulted. I'm never *not* recognized. Even when I try to go incognito and fly under the radar, I'm still eventually identified and photographed.

Katarzyna looks intriguingly from me to the magazine cover, her mind clearly following a direct path to the source of my tormented expression.

Then she leans in close to me and, in a tone that can *almost* be described as sympathetic, whispers the simple yet illuminating explanation that I couldn't come up with on my own: "No one notices the help."

CLICK HERE TO PLAY MESSAGE

Or read the free transcript from our automated speech-to-text service below.

[BEGIN TRANSCRIPT]

What up, Luke? Lucas. The Lukinator. It's me, Lexi. You said I could use any format to submit my status report so I decided to send it to you in a video message. I chose this format partly because it's how my generation communicates—e-mail is *soooo* last decade—but mostly because I really don't feel like typing. And even if I *did*, I don't think I'd be physically able to.

See this? See all these little white bandages on my fingers? Those are from the iron. Yes, the *ir-on*. As in what you use to remove wrinkles from clothing. Whoever invented that thing is a masochist. Here's a question. Why don't they just make clothes that don't get wrinkled? I mean seriously, how hard is that? We've landed a man on the moon and no one can invent a stupid shirt that doesn't wrinkle? What is wrong with this picture?

There. There's my insight for the day. Enlightening, isn't it?

And what else was it that I was supposed to include in these stupid little status reports of yours? Oh, right. My deep and profound life lessons. Okay, fine. You wanna know what I learned this week, working as a slave? Oh, sorry, I mean, a *maid*.

I learned how to clean out a refrigerator! Hoorah!

Now *there's* something that's going to come in handy in my future. If I'm ever at a party and there's a life-or-death refrigerator-cleaning emergency, I've got it completely under control. Everyone else will be running around screaming their heads off and I'll be like, *Don't panic! I've been properly trained!*

[Unidentified sound]

Oh. That's my cell phone ringing. I'm not going to answer it. It's probably my friends calling, asking if I want to go out. But can I go out? No. Because I've got these unsightly bruises all over my body. See this one on my arm? A coffee table did that. And see this scratch on my face? Right here under my chin? That's courtesy of a very hostile set of vertical blinds. Oh and don't forget these scabs I have on my knees from scrubbing four thousand square feet of Spanish-tile floors. Do you think I can honestly show up at a club like this?

Not to mention how sore I am after forty freaking hours of cleaning, scraping, squeegeeing, mopping, dusting, polishing, vacuuming, ironing, *and* laundering. I can barely walk, let alone get dressed. Let alone dance on tabletops.

So instead I'm just going to lie here in my room all weekend like a loser. I hope that makes you and my father very, very happy. I hope you're both pleased to know that your little Operation Let's Make Lexi's Life Miserable is a *huge* success.

So that's it. That's the official report on my status. I hope it exceeds your wildest expectations. I'm going to bed now. At eight o'clock at night. Like a two-year-old.

Wait. I just remembered something else. I do have one more insight to report. I realized something this week. I had an *epiphany*. Are you ready for this? Are you sure? Okay, here it goes:

It turns out I have not one, not two, but *fifty-two* reasons to hate my father, and Majestic Maids Cleaning Services is the first.

[END TRANSCRIPT]

BEDTIME

I CLOSE MY LAPTOP AND DRAG MY TIRED, BRUISED, and battered body to the bed, collapsing onto it like a sack of dirt. Holly hops up her custom-made, red carpeted staircase and lies down beside me.

Do people really do this *every* single week of their lives?

How do their limbs not fall off?

My phone rings again, and again I ignore it. The thought of my friends out there on the town having a blast without me makes me want to cry. I can't remember the last time (or the first time, for that matter) that I haven't been in the mood to go out. I'm Lexington Larrabee. Going out is what I do. It's who I am.

Not anymore, apparently.

I suppose the good news is now I don't have to worry about bumping into Mendi again.

The phone rings a third time. I finally locate it in the tangle of sheets and turn off the ringer. Then I crumble back into the bed with a whimper.

Holly picks up her head and stares at me curiously, her tall butterfly ears at full attention.

"I know," I tell her with a sigh. "It's pathetic."

She rises to her feet, pads over to me, and lies back down with her head resting on my stomach.

"Thanks," I say with a weak smile. "I knew you'd understand."

Twenty minutes later, I'm just drifting to sleep when there's a knock on my door.

"Go away!" I call to the unwanted visitor.

But the door opens anyway and in flounce Jia and T, dressed to go out. They skip over and plop down on either side of me. I groan and pull a pillow over my head. "Who let you in?"

"Señor Horatio," T answers cheerfully. "Now get your bum out of bed and put on something cute. We're going to Mist tonight."

"No," I say through the pillow. "I'm not going anywhere."

"Lex," Jia warns. "You can't hide from Mendi your whole life. This is *your* town, remember. You have to get out there and claim it!"

"This is *not* about Mendi," comes my muffled yet resolved response.

Jia lets out an exasperated sigh and pulls the pillow from my face and the covers from my body. They both gasp in shock at the sight of the bruised and battered shell of a person underneath.

"Bloody hell!" T exclaims. "What happened to you?"

"I cleaned houses for five straight days this week."

"That's what that smell is," Jia says with a satisfied nod, like she'd been trying to figure it out since she pranced through the door.

"Did you clean them or do battle with them?" T asks.

I manage a weak laugh. "A little of both, I suppose." I pull the covers back over myself. "So, as you can see, I'm in no condition to leave the house."

My two friends glance at each other and exchange consenting nods. "Have fun for me," I mumble to them.

There's a heavy silence in the room. I know they haven't left yet because I can still feel the weight of their slender frames sitting on either side of me. But there's something about the way the air moves around my head and the mattress shifts ever so lightly underneath me that tells me they're motioning to each other.

My eyes flutter open and I see T shaking her head, crossing and uncrossing her hands in an adamant gesture, and mouthing something that looks like *Not now*.

When she notices me looking up at her, her hands instantly fall to her lap and a fake smile hurries its way to her lips.

"What?" I ask.

"Nothing," T says quickly, reaching down to stroke my hair. I jerk my head away.

"She deserves to know," Jia argues in her infamous let's-get-down-to-business voice.

"Yes, but she can know tomorrow. After she's had a good rest. She's clearly knackered and—"

"She'll find out eventually!" Jia interrupts. "Better we be here for moral support when she does."

"Will you guys shut up and tell me already," I command.

T exhales loudly and turns her attention back to me. "It's your father, love."

"What about my father?" I ask, looking suspiciously between the two of them.

"He's . . ." T tries. "Well, he's . . ."

Jia eventually cuts her off with an impatient sigh, grabs the remote off my nightstand, and flips on the TV.

The familiar sounds and voices of *Access Hollywood* fill the room. On the screen, video footage of my father and his latest fling, Rêve, is playing. They're on the red carpet of some black-tie benefit. He's flashing his usual reserved yet respectable smile while his date, decked out in a long, sweeping red Valentino gown, beams and waves at the cameras like she's riding a freaking parade float.

The slick voice of the *Access Hollywood* host pipes in. "Spokespeople for the Larrabee family made the official announcement earlier today after the pair returned from a romantic two-day trip to Paris. The date is not yet set but the event is expected to take place later this year."

I feel a cold chill run down my spine.

Jia mutes the volume and tosses the remote back onto the nightstand. "He's engaged."

MOOD DE-HANCING SUBSTANCES

A HORN HONKS IMPATIENTLY OUTSIDE ON
Monday morning as I slip on my second Emilio Pucci espadrille. I
hum gleefully to myself as I go about my morning routine, taking
my time finishing my makeup and selecting my accessories. I riffle
through my jewelry box and hold up a long teardrop earring,
promptly ruling it out when I see how it clashes with my new wig.

After the close call last week, I've decided to purchase a new
one for every job. To keep my disguise fresh. And as a little treat to
myself each week. If I'm going to have to endure this torture for
an entire year, at least I can *try* to have some fun with it. Plus, I
figure it's a good way of mentally distancing myself from what I'm
being forced to do. For instance, today, I'm not Lexington Larrabee going off to work God knows where doing God knows what,
I'm *Cassandra*, the fiery redhead with long, luscious wavy locks
who looks like she's ready to race off to a newscaster audition at any
moment.

I found this awesome wig warehouse online and started or-
dering from it. Now it's like I get to be a different person every
week of the year!

The horn honks again.

I hum louder to drown out the noise and open one of my cabinets, rummaging through stuff until I find a bottle of clear nail polish. I give my French manicure a quick top coat, blowing on my fingertips, and holding out my hands to admire my work.

It took my manicurist nearly *three* hours to fix the mess that those cleaning chemicals made of my nails. And the masseuse who had to work on my tightly knotted muscles? She's probably undergoing hand surgery right this minute. The poor thing.

But the good news is I feel great. Refreshed and renewed.

My father can do whatever he wants. He can marry twenty-nine-year-old gold diggers and hire obnoxious liaisons to pick me up in the morning and drop me off at night but he can't (and won't) break my spirit. I got a nice little emergency pep talk from my shrink over the weekend and he kindly reminded me that I have total power over my own emotions. I can't control what other people do or say. I can only control how I react to those things.

And I realized that I've been reacting the *entirely* wrong way.

I've been so busy whining about my lot in life, I haven't even stopped to think about how I might be able to improve it. I've been so distracted by tacky uniforms and chipped manicures that I completely forgot about the *one* redeemable trait that I did manage to inherit from my father: the ability to think outside the box. The ability to *strategize*.

And strategize I have. Today I go into battle with a new plan of attack. A plan that is sure to get me through the next fifty-one weeks with my dignity, reputation . . . and manicure intact.

It's quite brilliant if I do say so myself. And so obvious, I'm honestly not sure why I didn't think of it before. Probably because I was so blinded and dazed by those toxic cleaning chemicals, I couldn't even think straight.

Hooooonnnnk!

It sounds like someone has laid a dead body on the car horn. I roll my eyes—some people are *so* dramatic—and toss a change of clothes into my bag. The weatherman on TV is going on and on about what a beautiful day it's going to be today. "Perfect beach weather," he chirps enthusiastically. "Don't forget to pack your sunscreen!"

There's a knock on my bedroom door. I zap the TV off with the remote and call casually, "Come in!"

Horatio stands in the doorway, looking quite perturbed (although it's so subtle, you'd have to have lived with him as long as I have to recognize it). Holly gives a happy little bark, runs over to him, and jumps against his shins. He lifts her up and tucks her under his arm.

"Yes, Horatio?"

He flashes me a tight smile. "It would appear you have a visitor waiting outside."

"Oh, would it?" I ask innocently, bending sideways to finger-comb my new red locks in the mirror of my vanity. "I hadn't even noticed."

I can see the reflection of Horatio's face in the mirror and I know that he's not buying my doe-eyed act for a second. I do feel bad that he has to be a casualty in this three-way battle between me, Luke, and my father, but as they say, all is fair in love and war.

Hoooooooooooooooooonk!

I wait for the cringe-worthy noise to stop before saying in a syrupy tone, "You can tell him I'll be right down."

Horatio nods and turns to leave with Holly still in his arms.

"Wait!" I call, and he stops. I rush over to him and lean down to caress Holly's precious face. "Bye-bye, baby," I coo softly. "Mommy will miss you today. Yes, she will."

Horatio waits patiently while I fawn over her before finally planting one long, parting smooch on the top of her head.

I stand up straight and address Horatio. "Thanks for taking such good care of her."

He bows and turns to leave, grumbling under his breath, *"Los perros no están en mi contrato."*

"I know it's not in your contract, Horatio," I reply sweetly. "That's why I appreciate it *soooo* much!"

He shakes his head and keeps walking.

"Aren't you glad you made me watch all those Spanish soap operas with you when I was growing up?" I call after him, but he doesn't respond.

After another neighborhood-shaking honk from Luke, I sigh, grab my bag, and head for the stairs.

"Good morning, Luke," I say politely as I strut down the front walkway of the house. "How are you today?"

"Thanks for getting out here so quickly," he mumbles.

I smile cheerfully as I slide into the passenger seat. "You're welcome."

His eyes glide over my outfit, lingering at my new hair for a moment before continuing to my feet. He shakes his head. "You might want to put on some more comfortable shoes for this week's assignment."

I glance down at my toes and can't help but smile at the cute little daisies my manicurist painted on my nails. "What are you talking about? These are Pucci *espadrilles*."

He gives me a blank look.

"Espadrilles are *known* for their comfort."

"Whatever," Luke mutters. "They're your feet."

I buckle my seat belt and continue admiring my pedicure. He's right. These *are* my feet. And thanks to my brilliant new strategy, I don't plan on being on them much today.

I can feel Luke's eyes boring into the side of my head and I turn to see him staring at me with a suspicious expression.

"What?"

His eyes narrow. "What's with you?"

I shrug. "I don't know. What's with *you*?"

"You're . . ." He searches for the right word. "Pleasant."

I chuckle at his baffled expression. "I'm always pleasant."

I can see an internal battle raging inside him. He's fighting back some kind of offensive remark—deliberating between taking advantage of this prime opportunity to insult me and holding his tongue in order to sustain my unexpected demeanor.

I could honestly care less what he does. He's not going to affect my mood. Not today. There's nothing he can do to spoil the good day that I have in store.

Not even when he starts that agonizingly long predeparture procedure that he does before he can go anywhere. Normally it drives me insane. The way he has to check every mirror three times, fiddle with air-conditioning dials to get the absolute perfect temperature, and verify that his windshield wipers are in proper working order—*twice*—before he can even put the car in drive. But today I sit patiently in my seat, humming quietly to myself until it's time to leave.

I don't even have to fight the urge to tell him that the chances his windshield wipers have stopped working or his mirrors have been mysteriously realigned between his house and mine are about five billion to one. Like I have to every other day.

Nope. Today, it's *all* good.

"So, what's with the good mood?" Luke asks once we're on the freeway, heading into the valley. "Did Louis Vuitton release a new overpriced, sweatshop-manufactured handbag?"

I smirk. "Not that I've heard. But if they do, I'll be sure to pick one up for you."

"A new club opening this weekend?" He ventures another guess.

"Nope."

"So, are you going to tell me, or do I have to keep guessing?"

I turn and face him. "Can't I just be in a good mood?"

He glances at me out of the corner of his eye. "No. *You* can't. Anyone else, sure. But not you."

I cross my arms over my chest in mock offense. "And why not me?"

"Because you're Lexington Larrabee. Lexington Larrabee doesn't simply wake up in a good mood. She has to have just cause. There have to be outside forces at work."

My mock offense quickly slips into real offense. "That's not true!"

"Of course it's true," he begins knowingly, like he's a college professor about to start his daily lecture to a hall full of eagerly awaiting students. "You're all about external motivators. Needing something on the outside to make you feel good on the inside. It's like some kind of modified codependency."

I scrunch my nose at him. "Well, thank you, Dr. Carver. I didn't realize you were also a shrink."

"I'm double majoring in psychology," he informs me. "I thought it would be a nice supplement to my business degree. If you're going to run large corporations one day, you need to be able to get inside your employees' heads."

I snort. "And where is this? *Harvard*?"

He suddenly looks forlorn and the arrogance in his voice drops out. "No. Harvard wouldn't give me a scholarship. USC offered me a full ride. Plus a chance to do a work-study program at your father's company this year. So I enrolled there. Harvard was my first choice, though."

"Of course it was," I mumble. "But regardless, you're wrong about me. I don't *need* external whatevers to feel good about myself. I feel good about myself all the time."

He shoots me a skeptical look. "Sure."

"I do!" I screech back. "And why wouldn't I? I'm Lexington Larrabee! In case you haven't heard, I'm worth twenty-five million dollars!"

"Well, not yet, anyway," Luke points out, his irritating smugness instantly returning.

"Fine. But I *will* be."

"And what if you weren't?" he inquires.

"What if I weren't what?"

"What if you weren't Lexington Larrabee? What if you weren't going to be worth twenty-five million dollars? Would you still feel good about yourself?"

"Yes," I say hastily, my chest burning with a familiar rage. "Not that it's any of your business what makes me feel good."

An awkward silence falls over the car as I quietly seethe in the passenger seat. Then Luke glances over at me and a sneaky smile appears on his lips. "Uh-oh."

"What?" I growl, my face flushing.

"Looks like I ruined your mood."

LEXI CAPONE

LUKE CARVER IS THE DEVIL. NO. WAIT. HE'S THE devil's *apprentice*. Which is way worse. Because the devil's apprentice *knows* how evil the devil is—he's heard the rumors about his immorality and heartlessness and cruelty—and yet he signs on to work for him just the same. He *chooses* to be like him. To dress like him. To talk like him. To follow in his callous footsteps. And that makes him even more wicked, even more abominable than the devil himself.

As we continue to drive, I tell myself to take deep breaths. I remind myself about the brilliant plan I've concocted and slowly my anger starts to subside. Just the thought of outmaneuvering Bruce, my father, and his annoying psychology-double-majoring protégé is enough to make the fire blazing in my chest simmer down and restore a blithe smile to my face.

Twenty minutes later we arrive in the remote suburb of Santa Clarita.

"What are we doing way out here?" I ask with a scowl.

"When appropriate your father has specifically chosen remote locations to minimize your risk of being recognized. He doesn't want the press involved in this."

I instinctively touch my wig. "Well, that's *one* thing we have in common," I remark with a snort.

"Studies have shown that people don't often recognize things when they're out of context," Luke explains, sliding right back into that annoyingly pretentious tone of his.

I think about that bratty little girl at the house last week with her dirty shoes and the *Tattle* magazine with my picture on the cover. I was right in front of her face and I might as well have been invisible. "So I've noticed," I murmur.

Luke navigates through the wide tree-lined streets until finally pulling into a giant parking lot housing a supermarket, an all-you-can eat Italian restaurant chain, a salon offering haircuts for twelve dollars, and one of those bargain clothing stores that has the nerve to call Liz Claiborne a designer label.

"So," I say breezily, "at which one of these fine establishments will I be spending my week?"

Luke nods at the anchor store in the center—an enormous Albertsons supermarket.

"Let me guess. Grocery bagger?"

Luke reaches into the backseat and pulls the file labeled *Job #2* from his briefcase and flips it open. "Actually you'll be doing a little of everything."

I smile enthusiastically and give him a thumbs-up. "Even better."

"Your assignment this week," he continues, "is to successfully complete a rotation through every department within the store. That includes bakery, deli, meat, seafood, produce, *and* dry foods."

"Sounds practical," I say, nodding with approval. "A very well-rounded schedule. Nicely done."

Luke flashes me a cut-the-crap look. "Okay. What gives?"

I open my eyes wide. "What do you mean?"

"Last week you moaned and groaned every single day and now suddenly you're little Miss Sunshine?"

"What can I say," I respond, with a shrug and a sweet smile. "I've decided to change my approach to things."

He's clearly not buying it but I don't really care. I click off my seat belt, grab my bag, and step out of the car. "What time will you be picking me up?" I ask.

"Six," Luke replies.

"Perfect."

"Ask for Neil when you get inside. He's the one who's supervising you this week."

I give him a quick salute and toss the bag over my shoulder. "Neil. Got it."

Luke shoots me one last distrustful look, which I respond to with a sugary smile before turning on the toes of my espadrilles and striding into the store.

Normally when I walk into a supermarket—or any other store for that matter—the world tends to stop spinning. People halt what they're doing, carts are absentmindedly released and left to run into giant displays of canned goods, and cash registers stop chiming. All eyes look up. Then the whispering starts, followed quickly by the requests for autographs. Cell phone cameras are whipped out and a frenzy of furious texting and Twittering begins.

Not today though. Today I get to experience what it's like for a normal person to walk into a supermarket. And I'll tell you, it's pretty anticlimactic.

Absolutely nothing happens. The world just keeps on turning.

I stand there for a few minutes, taking it in, before a tall, skinny, forty-something man in a black vest comes up to me and says, "You must be Lexi."

"Nuh-uh," I correct him, holding up one finger. "This week I'll be going by the name *Cassandra*." Then I give him a sly wink. "Aliases are important for protecting one's true identity."

He looks highly uninterested. "Sure. Fine. Whatever."

I squint at his name tag. "Neil?"

He nods. "Welcome to Albertsons. C'mon. We'll get you set up."

I follow him through the store to a small office in the back. He opens a metal locker behind his desk and starts flipping through a stack of white collared shirts and black vests like the one he's wearing. He stops long enough to peer around the locker door at me. "What size shirt do you wear? Small?"

"Actually," I say, taking command of the situation, "a uniform won't be necessary today."

"No?" he asks, genuinely confused.

I shake my head and reach into my bag, producing a large bundle of hundred-dollar bills (a generous loan from Jia) and setting it down on the desk between us. "No."

Neil jumps back slightly at the sight of it. As if I've just dropped a dead rat in front of him, as opposed to a giant wad of cash.

"What's that?" he asks in a wavering voice.

"Ten thousand dollars," I reply matter-of-factly.

Neil slowly sets down the black vest and reaches out to touch the tightly wrapped bundle with the tip of his index finger. As if checking to make sure it is real.

"What's it for?"

I shrug. "I don't know. To feed your children. Buy something nice for your wife. Whatever you want it to be for."

He looks anxiously at the open door behind me. "But Luke already paid me."

I turn and close the office door. "This isn't between you and Luke. It's between you and *me*." I look at him purposefully, holding his eye. "*Only* you and me."

Wow, I'm really good at this. I sound like I'm in a mob movie or something. I guess there's at least one upside to having Richard Larrabee's DNA running through my bloodstream.

Neil's face is still a giant question mark. I kind of feel bad for him. He looks so lost and out of his element.

"You see, I think there's a way we can help each other," I explain.

He nods, taking it all in.

I continue. "I need a report at the end of the week saying that I completed five days of working here. And you"—I glance around the small, cluttered office—"seeing that you work at a supermarket, I'm guessing need money."

I wait for the comprehension to register in his eyes. When he continues to hesitate, I push further. "Do you have kids?" I ask.

"Four."

I nod, trying to look contemplative. "Hmm. Sounds rough."

He blinks. No response.

"And expensive."

More silence.

"So, do we have a deal?"

I can see the gears in his brain clicking away but still he doesn't utter a single word. That's okay though. He doesn't have to say anything. As soon as I watch him slide the money off the desk and deposit it into his pants pocket, I know what the answer is.

It was an offer he couldn't refuse.

With a smug smile, I stroll out of the office, back through the store, and out the front doors. I slide my sunglasses over my eyes, whip out my cell phone, and call the number I programmed in last night.

"Yes, hello," I say cheerfully. "I need a car service from Santa Clarita to Malibu."

"Certainly," comes a friendly, accommodating voice. "Do you have an account with us?"

"No. I'll be paying cash."

"Of course. We can have a car out to you in fifteen minutes."

"Perfect." I give her the address of the store, click off the phone, and slide it into my pocket.

I pull a large straw sun hat out of my bag and place it on my head with a purposeful tap. I gaze up at the sky and squint gleefully into the beautiful southern California sun.

The weatherman was right. It's a perfect day for the beach.

NEVER UNDERESTIMATE
A LARRABEE

MWAHAHAHAHAHAHAHAHAHAHA!

In case you couldn't tell, that's my diabolical I-outsmarted-my-father-and-his-brownnosing-intern-page-boy laugh. I would do it aloud right here in the parking lot of the Albertsons supermarket but I don't really want to draw any unnecessary attention to myself. Not when I'm *this* close to getting the heck out of here.

That was easy. Almost *too* easy. I'm *almost* offended that my father and his minion think so little of me. That they so terribly underestimate me. Well, serves them right, then. They deserve to be duped.

When I told Jia and T my plan, they were more than happy to front me the cash to get me through the next fifty-one weeks. They know I'm good for the money. I mean, I *do* have a twenty-five-million-dollar check coming my way. I even offered to pay them interest on their investment but neither one of them would have it.

So all I have to do now is keep paying off struggling supervisor after struggling supervisor until the year is over and then it's *au revoir* Larrabee Family, *bonjour* trust fund!

I keep one eye on my cell phone to check the time and the other on the parking lot in expectation of my transportation. Cars come and go as the slew of suburban housewives tackle their weekly shopping lists. I told Jia and T I'd meet them at eleven at my father's beach-front condo in Malibu.

I quickly tap out a text message to Jia to let them know that my plan was a grand success. A horn honks just as I'm pressing send and I sling my bag over my shoulder and start for the curb. But when I look up, I'm dismayed to see that it's not, in fact, the black limousine with tinted windows that I ordered but rather a small silver sedan.

A very *familiar* silver sedan.

A silver sedan I was just riding in less than an hour ago.

Crap.

The passenger-side window rolls down and Luke's face appears. "Going somewhere?"

"No," I say, pretending to have absolutely no idea what he's talking about. "I was just getting some air." I wave a hand in front of my face for effect. "It's really stuffy in there!"

"Mmm hmm." Luke is clearly not fooled by my little hot-flash performance. "Get in," he commands.

I huff out a sigh and reluctantly slide into the passenger seat. "Yes?"

"I have something to show you." He reaches behind him and pulls his briefcase from the backseat. Then he takes out a Larrabee Media monogrammed laptop and opens it.

I feign impatience. "Will this take very long? I kind of have to go. I have a lot of work to do in there, you know? Bagging groceries and everything."

"Mmm hmm," he says again, tapping away at the keyboard.

I discreetly glance out the windshield for signs of my car service.

"It's not coming," Luke says, without looking up from the screen.

"What are you talking about?"

"Your car," he replies nonchalantly. "It's not coming."

I make a *pfff* sound with my mouth to indicate that he's clearly lost it. "What car?"

"The one you ordered and I canceled."

"What?" I cry. "Why would you do . . . How did you—"

He interrupts me by pushing the computer into my lap and pressing a button.

A grainy black-and-white image fills the screen. It looks kind of familiar. Then I gasp as I realize that it's the back office of the store that I left only a few minutes ago. And it's not just an image. It's a *video*. The door swings open and in walks Neil followed by me. I watch in horror as the scene I just lived replays right before my eyes.

"You were spying on me!" I scream in disgust.

"I find *monitoring* to be a more accurate term."

"It's *spying*," I protest. "And it's unacceptable."

"The store is already equipped with cameras," Luke explains. "We were just given access to the feed."

My eyes open wide with horror. "Does Neil know that?"

Luke nods solemnly. "Yes, which is why he called me the minute you left."

I can feel my stomach start to boil. "That rat!"

Luke laughs at my reaction. "Oh, Lex," he condescends. "Did you honestly think you could outsmart me? Your father?" He flashes me a patronizing smile. "Please."

I seethe in silence, my chest rising and falling in rapid, shallow breaths.

"Your father warned me that you'd try everything in your power to get out of having to work. Which is why I told all the supervisors in advance that they were to report any bribe attempts or other methods of evasion on your part. And which is why I got permission to tap your cell phone. It's also equipped with a GPS tracking device, so I wouldn't try to go anywhere if I were you." He cocks his head to the side, his expression suddenly pensive. "I guess now I understand your good mood this morning."

The anger is rising up. Just like it always does. I clutch the laptop in my hands and eye the open window next to me. With a distressed battle cry, I launch the computer up in the air and aim for the sidewalk. It leaves my hands and I watch anxiously for the collision. The satisfying crunch of Larrabee Media–issued technology smashing against pavement.

But it never comes. And that's when I realize that Luke grabbed the laptop from my hands right before I hurled it toward the open window.

I turn around to see him calmly closing the lid and returning it to his briefcase. As if removing computers from the hands of would-be electronics assassins is all in a day's work for him.

"Your father also warned me about your temper," Luke states in a composed tone.

With a furious grunt, I jerk on the door handle and push the door open with my feet. "You know," I screech as I scramble back onto the curb, "for someone who's never around, my father sure knows a heck of a lot about me!"

"Enjoy your shift!" Luke calls out.

I slam the door and stalk back into the store. I don't stop moving until I find Neil in the bread aisle, marking items with an electronic pricing gun.

I shove my open hand in his face and growl, "I want my money back."

CLICK <u>HERE</u> TO PLAY MESSAGE

Or read the free transcript from our automated speech-to-text service below.

[BEGIN TRANSCRIPT]

I know, I know. I haven't done a status report in over a month. Blah blah blah. You tell me every single time I get in the car. So fine. Here it is. Your new video message status report.

In case you couldn't tell from these horrific bags under my eyes, I'm a little tired right now. Can you see them? Can you see the bags? How about when I lean into the camera like this? Now can you see them? You shouldn't have a problem. They're epic.

That's probably because I spent the last month in hell. And I don't really feel like rehashing all the glorious moments of torture with you but I know, I have to. Because this is a status report. And I'm supposed to report on my status. And if I don't comply with your requirements, you'll have to report me to my father.

Did you like my impression of you just then? Pretty good, huh? I've been practicing.

So anyway . . . Wait, hold on . . . I have something disgusting under my nail. Ick! What *is* that? I don't even wanna know.

Okay. So job #2 was at Albertsons. What did I learn from Mr. Albertson? Well, I learned to always check for hidden cameras when you attempt to bribe someone. I learned that it's physically impossible to push a train of forty shopping carts through a parking lot in Pucci espadrilles . . . without falling on your face, that is. Oh, I also learned that you're not supposed to use cake icing to spell out obscenities or draw distasteful images on children's birthday cakes. And for the record, I don't know what Neil told you but that was not a picture of what he thought it was. It was supposed to be two people playing leapfrog. Just wanna clear that up.

Job #3 was . . . What was it again? Oh right. Cleaning horse stalls at that stable in Malibu. Sorry, I've tried to block that one from my memory. Although I found the experience very metaphorical. My life having literally turned to crap. Horse crap, that is. So there's my insight on that.

Then I worked at the doughnut shop where I learned how to wake up at 3:30 in the freaking morning. Every day. To do what, you might ask? Something exciting? Oh, yes! I woke up at the crack of dawn to knead dough! Thrilling, isn't it? And you wouldn't guess it just by looking at it, but doughnut dough is sticky. It gets places. Places I don't even want to talk about.

After that came the exciting week of washing dishes at that Chinese restaurant. And I learned that [unidentifiable word] in Chinese means hurry the [expletive deleted] up. At least that's what I could deduce from the context and the frequency of use. I guess that might come in handy the next time I'm in Beijing. So thank you! Thanks, Luke! Thanks, Daddy! I really *am* learning useful things.

That was sarcasm, by the way. In case they don't have that on your planet.

All right, where was I? Oh, yes. Job #6. Hold on, let me get my handy little list out.

Here it is. See? This is the official list. Kindly faxed over by my good friend Bruce. Here, I'll hold it closer to the camera. Can you see it now? If you'll notice, I've crossed out the original title and written in a new one. It's now called the 52-Reasons-to-Hate-My-Father list. And currently we're on reason #6. The cemetery. Digging graves for a week. Creepy. Very, very creepy. Although . . .

Oh, wait a sec. I just got an e-mail. It's from my friends Jia and T. Do you know where they are? They're where I'm supposed to be right now. On a private yacht, cruising around the Mediterranean. They left three weeks ago. Isn't that just the cherry on top of the whole yummy-delicious crap sundae that has become my life?

Ooh, they're in Santorini this week. How lovely. Look, they've even included a photograph. Check out that crystal-blue water? Isn't it beautiful? It says, *Miss you. Love you. Wish you were here.* Yeah, that makes three of us.

Wait, I have another picture to show you. Hold on, let me bring it up on my phone. Okay, here it is. Here's me, after working the graveyard shift . . . literally . . . *at* the graveyard. Notice the shovel in my hand and the dirt. It's pretty much everywhere, isn't it? Notice the expression on my face. That's the face of misery. In case you couldn't tell.

So what did I learn from that experience? I learned that I would like to be cremated.

[END TRANSCRIPT]

COLD FRONT

I'M NOT GOING," I VOW AS I LIE FACEDOWN ON my unmade bed. This is generally what my weekends have become, by the way. Forty-eight hours of lying motionless on my bed (or in the bathtub) while my muscles and joints attempt to recuperate from the horrors of my most recent job.

And with my friends off cruising around the Mediterranean without me, there's not much else for me to do. The day they left was pretty much the worst day of my life. They offered to stay but I wouldn't let them. What would be the point? Just because I have to suffer doesn't mean they should have to also.

But I'm seriously starting to regret that heroic decision of mine because now I have no one. I'm utterly alone. And the last thing I want to do right now is be social. Especially at an event like this.

"It's your father's *engagement* party," Caroline reminds me with an impatient *tap tap tap* of her foot.

"Exactly."

She huffs and pulls another dress from the wardrobe rack my stylist wheeled in last night. "What about this one? This one looks nice."

I don't look up. "I said I'm not going."

"You have to go," Caroline insists in her nasally French accent. "The entire press corps will be there."

"How romantic," I mumble.

"It is your duty to this family to be photographed next to your father and his fiancée on the day of their engagement party."

"Will I also have to be photographed next to them on the day of their divorce?"

Caroline sighs and returns the dress to the rack, exchanging it for another. "Now, this one is *gorgeous*. You will look fantastic in this!" Her fake enthusiasm is so transparent I nearly gag.

I roll onto my back and pull the covers to my chin. Holly emerges from the balcony where she's been stalking a squirrel, bounds up her red carpeted staircase, and curls up next to me. "Spare me the flattery, Caroline. I'm not getting out of this bed."

"But the guests are going to start arriving in an hour. The twins are flying in from New York. *People* wants an exclusive with you and your brothers, and we're setting up a beautiful shot of the whole family in the gardens."

The thought of that bimbo being photographed in my *mother's* gardens makes me want to hit something. Or some*one*.

"If Cooper doesn't have to be there, then neither do I."

"Cooper," Caroline growls back, "is feeding starving children in the Sudan. He gets enough good publicity for this family. You, on the other hand, after that little stunt you pulled with the convenience store, are in serious publicity deficit. Your father's working on a big upcoming merger and we need all the good press we can get to make sure the stockholders are on board. So why don't you get up, put on something the photographers will like, get your butt downstairs, and do your part, okay?"

I pull my cell phone off my nightstand and start scrolling through the latest tweets on my Twitter app. "Thanks, but I'll pass."

"Fine," Caroline snaps, brusquely returning the hanger to the rack. "Lie there all night. See if I care." Then she storms out the door.

I should have known she wouldn't give up that easily. I should have known she'd send in reinforcements. I just didn't realize she'd go all the way to the top to get them.

Ten minutes later, my father stalks through the door. He doesn't even knock. He just comes right in and stands in the middle of the room with his arms crossed over his chest. I jump at the sight of him. I can't even remember the last time my father set foot in my bedroom. He looks terribly out of place. Like a skyscraper in the middle of a meadow.

"Lexington, quit the performance. Get up and get dressed," he commands sternly.

I don't respond. I conceal my shock at him being there with stubborn silence.

"Rêve is waiting to meet you downstairs," he continues, his tone void of any emotion.

"Why?" I ask simply.

"Why?" he echoes back in annoyance. "Because she's going to be your new stepmother, that's why."

I snort at this, and my father's nostrils flare in response. "Look," he warns, "I'm in no mood for your antics." (Is he *ever* in the mood for my antics?) "You'll get up and you'll get dressed and you'll go downstairs and you'll smile for the press. And after that, I don't care what you do."

He starts toward the door and I feel an unexpected boldness come over me. I'm not sure where it's coming from but for the life of me, I can't seem to keep it from bubbling forth like the champagne they're undoubtedly starting to serve downstairs. "Because as long as I put on a good show for the cameras, nothing else matters, right?"

He slowly turns back around. "Excuse me?"

I know I should probably shut up now. I should just slink out of bed, throw on one of those twenty-thousand-dollar designer dresses, and do what I'm told. Because that's what I've always done. Because it's easier than trying to fight someone who never loses. It's easier than going into battle against a stone wall.

But that's the difference between the me from the past and the me now. The old Lexington was afraid. Because she had something to lose. Her livelihood. Her lifestyle. The safety of her comfort zone.

But I've already lost all of that.

So what do I have to be afraid of now?

"As long as it looks good from the *outside*," I press on, "the inside is irrelevant. Right, *Daddy*?"

I can see the vein in my father's neck start to bulge. It's one of his very few "tells." But it's so subtle, most people miss it.

"I'm not sure what you're getting at, Lexi," he says darkly, "but I don't have time for it. I have an engagement party to attend."

"Oh, right," I say sarcastically. "Sixth time's a charm, huh?"

He remains silent but the vein pulsates in response.

I sit up, feeling more daring than I ever have before. "Do you love her?"

Again, my father doesn't respond. But I think we both know the answer.

"Then why are you marrying her?" I challenge his silence.

When he speaks his tone is once again flat and empty. "Marriage, like any relationship between people, is a business arrangement. A negotiation." My father straightens his tie and tugs at the lapels of his suit jacket. "Love has nothing to do with it. And the sooner you come to realize that, Lexington, the better off you'll be."

I've spent nearly my entire childhood building up an immunity to my father's callousness and icy approach to life. But no matter how long you work at it, how many years you practice, you are never immune to everything. Because you can't predict when the next frost will hit. Or how hard it will bite.

As much as I want to lie down and let the arctic mist roll right over me, I feel a stabbing sensation in my chest. The icicles have fallen. They've pierced through the skin. It's a direct hit.

And I loathe myself for being so weak and susceptible. I despise my own vulnerability.

"You don't really believe that, do you?" I ask in a feeble voice.

My whole body is now trembling from the cold and the anticipation of his response. I pull the blanket from my bed over my knees to keep them from knocking together. I hold my breath in fear that he might be able to see it.

I wait in the frozen tundra for his answer.

Then, as swiftly and sinuously as he entered the room, my father exits without another word, taking the chill with him. And I slowly peel the covers from my lap, pull a random dress from the rack, and start getting ready.

THE STAGE IS SET

WELL, LOOK WHO DECIDED TO GRACE US WITH
her presence," Caroline sings as I emerge from the back door of the
house and linger at the top of the staircase that leads down to the
gardens. There are cameras and equipment and activity everywhere. Photographers are setting up their shots, event planners are
putting the finishing touches on decorations, and waiters dressed
as cupids (seriously?) are passing around trays of hors d'oeuvres and
champagne.

I manage to grab a flute off a tray just as one floats by me.

Thank God. Something to take the edge off.

But I'm barely able to get it to my lips when Caroline whisks
it from my hands and glances nervously over her shoulder at the
flittering press. "Are you crazy?" she hisses at me. Her teeth are so
tightly clenched I'm worried she might break her jaw. "We finally
got them to stop talking about your *last* drinking fiasco."

She flashes a big smile at a passing reporter and holds up the
glass to him, as though she's offering him a toast.

Cheers to you for believing all the crap I tell you.

Then she takes a tiny sip before dumping the rest of the champagne onto a nearby shrub, depositing the empty glass on another passing tray, and asking the waiter to bring me a seltzer water. He returns a moment later with a glass full of fizzing clear liquid garnished with lime and a sprig of mint.

I take a small sip and grimace at its useless aftertaste. So much for taking the edge off.

I swirl the ice cubes in my drink and stare down the staircase toward the main fountain, where a young blond woman is showing off a long, nude-colored, open-back Galliano gown with a thigh-high split to a group of eager photographers, basking in her fifteen minutes—or in this case, approximately two years—of fame. I can see the five-carat Harry Winston sparkling on her left hand all the way from here. I swear my father must be on some kind of frequent-buyer program there.

According to *Access Hollywood*, "Twenty-nine-year-old Rêve Rodiccio was a struggling executive assistant at Larrabee Media's New York offices when the pair first locked eyes across the employee break room."

Yeah, I'm sure she was. A struggling executive assistant/wannabe actress/wannabe model/wannabe with anyone who can take care of her and ensure she doesn't have to work another day in her life. Well, didn't she strike the jackpot? She was probably aiming for some VP or board member—five hundred thousand a year or more—and, lo and behold, as luck would have it, she snagged the CEO himself.

I watch her bat her eyes flirtatiously (and skillfully) at the cameras, giving each and every single reporter her undivided attention in turn. As though there were no one else in the world she'd rather be talking to.

Perhaps I underestimated her. She might have had her sights on the grand prize from the very beginning.

"Are you ready to meet your new stepmother?" Caroline asks me out of the corner of her mouth.

"No. But when does that ever matter?"

"Remember," she cautions me, hiding her rapidly moving lips behind her hand, "according to the press, you two have already met and have spent lots of quality time together."

"Of course we have," I grumble. "Let me guess, we're BFFs?"

Caroline's head teeters from side to side as she tries that on for size. "That's good," she concludes. "I like it."

"Well, it's fitting. Since we're practically the same age."

I return my gaze to the fountain. My father has joined the circle now. He has his arm wrapped tightly around Rêve's nonexistent waist as he politely fields questions from the press. He's decidedly less enthusiastic as he delivers his responses, but that's to be expected. My father doesn't do enthusiastic. Plus, she's plenty enthusiastic for the both of them.

"Well, it's showtime," Caroline says quietly to me before mumbling something unintelligible into an earpiece that's hidden from view behind her hair. Seriously, is she a publicist or a member of the president's security detail?

The message is delivered to an assistant down at the fountain and he ducks his head to indicate receipt. Then I watch him tap

Rêve on the shoulder and whisper something into her ear. Her eyes illuminate, her head wheels around, and her gaze lands right on me.

"Lexi!" she calls eagerly, waving her arm above her head. I half expect her to kick off her heels, jump *into* the fountain, and start wading through it to get to me. Like some overly dramatic scene from a movie.

Showtime indeed, I think to myself as I launch my hand into the air and wave back, matching her animated smile.

I start down the stairs and she hurries across the garden until we meet in the middle and embrace.

Click. Click. Flash. Flash.

The photographers eat it up.

"It's so great to see you again," she gushes.

"Love the dress," I gush back.

She beams and smooths the fabric against her slender frame. "Thanks! Yours too! Is that the dress we found last time we went shopping?"

"It is, actually!" I reply, painting on a look of nostalgia for a beautiful day that never happened.

Rêve sighs and reaches out to tenderly finger a lock of my hair. An affectionate gesture only done between friends. Between two people who have shared numerous cups of coffee and intimate details of their lives.

"Oh, Lex," she croons. "I'm so thrilled to be joining your family."

I hide my gag reflex behind a sip of my drink. "Not as thrilled as I am, Rêve." I lay it on thick.

Caroline pantomimes *cut it out*, indicating that I've wandered too far off the preapproved script. But I just shoot her a goading grin in return.

"So, Lexi," one of the reporters begins. "What do you think of your father getting married for the sixth time?"

"What can I say?" I jest. "He's a regular Henry VIII!"

The press corps chuckles and the humming sound of pens scratching against notepads fills the air as my precious sound bite is recorded for all eternity.

"Hey, at least he hasn't beheaded any of them!" one reporter quips back lightheartedly.

"Only metaphorically," I reply, evoking another round of sniggers and scribbling.

An unspoken message is sent from my father to Caroline with a single menacing look and she quickly jumps into the center of the circle and starts clapping her hands to get everyone's attention and regain control of the situation. Then in her best bubbly publicist voice she announces, "Mark your calendars, everyone, because the wedding date has been set for February 17 and I believe Rêve has something very important to ask Lexington."

She nods pointedly to Rêve, indicating that they've already rehearsed this.

"Oh right," Rêve replies giddily, looking somewhat bewildered by the former exchange. I wouldn't be surprised to find her in the bathroom later Googling *Henry VIII*.

She turns back to me and takes my hand in hers. For a minute, I wonder if she's going to get down on one knee and propose.

"Lexi," she begins wistfully, moisture appearing in her eyes.

Oh, she's good. Crying on cue. That takes some serious talent. Either she's a natural born liar (in which case she'll fit into this family perfectly) or Caroline's been coaching her well.

"I know we've only just recently met," she goes on, squeezing my hands. "And we still have lots of getting to know each other to do. But you already feel like a daughter to me and I would be so delighted—no, *honored*, if you would be my maid of honor for the wedding."

Click. Click. Flash. Flash.

I'm biting down so hard on my tongue I'm sure that the next time I open my mouth blood will come spilling out like in a scene from *Dracula*. The cameras are snapping away again and I have to fight the urge to flick her bony little hands from mine and stalk back into the house. My father appears next to Rêve and puts a reassuring hand on her bare shoulder, stoically showing his support in a decision that was more than likely never hers. She probably wanted some cousin or sister or best friend from high school to be her maid of honor but I'm sure she's learned by now (or will soon enough) that when you marry Richard Larrabee, you forfeit personal preferences. There's only one way things are done around here. The way that makes Richard Larrabee look good.

The way that makes Larrabee Media continue to be a successful, multibillion-dollar corporation. And if you can't get on board with that, then you might as well jump ship now.

Caroline gives me another look of death and gestures subtly for me to hurry it up and answer. My father's dark eyes narrow ever so slightly in my direction.

I know what's expected of me. It's the same thing that's been expected of me since the day I emerged from the birth canal.

Compliance.

Just another pawn in one of my father's strategic negotiations. A business arrangement wrapped up with a bow and a truckload of rented cupid costumes and made to look like love. Like happily ever after.

Everything this family does is a front. A costume. A wizard's curtain to hide the rest of Oz from the truth. And with scabbed knees concealed behind a twenty-thousand-dollar dress, bruised arms masked in layers of the most expensive makeup money can buy, and a box of wigs stashed in my closet, I suppose I'm no different.

I turn back to the twenty-nine-year-old woman standing before me with the nerve to call me her *daughter* and with a deep, regretful sigh say, "No, Rêve."

A collective breath is sucked in. Eyes widen. Caroline's face starts turning a very interesting shade of red.

"*I* would be honored," I finish.

TROUBLED WATERS

THE TWINS, HUDSON AND HARRISON, MAKE THEIR grand entrance a few moments later, and I'm barely even able to say hello before we're shoved together by Caroline and her assistant for the big family photo.

Rêve and my father are positioned in the middle with RJ next to my father, and me, the newly crowned maid of honor (for the third time running), next to his blushing bride to-be. Hudson and Harrison are then placed on either side of the group.

"We apologize for being one member short today," Caroline announces to the press. "As you know, Cooper Larrabee is still traveling with the Peace Corps. He's currently in the Sudan feeding the hungry and wasn't able to make it today. But he sends his love and best wishes to his father and his future stepmother."

Rêve looks touched as she places her hand to her heart and murmurs, "I love that boy."

We pose for what feels like hours while the photographers take their turns capturing this truly joyful day in the Larrabee family as we welcome the newest member into our happy clan.

Soon afterward, like clockwork, the press pack up their stuff and head out to their vans as the guests start arriving.

My brothers' graduation from Yale Law School is the hot topic of the party. Probably because it's the only conversation topic that's safe . . . and permanent. No one dares say anything about my father's imminent marriage to Miss Executive Assistant Turned Gold Digger, beyond the obvious enthusiastic offerings of congratulations and superficial remarks about her dress and flawless skin. Everyone knows anything more profound than that is treading through dangerous territory. Because it can and will be used against you in approximately two and a half years when the two parties are sitting on opposite sides of a conference table, reviewing my father's standard watertight prenup.

But Yale law degrees and graduating at the top of your class is eternal. Something that can't be reversed. So people are smart and just stick to that.

In fact, my brothers are so monopolized throughout the entire party, I don't even get a chance to talk to them. Not that I really have anything to say. And with RJ and his wife refusing to leave my father's side, Cooper (my usual partner in crime at these sorts of things) off spreading good Karma in the Sudan, and my friends having the time of their lives in the Mediterranean, I'm pretty much a loner.

Looks like my only friend tonight is the vodka I managed to sneak into my seltzer water. I meander from cluster to cluster, eavesdropping on conversations and listening for something interesting enough to warrant my attention.

A group of my father's executives are gathered around the bar yammering about some French media corporation that they hope to merge with. Yawn. Next.

There's a gaggle of teens huddled in a corner gossiping about a website that some fifteen-year-old girl started, where you can vote on various aspects of her life. Lame. Next.

I wander over to the pool and sidle up to a table of gourmet appetizers. I select a canapé from a tray and pop it into my mouth, washing it down with a large gulp of my "seltzer water."

"Now, see, I remember when he was married to Elizabeth," comes a slurred, booming voice behind me.

My ears perk up at the mention of my mother's name. At least, I assume it's my mother he's talking about. It makes sense, given that this *is* an engagement party for her widower. Although I suppose there are a lot of Elizabeths in the world.

"Really?" a female voice responds with interest. "I never had the chance to meet her but I've heard such wonderful things about her."

"Well, sure," the slurrer continues. "That's what they pay publicists for. But I knew Lizzie a long time and I'm telling you she was no picnic. Extremely troubled."

Well, I guess that settles it. They couldn't be talking about my mom. I've never heard anyone describe Elizabeth Larrabee as "troubled."

I attempt to zone him out, concentrating on the selection of my next canapé until I hear him say, "And it seemed like the more successful Richard became, the worse she got. I felt sorry for the poor guy. He put up with a lot of drama."

Suddenly I'm on full alert again. Did he just say *Richard*? As in

Richard Larrabee, my father? No, that's impossible. He couldn't be talking about *that* Richard because that would mean the Elizabeth he was referring to really *is* my mother.

I subtly turn my head toward the source of the voice and catch sight of a paunchy, clearly intoxicated red-faced man who I faintly recognize. He's talking to a woman who looks like she's trying to find a way to politely bow out of this uncomfortable (not to mention *inappropriate*) conversation. And she's smart to do so. Only someone as wasted as that guy would be stupid enough talk about my mother at an event like this. Let alone openly *insult* her.

"I'll tell ya"—the intoxicated man waves his hand dramatically across his body, sloshing ten-thousand-dollar-a-bottle scotch down the front of his shirt—"ya can't really blame the guy for marrying a string of brainless supermodels after that whole mess."

The canapé drops from my hand and tumbles into the grass.

I stand frozen in place, literally *stunned* at what I'm hearing. How dare he spread such nasty not to mention *false* rumors about my mother! And in her own backyard!

I'm about to march right over there and kindly ask him to take his lies somewhere else when I feel a warm hand on my arm.

"Hey," a familiar voice says behind me.

I swivel around and come face-to-face with Luke, who's holding a barely touched flute of champagne in one hand and an empty appetizer plate in the other.

"Hi," I mumble distractedly, darting vicious glances behind me.

"What's the matter?" Luke asks, peering in the direction of my gaze.

I grunt. "Just some drunk idiot saying rude things."

"Well, ignore him," Luke suggests.

I take a deep breath. Luke is right. I *should* ignore him. He's obviously sloshed off his face and making no sense. This certainly wouldn't be the first time I've had to ignore vicious gossip about members of my family and it definitely won't be the last. I'm not sure why this particular conversation is affecting me more than normal. Maybe it's because, of all the times I've had to ignore vicious gossip, it's never been about my mother.

Or maybe it's because that particular man is so much more annoying than most.

But when I steal another glance in his direction I see that the woman he was talking to has left and now he's standing alone, staring forlornly into his empty scotch glass.

Serves him right.

Loser.

With a swift sip of my drink, I manage to shake off my infuriation and focus on Luke. It's only now that I notice how terribly out of place he looks. And that's probably because he's wearing this really strange combination of pleated-front khakis, a white-button down with an argyle sweater tied around his shoulders, and dark brown loafers with tassels. He looks like he just walked out of a glossy country club brochure.

I shake my head critically.

He glances nervously at his outfit. "What? No good?" From the panic in his voice, it's obvious he spent about an hour deliberating before finally selecting this.

I give him a pitying look. "Next time you need help picking out something to wear, call me, okay?"

He breathes out a laugh. "Okay." And then after a minuscule sip of his champagne, he adds, "I'm relieved to have found a familiar face here." He flashes me a warm smile and I can't help feeling just a tad bit sorry for the guy. I mean, how sad is it that *I'm* the person he's relieved to see?

He peers around at the mass of guests that have filled almost every corner of our backyard. "Do you *know* all these people?"

"No. Not even half."

"Does your father know them?"

"Probably not."

He seems to be lost in thought for a moment, taking in his surroundings with an awed expression. "What was it like growing up with this?"

"With what?"

He motions to the grounds. "With . . . all of this! The cars and the houses and the"—he holds up his drink—"champagne that costs more than my monthly rent."

I stifle a giggle, suddenly realizing why his glass has remained relatively untouched. He's *afraid* to drink it.

"Well," he prompts me, "what was it like?"

I shrug. "I don't know. I mean, I don't know any different. That's like me asking you what it was like to grow up in *your* family."

"It sucked," he answers so swiftly it makes me blink.

"Oh," is the only thing I can think to say.

"We never had any money. We were always moving from place to place. We kept getting evicted from our apartment because my dad kept losing his job. My parents fought about finances constantly. It was awful. Then finally one day my dad left to find a new job and never came back."

"Oh," I mumble again, suddenly feeling extremely uncomfortable. I gulp down the remainder of my drink and set the glass on a table. "Sorry."

Luke shrugs away my apology. "I managed to escape relatively unscathed."

He continues to marvel at everything around him. Like he's a character from a black-and-white movie and this is his first time seeing the world in color. He walks in a slow circle, taking it all in, until he's finally facing the back of the house again. Then he stands there, shaking his head in amazement. "I can't even imagine what's it's like inside there."

I let out a laugh. "Well, fortunately, you don't have to." I grab his elbow and start pulling him toward the stairs. I take the empty appetizer plate from his hand and toss it haphazardly on the bottom step before climbing up to the first landing. But my eyes slowly drift back down to the abandoned plate and an unsettled feeling creeps into my stomach. I let go of Luke's arm, skip back to the grass, snatch up the plate, and run it over to the nearest trash can.

Then I catch up with Luke, link my arm through his, and say, "C'mon. I'll give you the grand tour."

MR. CARVER, IN THE BILLIARD ROOM, WITH THE POOL CUE

LET ME GUESS, THIS IS YOUR FIRST PARTY," I SAY to Luke as we leave the formal dining room and enter the library.

Luke whistles as he gazes up at the floor-to-ceiling mahogany bookshelves. "Well, my first party on this scale, I guess you would say. I'm certainly not used to this kind of thing."

He hops onto the rolling book ladder, pushes off with one foot, and rides it across the far wall. With that huge toothy smile on his face, he looks like a little kid at a playground. It's almost sort of endearing. "I've always wanted to do that," he explains as he steps off.

I laugh. "What kind of parties *are* you used to?"

"I don't really go to parties," he replies with a shrug.

"Oh, c'mon!" I urge him with a poke. "At USC? I know for a fact that they have some off-the-hook parties there."

"I'm sure they do," he says casually, leaning over to examine a set of original classics displayed in a glass case. "But I don't have any time to go. I'm always too busy working. My scholarship doesn't cover room and board."

"Oh," I say, biting my lip.

"What about you?" he asks, looking up and staring at me from across the room.

"What *about* me?" I shoot back defensively.

"College," he prompts, taking a few steps toward me. "You have no desire to go?"

I laugh at this. "What for?"

"I don't know. To learn things. Study. Become more worldly."

"I spent my childhood hopping around Europe. I've visited thirty-two countries in eighteen years. I think I'm plenty worldly."

Luke raises his hands in the air in a gesture of surrender. "Sorry. I'm only wondering if you've ever given any thought to what you want to do with your life."

I put my hands on my hips. "And what's wrong with my life now?"

He stifles a smile. "Do you honestly want me to answer that?"

"Yes," I challenge, "I do."

He takes a few more steps in my direction until he's almost an arm's length away. He looks me directly in the eye. For some reason, I feel my face grow hot but I'm not sure if it's because of my sudden irritation or something else. He holds my gaze tightly and I feel my breath start to quicken. I even feel myself leaning forward slightly.

"No you don't," he says at last, breaking eye contact and turning away from me. He wanders to the fireplace and stares at the giant framed photograph of my father hanging over the mantel. It was taken right after my mother died. When I was younger I used to come in here after school and tell my father's portrait about my day. I would pull one of the large upholstered reading chairs from the center of the room, position it directly in front of the fireplace, and climb into it. The chair would swallow up my tiny body. My feet would barely reach the edge of the seat. But I felt safe sitting there. With my father standing guard above me. His serious expression and watchful eyes looking down on me.

Now the portrait just freaks me out. His eyes don't watch over me anymore. They judge me. They condemn me. Funny how over the years the exact same portrait can grow to depict such a different person.

"Someday I'm going to have all of this," Luke vows quietly, and for a minute I wonder if I'm even supposed to have heard it. Or if he was talking to himself. But then he speaks slightly louder. "Someday I'm going to be exactly like him."

I snort. "Have fun with that."

"Your father is the reason I'm interning at Larrabee Media, you know," he goes on, ignoring my sarcasm. "He's the reason I'm struggling to put myself through college. The way he started out with nothing and then became the icon that he is. He's an inspiration to a lot of people, you know."

I roll my eyes. "How lucky for them," I mumble, glancing briefly up at the portrait. A chill runs through my body and I drop my eyes to the floor.

"Why are there no pictures of your mother anywhere?" Luke asks, gazing around.

"My father took them all down when she died," I reply, trying to keep my tone as neutral and impassive as possible. But after the infuriating conversation I overheard outside, it's decidedly more difficult than usual.

"I read that he took her death very hard."

"Yeah," I grumble, staring down at my fingernails. "So hard that he continues to honor her memory every three years by marrying another bimbo."

I can feel Luke's gaze flicker over to me momentarily. "Maybe he likes the bimbos."

"He doesn't," I answer with certainty. "They're just a distraction."

"Some people need to be distracted from things they don't want to think about," Luke offers gently.

I know what he's trying to do. And I don't really feel like getting into a heart-to-heart about my mother's death right now. Especially not with Luke Carver, of all people.

"Yeah, well, it happened a long time ago and everybody's over it now," I say dismissively. I take hold of his elbow and lead him toward the door. "Come on. Let's continue with the tour."

He seems to pick up on my attempt to evade the subject and follows me willingly back into the hallway, where the temperature is noticeably warmer.

I lead him to the room directly across from us but Luke stops just short of the entrance and points to the closed door at the end of the corridor. "What room is that?"

"That's my father's personal study. No one ever goes in there. He keeps it locked year round." I keep moving into the next room, and eventually, after a lingering glance down the hall, Luke follows. "And obviously this is the billiard room," I say uninspiringly, motioning toward the large, handcrafted, red-felt-covered pool table in the center.

He hoots with laughter. "This place is like walking through a game of Clue!"

I run my finger over the smooth oak. "I wouldn't know. I've never played it."

Luke's mouth falls open. "What? How could you never have played Clue? It's only one of the most popular board games of all time!"

I shrug. "I don't know. I just never did."

"That's a shame. It's one of my favorites." Luke nods toward the table. "Do you at least play pool?"

I grab a pool cue and skillfully run a cube of chalk over the tip. "Very well, actually."

He flashes me a sly smile and accepts my challenge by grabbing a second cue and chalking it up. "Well, game on, then."

I rack the balls and Luke breaks, sending the six ball into the corner pocket.

"I guess I'm solids," he says, lining up his next shot. He tries to sink the three ball into the side pocket but misses by a few inches.

I finish chalking up my cue and get down to businesses, sinking seven striped balls in a row before finally calling the eight ball in the corner and knocking it in with ease.

Luke stands off to the side with a baffled look on his face. Like a ghost just swiped his wallet. "So *that's* what it feels like to be hustled," he jokes.

I laugh and cock my head to the side. "Sorry!" I sing insincerely.

His mouth is still hanging open. "Where'd you learn how to play pool like that?"

"Horatio," I say with a smile, leaning on my pool cue. I feel a quick burst of nostalgia as I remember when I was a kid and Horatio had to lift me up to the table so that I could make a shot.

"Who's Horatio?" Luke asks.

"Our butler."

"Of course." He shakes his head and laughs, his tone slipping into an obnoxious over-the-top British accent. "The *butler* taught you to play pool. Isn't that lovely?"

"Hey!" I shout at him from across the table, feeling my cheeks start to burn with rage again. "You have no idea what you're talking about."

"Jesus," he swears. "Calm down. I was only joking. You're so easily triggered."

"Oh and there he goes again with the psychology-major crap. Thanks, but I have a shrink for that."

"Okay, okay," Luke says, throwing his hands up in the air. "Lighten up, okay? I'm sorry I said anything." He takes a hesitant step in my direction but I quickly move away, tossing my pool cue down on the table.

"You shouldn't make jokes about things you know nothing about." I storm out the door, not even bothering to tell him how to get back to the party. Luke's a big boy. He goes to college. I'm sure he can figure it out himself.

DISAPPEARING ACT

I HAVE TROUBLE FALLING ASLEEP THAT NIGHT. THE events of the day are replaying in surround sound in my brain. No matter how hard I try, I can't seem to shake anything anyone said. My father's heartwarming sermon about love and relationships, Mr. Too Much Scotch's harsh allegations about my mother being some kind of disturbed drama queen, and even Luke's relatively harmless attempts to get to know me better.

When I've tried all my usual tricks to clear my mind, I grab my iPad off my beside table and switch it on. Holly, who's been asleep on the other pillow, picks up her head momentarily to check out what I'm doing and then after evidently deciding that it's not something to be concerned about, goes back to sleep.

Since I have no idea where my father keeps the old photographs of my mom, the only place I can see her is on the Internet. I type in the familiar search term *Elizabeth Larrabee* and wait patiently as Google spits back several pages of results. I click on *Images* and scroll through all the photographs of my mother from various newspaper clippings, magazine articles, and promotional photo shoots.

My parents married young. My mom was nineteen and my

father was twenty. He had only just started his first company and his headquarters were still located on the kitchen counter of my parents' tiny apartment in Fresno.

RJ was born two years after they got married and my father made his first million a year after that. By the time I came into the world, a little less than nine years later, Larrabee Media was a billion-dollar corporation and my father was already the poster child for success.

Which is why most of the photographs that now stare back at me were taken in the last few years of my mother's life, when the Larrabee family started to become a recognizable household name.

I glimpse past the several red-carpet photos and promotional family portraits until I find my favorite picture. It's from a sixteen-year-old issue of *Better Homes and Gardens*. The magazine dedicated an entire six-page spread to the Larrabee family's brand new Bel Air mansion and the custom backyard my mother had designed to resemble her favorite French gardens at the Château de Villandry.

The photo was taken shortly after my first birthday. My parents are teaching me how to walk, in the garden.

I don't have any reliable memories from the time my mother was alive—and no one in this family likes to talk about her—but I have to think that things used to be different back then. That there once was a time when we actually *were* a family. Maybe not a normal one, but at least a real one. Not this over-the-top propaganda that Caroline feeds to the press.

I glance over at the gold-silk-covered chaise longue in the middle of my bedroom. The dress I wore to the engagement party is still slung haphazardly across the back from when I stripped it off in a mad rush to shed any and all reminders of the circus act that was going on downstairs.

Then I look back at the little girl in the photograph in the frilly pink dress, matching bow, and white patent leather shoes. Taking those first wobbly steps while her parents crawl behind her with open arms, ready to catch her if she falls.

I scrutinize every single detail of the picture-perfect composition and suddenly a cold chill creeps its way up my arm.

What if I'm wrong?

What if it *has* always been like this? And I was too young and naïve to realize it? What if I believed the lies and ate them up just as hungrily as the reporters that follow us around?

Is that tiny dress not just another costume? Essentially identical to the one I wore tonight? Could this flawless family moment captured on film be just another show? Another dazzling performance for the press?

After the photographer went home, did my mother and father stand up, dust the grass stains from their knees, and hand me off to some nanny so they could go their separate ways and live their separate lives?

How well do I even know the woman in this photograph? The infamous Elizabeth Larrabee. Everyone tells me she was wonderful. Everyone gushes about how beautiful she was. How loving and supportive and maternal. The perfect wife. The perfect mother.

But how do I know that's not another script? Carefully constructed by a crafty publicist. Designed to make my father look good and the Larrabee family continue to shine in the spotlight.

How do I know that drunk fool at the party isn't the only one with the guts to tell the truth?

The only one not being *paid* to lie.

I set the iPad aside and reach for my cell phone, unplugging it from its charger. I find the toll-free, in-case-of-emergency-only number in my contact list and press call.

It rings once before a friendly receptionist answers. "Thank you for calling Peace Corps. How may I help you?"

"Hi," I say, my voice fragile and thin. "I need to get in touch with Cooper Larrabee. I believe he's in the Sudan."

"Is this an emergency?" she asks.

I hesitate for a moment. "Yes. It's a family emergency. I'm his sister."

I hear her typing furiously into a keyboard before she returns to the line. "I've sent a message to the local office there. They will get in touch with him and have him call you as quickly as possible."

I feel somewhat bad about lying but I really need to talk to someone right now and I can't think of anyone else to call. My three other brothers are practically strangers to me. RJ is too wrapped up in my father's company to bother himself with anything I have to say. The twins have always kind of stuck together in their own little clique, as I've heard twins often do. Cooper is the only one I've ever been able to talk to. Being a mere two years older than me, he's the only one who gets me. Who's *ever* gotten me. After our mother died, he was the one I crawled into bed with when the nightmares haunted me. He was the one who told me reassuring stories about angels and fluffy white clouds as I fell asleep.

My cell phone trills beside me a few minutes later, causing me to jump. The caller ID says *Unknown*, and I scramble to answer it.

"Hello?"

"Lex," my brother says, panicked, "what's wrong?"

The sound of his voice—even muffled by static and affected by a slight delay—instantly soothes me.

"Hi, Coop," I say softly.

"They said it was an emergency."

"I know," I begin regretfully. "Sorry. I might have exaggerated a bit. I just really needed to hear your voice."

He exhales in relief and I half expect him to berate me for pulling this kind of stunt but he doesn't. Instead I can hear the playful smile in his tone as he asks, "What's wrong, baby sis?"

"Things are just . . . hard."

"I heard about your new job. Or shall I say, *jobs*." He chuckles. But I don't get offended by his amusement. Anyone else, yes. But not Cooper. He always means well and I always know it.

"Yeah," I say with a sigh. "But actually I called to ask you about mom."

"Mom?" comes his confused reply. And I suppose I should have anticipated that. It's not a conversation we broach often. It's always been one of those unspoken rules between us. Between all of us.

"How well do you remember her?" I ask.

"Not that well," he replies. "I remember she was wonderful. Loving and supportive and maternal."

Frustrated, I press my fingertips against my temple. "Do you really remember that or do you just remember people *telling* you that?"

He falters for a moment and even from eight thousand miles away, I can almost hear the gears in his mind turning, trying, exactly as I have been doing, to sort the real memories from the implanted ones.

"I'm not sure," he finally admits.

"Well, do you remember anything other than that? Anything . . . I don't know . . . maybe unusual or strange or even . . . *disturbing* about her?"

"Lex," he warns. "What's going on?"

"Nothing," I reply quickly, although I'm almost positive he won't buy it. "I've just been thinking about her."

"Maybe you should call RJ. He would remember that kind of stuff. He was fourteen when she died."

"You know I can't talk to RJ about anything."

He sighs. "Well, I do remember her being gone a lot. Especially at the end. You know, before she died."

"Gone?" I repeat skeptically.

"Yeah," he confirms. "Like on vacations."

"What kind of vacations?"

There's an extended silence as Cooper reflects. "Cruises, I think."

"Really?"

"Yeah," he says, gaining momentum, as though he's opened some kind of doorway and now he's anxious to run through it and see what's on the other side. "I remember now. She would go on these cruises for like a week or two. Sometimes longer. Horatio said it was so she could relax from the stress of raising five kids." Then he lets out a jovial laugh. "I guess I can't really blame her."

"I don't remember any of that," I marvel quietly.

"Well you were five," Cooper states. "I'm not surprised."

"How often did she go?"

"I don't know," he replies nonchalantly. "But I remember she had just gotten back from a really long one when she had the accident."

I struggle to see through the fog in my mind as I think back to the day we got the news. I've worked so hard to block that day from my memory. Cooper and I were playing in the backyard with Horatio. Bruce appeared at the top of the stairs. He called us inside. RJ and the twins were already there. Bruce sat us down on the couch—or was it at the dining room table?—and told us that our mother had died in a car crash on the way home from the airport. I never thought to question why she was at the airport to begin with. I suppose the cruise story makes sense.

But what if that's all it was? A story. Some kind of cleverly concocted tale designed to cover up the truth. And if that's the case, what exactly was it covering?

"Lex." Cooper's voice snaps me back into the moment.

"Huh?"

"Are you going to tell me why you're asking these kinds of questions?"

All this hypothesizing is starting to make my brain hurt. I suddenly feel very tired. And foolishly paranoid. I'm probably blowing this whole thing way out of proportion. So my mom liked to go on cruises. So what? Raising five children *is* very stressful. And that man at the party *was* really wasted. It was probably the scotch talking. He said he'd known my mother for a long time so maybe he'd always had some secret crush on her that was never requited. Maybe this was his way of getting back at her. By spreading rumors.

In any case, there's no point in getting Cooper worked up about it. Especially when he's halfway across the world trying to deal with *real* problems.

"Never mind," I reply quietly. "It's not important." I transfer the phone to my other ear and sink farther down into the bed. "Tell me the latest about your trip. How is saving the world treating you?"

Cooper laughs and launches into several stories about his adventures in the Sudan, including one about a boy named Chiumbo who has been teaching him how to rap. I smile as his warm, familiar voice envelops me and allow myself to drift away, if only momentarily, to the other side of the earth where my problems cease to exist and my mind is empty.

Sent: Friday, August 10, 10:40 p.m.
To: Luke Carver
From: Video-Blaze.com
Subject: You have received a video message from
Lexington Larrabee

CLICK <u>HERE</u> TO PLAY MESSAGE

Or read the free transcript from our automated speech-to-text service below.

[BEGIN TRANSCRIPT]

Hey. Me again. This is going to be a short video because I have nothing official to report. I could show you some more bruises but I'm sure you're over that by now.

I know you want me to talk about what I've learned in the past few weeks but honestly there's not a whole lot to say.

Hold on, let me get out the list.

Let's see here. Where are we? Oh, right. Job #11. I milked cows at a dairy farm. Before that, I held up a stop sign while kids crossed the street on their way home from school. And I also gutted fish at a seafood market.

That's it. *C'est tout.*

It's probably going to be a while before I eat sushi
again, but that's about all I got.

So . . . yeah. See ya.

[END TRANSCRIPT]

I GET THAT A LOT

TODAY IS MY FIRST DAY WORKING AT THE FINE establishment of Don Juan's Tacos, a popular fast food chain famous for their creative use of nacho cheese. Not to mention an entire menu of delectable food items available for under a dollar. As if that's supposed to be a *good* thing.

The uniform is a whole other issue. Let's start with the color of this shirt. Hideous. Fashion rule number one: No one looks good in mustard. Not even me. And I've been known to pull off some pretty risqué colors in my day. And what's with the elastic waistband on these pants? Are they maternity pants? Or have they just been designed to stretch to accommodate the weight you're guaranteed to gain from working at this place and eating the food?

And don't get me started on the sombrero.

Not even my beautiful blond wig with its sleek, straight, shoulder-length layers can improve this thing.

I've never actually been *inside* a Don Juan's Tacos before but I'm somewhat familiar with at least a few of their menu items from the never-ending string of commercials on TV. Although apparently not familiar enough to *make* any of the items from scratch.

Javier, the supervisor who is training me on the food line, is getting really frustrated at my burrito-building ineptness. So far, I've proven myself completely incapable of wrapping a tortilla around half a pound of beans and cheese without ripping it.

And judging by the way he's yelling at me, he seems to be taking the whole thing *very* personally. I'm not sure what that's about but it's giving me a serious headache.

I grab a handful of lettuce and dump it into the open tortilla in front of me.

"Oh *dios mio!*" Javier screams again, throwing in a few random Spanish curse words that I recognize from eighteen years of witnessing Horatio attempt to repair things around the house.

"How on earth are you going to wrap it with that much lettuce in there?" he asks. "Huh? Huh?"

He's glaring at me now as though he really expects me to answer.

I'm starting to think this guy might be related to Fidel Castro.

"You can't!" he bellows back before I can utter a single word. "That's how."

He scoops up half of the lettuce and violently throws it back in the bin. Then he shoves me to the side, mumbles for me to go up front and have Jenna train me on the register, and hastily wraps the burrito in waxed paper and drops it onto the tray.

It's hard to believe, after all I've been through so far, that I'm only on job number fifteen. Which means I have thirty-seven weeks left to go.

I stagger out to the front of the store and find a small blond girl with dramatic aquamarine eyeliner, a bad perm, and a name tag that reads: JENNA. I introduce myself with my code name for the week—Alicia—and unenthusiastically inform her that she's supposed to train me on the register.

"Don't worry about Javier," she says, reading my defeated expression. "He's like that with all new people. But he's actually pretty nice once you get to know him."

"Oh yeah," I jest. "I can tell we're gonna be BFFs."

She giggles and then stops suddenly as a strange expression comes over her face. She's staring at me really curiously and I feel my heart start to accelerate.

I know that look.

I've seen it a million times. In a thousand different places. It's that bewildered expression people get when they think they recognize you but can't quite figure out why. And now it'll only be a matter of seconds before the gears click into place, the lightbulb goes off, her face lights up with recognition, and she goes . . .

"Oh my God!" she exclaims, pointing at my face and jumping up and down excitedly.

I close my eyes and swear under my breath.

So this is going to be my ultimate undoing, huh? Don Juan's Tacos is going to be my Waterloo. So much for flying under the radar. For being "out of context." I knew it was wishful thinking. That someone was *bound* to recognize me eventually.

"Do you know who you look like?" the girl bubbles excitedly.

I cautiously open my eyes. "Huh?"

"I bet you get it all the time."

I squint inquisitively at her. "Get *what* all the time?"

"That you look exactly like Lexington Larrabee!"

The tall and lanky employee cleaning up the salsa bar stops wiping for a moment and curiously shifts his gaze toward us.

"You know," Jenna prompts, "that spoiled-brat heiress that's always in the tabloids."

I exhale loudly and force a smile. "Oh. Right. *Her.*"

"You look *exactly* like her," she compliments, like she's expecting her comment to make my day. Although, to be honest, it did. Only not in the way she would think.

She turns to the teenage boy at the salsa bar. "Rolando, doesn't she look *exactly* like Lexington Larrabee?"

He nods hurriedly and then goes back to wiping.

"You could totally, like, *be* her," Jenna continues. "Except for, you know, the hair."

I reach up and stroke a lock of my ash-blond wig, saying a silent prayer of thanks to the online wig warehouse that supplied it. "Yeah." I nod vehemently. "I get that a *lot.*"

"You know who I get?" she asks.

"Um . . ." I begin, staring intently. Truthfully, with that crunchy, over-gelled perm on her head, I can't imagine people thinking she looks like *any* celebrity. "Hmm." I attempt to buy time while I rack my brain for a name. Fortunately, I'm saved when two customers walk through the door and she turns to greet them.

"Welcome to Don Juan's!" she says with a slight bounce. "What can I get for you today?"

The man holds up one finger as he and his wife quickly scan the menu, whispering to each other. I can tell immediately from the way they're dressed that they're not American. Having spent the majority of my childhood traipsing around Western Europe, I have a very finely tuned radar for foreigners. Especially of the European variety.

The woman makes a disgusted face and turns away from the menu, muttering to her husband, *"Je n'arrive pas à croire que les Américains mangent cette nourriture dégoûtante. Je ne peux pas manger ici."*

I was right. They're French. And that woman just expressed her utter disbelief that Americans can call anything on this menu *food.* It's the exact same thought I had when I walked in here this morning.

"I assure you," I reply in French, without thinking, "not *all* Americans eat this crap."

The couple laughs and the woman murmurs something about trying Mimi's Café next door instead. I tell her it's probably a safer bet.

As soon as they exit, Jenna turns to me with a look of pure awe. "You speak French?"

I blink back at her in surprise, taking a moment to figure out why she looks so astonished. Even Rolando, the guy cleaning the salsa bar, has looked over here again to wait for my answer.

Whoops.

I guess employees of Don Juan's Tacos aren't usually fluent in French.

"Oh," I say quickly, waving my hand in the air to downplay the situation, "just a little."

Jenna laughs. "Sounded like more than a little." She turns toward the salsa bar again. "Rolando, did you hear that? She was like, *Bloodidoo bla bloo bla.*"

He laughs. "Yep. Pretty impressive."

"Well . . ." I fidget with the stack of plastic trays on the counter. "My mom is French."

As soon as the lie is out of my mouth, I wish I could take it back. I immediately feel guilty about mentioning my mother. Especially when what I said is not even true.

"Cool," Jenna says. "My relatives are from, like, Norway or some-thing. But that was, like, thousands of years ago. You know what's kind of weird? I think Lexington Larrabee speaks French too! I'm pretty sure I read that somewhere. She has, like, five houses in France or something."

Actually it's only two. An apartment in Paris and a château near Aix-en-Provence but I'm not about to correct her.

"I don't think her mom is from France, though." Jenna keeps babbling. "I'm pretty sure she's dead. Some tragic car accident or something. It's kinda sad when you think about it, huh? Losing your mom like that?"

"We should probably finish the register training," I interject quickly. "You know, before Javier comes out here and murders me with a taco shell."

Jenna laughs, seemingly oblivious to my skillful topic-dodging. "Good thinking," she says, tapping her forehead.

Thankfully, Rolando goes back to filling salsa bins, Jenna goes back to pointing at random buttons on the computer in front of us, and I slowly go back to breathing normally again.

CULT CLASSIC

I THOUGHT WORKING IN FAST FOOD WAS SUP-
posed to be easy. But it's actually ridiculously hard. Like brain surgery or something. The drive-thru headset requires a PhD to
operate. In one shift I manage to accidentally cuss out three customers because I thought I was pressing the off button when really I was
pressing the broadcast-my-voice-to-the-world button. And since
every employee in the restaurant wears a headset pretty much everyone heard me.

The order screens positioned above the food line are even worse.
I swear the incoming orders are displayed in some kind of top-secret
government code. What the heck is *SDT wo ch +so* supposed to
mean? I need a translator just to figure out what item to make and
there are so many freaking ingredients, even then I don't get it right.

Plus the deep fryer is out to get me. I'm convinced of it. It bubbles and boils in blistering hot rage and lashes out at me every time
I attempt to submerge a basket of fries. And don't even get me
started on the nacho cheese sauce. This lethal substance is dangerous, volatile, and should be kept far away from living creatures. Its
creamy and inviting texture is but a ruse to reel you in and gain

your trust. But turn your back for only a few minutes and it morphs into a crusty, gelatinous, fluorescent yellow sludge. And once it's touched the surface of any object it's virtually impossible to remove.

By the end of my first day, my feet are swollen, my back is throbbing, I have burns on my arms, and I smell like I've been rolling around in french fries all day. I swear the stench of grease has seeped into my clothes and skin.

So I think it's safe to say that the very *last* face I want to see at ten o'clock at night after coming off my hellish eight-hour shift is my father's. And yet, there it is. The second I open the door of Luke's Honda Civic, I see it. Lying on the passenger seat. That infamous I'm-going-to-eat-you-alive-and-enjoy-it half smile staring up at me.

It's a copy of my father's autobiography. Although the "auto" part is yet another brilliant Richard Larrabee deception. I know for a fact that he hired a ghostwriter to write the stupid thing.

I let out a loud groan. "What is *that* doing here?" I ask, glaring at the hardcover. I lower myself into the car, trying to aim my butt *right* onto the image of my father's smug face. Luke saves the book just in time and holds it protectively to his chest.

"I bought it today," Luke says proudly. "I'm going to take it into the office tomorrow to get it autographed."

I roll my eyes and buckle my seat belt.

"We're studying him in our entrepreneurship class," Luke continues eagerly. "I'm reading about how your father started out with no money, no higher education, working in the mail room of a small newspaper."

"*Copy* room," I correct begrudgingly.

"Right," Luke says. "It's amazing how in only a few short years, he went on to form one of the largest media corporations in the world."

I scowl in disgust. "Spare me the book report, okay?"

Luke shoots me a scolding look and shoves the book in my face, tapping the cover brusquely. "This man is a legend. He has changed lives."

"I'm living proof of that," I grumble.

But Luke hardly hears me. He stares wistfully at the cover like he's a twelve-year-old girl staring at a photograph of her latest heart-throb crush and is about to start making out with it.

"He certainly changed mine," he muses, and I marvel at how much he sounds like a member of one of those crazy cults that go off to live together in the woods somewhere.

Good. I hope they serve Kool-Aid.

"You should read it," Luke suggests, coming out of his love trance and tapping the cover again.

I snort. "Sure. That's *exactly* how I want to spend my free time."

"You might learn a few things about the man who raised you."

"That man did *not* raise me."

"You know," Luke begins pensively, "I don't think you appreciate what you have. Who you are. How fortunate you are to have been born into your family. The rest of us actually had to *work* to get to where we are."

I cackle with fake laughter. "And I don't think *you* appreciate what the reality of being born into my family truly is."

He ignores me. "You have been given so many amazing

opportunities and all you've chosen to do with any of them is get drunk and party and crash cars into convenience stores."

"Well, at least I have *fun*," I snap back at him viciously. "At least I know *how* to."

"I have fun," he defends, sounding insulted.

"Oh yeah," I mock. "I'm sure spreadsheets and status reports are a whole barrel of laughs."

"My entire life is not just spreadsheets and status reports, I'll have you know."

"Oh please! You're so uptight about everything!" I press on. "You can't even start a car without analyzing the process. I bet your idea of fun is organizing the pens in your desk drawer. Don't you ever let loose? Throw caution to the wind? Do something reckless?"

There's a long silence on the other side of the car and suddenly I feel like we're separated by a football field instead of a mere six-inch center console.

"Yes," he finally replies meekly. "Yes, I do."

"Oh really?" I challenge. Then without another word, I open the passenger door and step out of the car.

"What are you doing?" Luke calls after me, but I don't answer. I march over to the driver's-side door and yank it open. Luke looks up at me like he doesn't even know me.

"Out," I command, beckoning harshly with my hand.

He gives me a guarded look but eventually steps out of the car. "Why?"

I immediately slide in behind the wheel and buckle my seat belt. "I'm driving."

"Okay," Luke stammers, still looking extremely unsure as he runs around and gets into the passenger seat. "Where are we going?"

I move the seat forward so that my feet can reach the pedals and rev the engine. "You say you know how to have fun?" I begin, shifting the car into drive. "I'm taking you somewhere you can prove it."

THE ART OF NEGOTIATION

I SCREECH UP TO THE CURB OF CLUB SHADOW ON Sunset. Luke looks positively green from my reckless driving and I half expect him to open the car door and start vomiting. I hop out and toss the keys to the waiting valet. Luke follows warily behind me, staring blindly into the flashes of the dozen paparazzi who are staked out front.

"Lexi!" they call desperately, trying to get me to turn around and give them a clean shot of my face. But I pay no attention and continue into the club with my head down, hauling Luke behind me by the sleeve of his suit jacket.

Inside we're ushered straight to the VIP room and escorted to a private booth in the back. I order a vodka on the rocks and Luke mumbles something about having a diet soda.

I roll my eyes. Even his drink choice is boring. I stop the waitress on her way to the bar and tell her to skip the soda and the vodka and just bring us a round of tequila shots. She nods and winks at me.

I peer across the booth at Luke who's staring wide-eyed at his surroundings, taking in the scantily clad waitresses who pass with trays, two girls making out passionately in the next booth, and a mosh pit of recognizable celebrity faces grinding up against each other both on and off the dance floor.

Watching his deer-in-headlights expression makes me feel quite pleased with myself. This guy has been living in a bubble for far too long. It's about time someone popped it.

"I can't believe they didn't even card you," he says after the waitress delivers our shots.

I shrug. "They know who I am."

"Exactly," he replies, sniffing his tequila and grimacing. "They know you're only eighteen."

"The rules are different for me."

He lets out a short laugh and shakes his head. "So I've seen."

I hold up my shot glass and motion for him to do the same. But he just stares numbly at it. "C'mon," I coax. "Live a little."

"I live plenty, thank you."

"Oh, I doubt that." I flash him a coy grin. "I bet you've never let yourself lose control. Even for a second."

He shakes his head again but doesn't say anything.

"I'm right, aren't I?"

His body stiffens. "You don't have to get drunk off your face to have fun, you know."

"True," I admit with a smile. "But it helps."

He leans back in his seat and crosses his arms over his chest. "I think I'll just chill here and make sure you get home okay. We both know you have some trouble with that."

"Suit yourself," I say contentedly, downing my shot and then reaching across the table and grabbing his. I quickly swallow that one too and bristle at the aftertaste.

"Woo!" I cry out. "It's good to be back!"

Luke looks at me and shakes his head one more time.

I stifle a giggle. "You can stay here and be boring all you want," I say playfully, reaching out to stick my finger in his face. He jerks his head away and I scoot to the edge of the booth. "I'm going to dance. Come join me when you get tired of living in that shell."

An hour and several more shots later, I'm still on the dance floor and Luke is still presumably sulking in the booth. Although I haven't seen him since I left so there's a high probability he's already pouted his way home.

But I vow not to think about him. He's a total buzz kill and right now I feel incredible. It's so amazing to be back here. The alcohol pumping through my veins. Warming me. Loosening me. Erasing me. The music numbing my brain and silencing my thoughts. I can feel it thumping through my core, taking control of my body and whipping my limbs this way and that. I can feel my head lightening. Opening. Floating.

I let my eyes close and the rhythm take me over.

This is exactly what I needed. An escape. A diversion. A way to press reset and make the last three months disappear.

There's a brusque tap on my shoulder and my eyes flutter open to see Luke standing next to me. He's not dancing. He's not even attempting to move to the music. He's just standing there, looking drearily sober and very irritated.

"I think we should go!" he shouts over the music.

"What? Why?" I shout back. "It's not even midnight."

He looks around anxiously, his discomfort in the surroundings evident on his face. "You have to work tomorrow."

I laugh loudly. "So?"

"So, maybe you should get some rest."

"Maybe you should *give it* a rest!" I call back.

I grab Luke's waist, forcing him to move with the music. "Come on! Lighten up. It's easy. You just have to disengage from your mind."

He steps nervously out of my reach. "C'mon, Lexi. It's getting late. You've had your fun. I think I should take you home."

"Why? Are you worried about what *Daddy* will think? His intern out partying with his only daughter? Are you worried he'll disapprove?"

I can tell by the way the corners of his mouth tug downward that I've hit the nail right on the head. But still he doesn't respond.

"Look—" I start to say, but my voice catches in my throat when I see a figure in the distance, moving toward me, making his way through the crowd seemingly in slow motion. My vision is hazy from the alcohol but I recognize the shape of his broad shoulders. The slight swagger of his frame as he walks—no, *struts* through a crowd. The sexy smile that parts his lips as he recognizes me and approaches.

Luke turns to see what's snagged my attention. "Hey," he says. "Don't I know that guy from somewhere?"

I can feel the oxygen abandoning my lungs. The muscles in my legs suddenly turn to mush. My voice is hoarse and almost trembling when I answer, "Yes. That's Mendi Milos. The heir to the Milos real estate empire . . ." I pause and take a deep, stabilizing breath. "And my ex-boyfriend."

Before I can think of what to do or how to react, Mendi is suddenly next to me, his lips brushing against my cheek. "Hi, Lex," he says, that smooth accented voice slicing through the music. "I haven't seen you around in a while."

I swallow hard. "I've been busy. Taking some time off from the scene."

He smiles, causing my knees to buckle. "I don't blame you," he says. "It can get rather . . . I don't know, repetitive." He glances behind me. "Who's your friend?"

"Oh," I say in surprise. For a moment I'd forgotten Luke was even there. Mendi has always had that effect on me. Making me feel like there's no one around but us. For a dozen miles. Even in a crowded club. "Sorry. This is Luke Carver. Luke, Mendi Milos," I introduce them politely, and then quickly add, "Luke works for my father."

They shake hands, subtly sizing each other up the way only guys know how to do.

Mendi immediately turns back to me, as though Luke has simply vanished in a puff of smoke and we're back in our own little world built for two. "It's good to see you, baby. I've missed you."

I can feel my vital organs melting. Stomach first. Then lungs. Then heart. That voice used to lull me to sleep at night. It's a delicious recipe of about six countries beautifully melded together in one lilting accent. The result of growing up in hotels across Europe. And it's still, much to my dismay, the most breathtaking sound I've ever heard.

Instinctively I open my mouth to speak, to tell him that I've missed him too, when I see the girl sidle up next to him. She tucks her hand casually into the back pocket of his designer jeans and gives me a less-than-subtle once-over the way only girls know how to do.

I recognize her immediately. The long extensions of stringy blond hair. The twelve-inch waist. The D-cup chest stuffed into a B-cup bra.

My heart leaps into my throat and continues to beat there, choking me up, rendering me utterly speechless.

I watch helplessly as his arm drapes around her thin, frail shoulders. The same arm that used to hold me. That used to drape around me when I was cold. That used to shield me from the imposing flashes of nosy photographers.

"This is Serena," he says. As if I didn't know. As if the entire world hasn't been watching her on that sleazy MTV reality show for the past two years.

The infamous Serena Henson. Otherwise known as the ditzy, overprocessed backstabber.

I've never had anything against her personally. That is, until she walked into the club with my ex-boyfriend.

I simply can't believe he would actually date someone like that. A prominent European heir isn't supposed to date trashy American reality-TV stars. It simply isn't done.

"You look good," he coos to me. "What have you been up to?"

Mendi may want to hang out and chat like nothing ever happened between us—like we didn't spend the last two years running in and out of each other's lives—but I can't stand there another second. Not if I want to keep the alcohol in my stomach from coming back up. So I spin around and bolt from the dance floor, pushing my way through the crowd of people and heading for the door.

I feel a hand grip my upper arm, slowing me to a stop. I turn and once again come face-to-face with Luke. He no longer looks irritated. Now he looks genuinely concerned.

"What was that about?"

I don't answer. I wouldn't know how to respond even if I could. Because the truth is, I have no idea what that was about. I've never known what my inescapable attraction to Mendi was about. If I did, then maybe I could stop my limbs from liquefying the moment he touches me.

Without thinking, I lunge toward Luke, throwing my arms around him and planting my lips directly on his. He stumbles and falls back into an empty booth. I land on top of him, keeping my mouth pressed against his.

I clasp my hands around the back of his neck and hold his face captive. For a moment, he's frozen, clearly unable to figure out what to make of this unexpected and rather sudden turn of events. Then he starts kissing me back. His lips moving in sync with mine. His hands pressing into my back. The intensity mounting.

His participation is short-lived though. His instincts can only survive for so long. Eventually that annoying analytic brain of his catches up and after it's been given ample time to sort through all the variables and calculate the consequences, his lips fall still. His hands move from my back up to his neck, where he grabs onto my wrists and slowly disengages my grasp. Then he pulls his head back.

"Whoa, Lexi," he says, staring up at me. "What are you doing? You're not in the right mind to—"

I wave away his stupid logic and thrust myself back onto him. This time, I force my tongue into his mouth and position my body more squarely on top of his, making it harder for him to pull away.

But still he manages. He slides out from under me, causing me to fall flat against the bench seat of the booth, my protracted tongue getting a big fuzzy taste of velvet.

I struggle angrily back to a seated position. "What's your problem?" I yell. "Do you know how many guys in this club—in this *city*—would kill to be in your position right now?"

"Lexi," he cautions calmly, "you've had a lot to drink. You're not thinking clearly."

"Oh, Jesus!" I swear. "All you ever do is think clearly! It's so boring I'm going to fall asleep!" I quickly collect my emotions and replace my irritation with a flirtatious smile. I inch my way back toward him. "C'mon," I urge seductively. "Don't you ever just wanna do something without thinking?"

I lean in closer, pressing my palm against his chest. I can feel his heart racing. I can smell his faded aftershave. I start to slide his suit jacket over his shoulders and lean down to kiss his neck. His Adam's apple expands and contracts as he swallows.

"Lex," he says, his voice distressed. He gently pushes back against my shoulders. "Why are you doing this? You don't even *like* me."

"So?" I say, squirming away from the pressure of his hands. "I don't have to like you to do things to you." I run a fingertip slowly down the front of his shirt, fingering the tip of his tie and then finally gripping it and pulling him toward me. I can feel his body yielding. His defenses crashing. His inherent male instincts kicking in once again.

I stop with my lips inches away from his. "Besides, in the end love is just a business negotiation between two people."

His hands are suddenly back on my shoulders, forcing me to arms' length. "What?" he spits out.

"You heard me."

He fixes his gaze on me. "Do you really believe that?"

I shrug and look away. "Yes."

I can feel his eyes focusing intensely on my face, burning a hole into my cheek. After a long moment, he breathes out a disbelieving chuckle and shakes his head. "You're drunk," he concludes, sliding out of the booth and holding out his hand for me to take. "C'mon. I'll drive you home."

OFF WITH HIS HEAD!

I'M BEYOND HUMILIATED. AND SURPRISINGLY, IT has nothing to do with the huge straw sombrero strapped to my head. I'm trying to block out the splintered memories from last night but they keep burrowing their way back into my mind.

Luke Carver.

I kissed Luke Carver!

What the heck was I thinking?

And I'm sorry but being drunk is not a good enough excuse this time. I mean, I've done some pretty embarrassing, front-page-worthy things under the influence of alcohol before but this is something else. This is in an entirely new category of shame.

Fortunately, when I get into the car on Tuesday morning, he seems just as averse to talking about it as I am. So when I plop down in the passenger seat, I mumble something that sounds like *Good morning*, then stick headphones in my ears and blast my music. Luke fumbles to get a CD into the car stereo and then peels out of the driveway.

For the first time in the three months that we've been doing this same routine, he doesn't take five minutes to check all his knobs and buttons. He just goes. I imagine we're both equally eager to get this car ride over with.

And I'd be willing to go out on a limb here and say that we're also probably equally eager to get this *year* over with.

I guess we *do* have something in common.

Well, how do you like that?

There seems to be a universal sentiment of surprise when I walk back through the doors of Don Juan's Tacos. Everyone gives me the same bewildered look, like they've never seen me before.

"Hey." Jenna approaches cautiously as I hang my bag on a hook near the door. "You're back."

I glance down at my god-awful uniform. "Unfortunately."

She peers back over her shoulder at the room full of inquisitive faces looking in our direction. "Some people thought you might have quit after yesterday." Then softer, in a whisper, she hastily adds, "Or gotten fired."

I wish.

I paint on a bright smile and announce to the rest of the kitchen, "Nope. I'm still here!"

I see one of the employees sourly slip a twenty-dollar bill to the guy named Rolando, who grins and pockets it.

"Good!" Jenna sounds like she's trying to be bright and upbeat about it. "I hate being the only girl here."

"Where should I go?"

She glances around the kitchen. "Why don't you help with the prep work?"

I reluctantly trudge over to the counter where Rolando is dicing tomatoes with a large metal contraption. He's tall and slender with a boyish charm about him. His hair has been sheared short. Like a marine's.

"Hey," I mumble, sidling up next to him. "I'm supposed to help you."

He offers me a kind, genuine smile and pushes the carton of tomatoes toward me. "Okay, why don't you finish dicing and I'll start on filling the lettuce bins."

"So you bet I would make it past the first day, huh?" I ask as I grab a tomato and place it under the blade.

He blushes, evidently realizing that I witnessed his little cash exchange. "Oh, yeah. Sorry about that."

"Don't be," I tell him. "You're the only one who seems to have any faith in me around here." Then under my breath I add, "Or anywhere, for that matter."

I lower the lever of the dicing machine and press my weight onto it. Instead of dicing the tomato, it ends up splattering, sending seeds and juice everywhere, including all down the front of my uniform.

"Fantastic," I gripe, grabbing a towel and wiping myself down.

Rolando laughs and scurries over to help me. "Here," he says, taking another tomato and positioning it in the dicer. "Let me show you. You've got to be hard and quick. You know, like a guillotine."

I laugh at his analogy. "A guillotine?"

"Yeah," he replies, grinning from ear to ear. "You know, what they used to use to chop off heads."

"I know what a guillotine is. I was just surprised to hear it used in that way."

"It works really well, actually," he tells me. "I think of someone I dislike and pretend that the tomato is their head." He yanks the lever down firmly and swiftly. The tomato chops into a hundred smoothly cut pieces and falls into the bucket below. "See?"

I laugh again. "Looks violent."

He waves away my concern. "Not really. But it *does* make it more fun."

I grab another tomato and secure it under the blade.

"Now," Rolando prompts, "who are you going to imagine as the tomato?"

A sly smile creeps its way across my lips. "Don't worry, I have a few people in mind."

My fingers curl tightly around the black rubber handle of the lever and I use all my strength and emotion to yank the blade down fast and furiously. A small, martial-arts-style grunt even comes out involuntarily in the process. And to my surprise, the blade cuts through the tomato with ease and several more pieces tumble into the bin.

"There you go!" Rolando cheers. "Well done, girl."

I stare at my handiwork in amazement. Rolando was right. That *was* fun. I eagerly move on to my next victim and the one after that, until I'm annihilating tomatoes at record speeds.

It's amazing how good I feel. How much anger is released. How even the tension in my neck and shoulders starts to fade. When I reach the bottom of the carton and there aren't any tomatoes left, I feel better than I normally do after a five-hundred-dollar-an-hour therapy session with my shrink. I feel strong. Powerful. Almost *reformed*.

"Wow, girl," Rolando says as he gazes into the bin which is now nearly overflowing with the fruits of my wrath. "You must *really* hate someone."

I let out a weak giggle. "You have *no* idea."

LET THE GAMES BEGIN

ROLANDO IS HILARIOUS. HE HAS A WAY OF turning every single task in the restaurant into a game. In addition to Tomato Guillotine there's Prime-Time Food Line where you get points based on this complicated calculation that combines how fast you can assemble a food item with how much it weighs on the scale compared to the suggested weight printed in the Don Juan's employee handbook. Rolando is the reigning champion for the Deluxe Taco, the Grande Burrito, and the Grande Nachos.

Then there's a game called Drive-Thru Guess Who where you get points for correctly identifying character traits of people in the drive-thru line based solely on their voices. Like red hair, big boobs, or wearing a baseball hat. And since the drive-thru cameras only show the car's exterior, you get extra points if you can predict specific details about the interior. Like manual transmission or empty Starbucks cup in the cup holder. I happen to *rock* at this game. And I blew the competition right out of the water and soared to the top of the scoreboard when I correctly predicted that the woman with the sex-phone-operator voice, driving the giant black Range Rover, would be wearing a Juicy Couture sweat suit with a Tiffany heart-charm bracelet and would pay for her kids' meals out of a last-season Fendi bag. No one was able to confirm that the bag was actually last season except me but I still got like a thousand points for that one.

I don't know where Rolando comes up with some of this stuff but it's brilliant. And it makes the time go by so much faster. Normally I'm watching the clock like a hawk throughout my entire shift but today Javier actually has to tap me on the shoulder and tell me it's time to go home. Then, get this, honest to God, he says to me, "Good work today."

For a second, I think he must be joking (or talking to someone else) and so I wait for his face to give him away. But after a few moments of staring at his blank expression, I try to verify, "Really?"

And he replies earnestly, "Really. Keep it up."

I'm so shocked, I nearly faint. I thank him profusely and then prance into the employee dressing room. I grab my bag, bid the crew of the late shift a bubbly and cheerful farewell, and then float out the door.

But my good mood vanishes as soon as I remember what's waiting for me outside.

Luke.

I'm going to have to face him again. I'm going to have to share a confined space with him for the entire drive home. And then suddenly all the horrifying memories of last night start flooding back.

Mendi showing up with that reality-show tramp. Me running

from the dance floor. Throwing myself on top of Luke. Sticking my tongue in his mouth.

Yuck! Stop!

If I'm ever going to survive the next eight and a half months, I'm going to have to learn how to block out nauseating thoughts like that.

I hesitantly step out into the parking lot and cringe in anticipation of seeing his car, his face, and all the humiliation that comes along with it, but there's no sign of him. I breathe out a sigh of relief until I realize how odd it is that he's not here yet. Normally he's waiting for me at the end of every shift, like the good little brownnosing babysitter that he is.

I check my phone and find a text message saying that he's running late because my father's in the middle of some huge merger and he had some extra work for him at the office. This infuriates me. That he honestly expects me to wait around for him to show up like the last kid left at day care.

My father always says the only reason people are late is to assert a position of power. It used to annoy me when he said that. Mostly because I had no idea what he was talking about. And because he was almost always talking about me when he said it. But now I'm starting to understand what he meant.

Irritated that Luke seems to have the upper hand in every aspect of this stupid arrangement, I decide to busy myself by reading e-mails. There's one from Jia and T gushing about how they found this marvelous villa in the south of France that they're going to rent for a few months after the yachting adventure is over. Unless, of course, I need them back in LA. Then obviously they'll come running home.

Of course I need them back here. What kind of stupid question is that?

But it's not like I can actually answer it truthfully.

I sigh, swallow down a lump forming in my throat, and move on to the next e-mail. It's from Caroline. She's been trying to set up some stupid maid-of-honor brunch with Rêve and the Los Angeles press corps for weeks. I don't bother reading it. I just mark it as spam and move on.

"Great job today, girl!" A voice interrupts my e-mail scrolling and I look up to see Rolando sauntering out the back door. He slips a ragged black hoodie over his head and a red backpack onto his shoulder. His light and friendly tone immediately refreshes my smile.

"Thanks to you," I commend.

He reddens and waves away the compliment. "Nah. You did it on your own."

"Nuh-uh," I insist with an adamant shake of my head. "I never could have done that on my own. In case you haven't figured it out, I'm pretty useless when it comes to"—I wheel my hand around—"well, everything."

"I don't believe that," he says, walking over to me and bumping playfully against my shoulder. "You're just out of your element, that's all."

"You can say that again."

"Pretty different from life in Bel Air, huh?"

It takes me a moment to realize what he's said and once I do, my head reels and I gape at him, openmouthed. "What did you say?"

But he just laughs at my reaction and pulls the hood of his sweatshirt over his head. "I know your name is not Alicia," he says matter-of-factly, as if it's no big deal. As if he's simply talking about knowing how to get to the supermarket around the corner.

"W-w-wha—I don't know what you're talking about," I stammer.

He chuckles again. "Lexington Larrabee. The infamous daughter of Richard Larrabee. I know who you are. I'm just a little confused at what you're doing *here*. Some kind of social experiment?"

When I can finally form words, I stutter, "H-h-how did you know?"

He chuckles at my dumbfounded expression. "I figured it out as soon as you got here. My girlfriend is a huge fan. She has posters of you on every wall of her bedroom. I was pretty sure I knew who you were right away but then when you broke out with the French, that's when I was sure. My girlfriend is taking French next semester so she can be more like you." He nods at my hair. "It's a wig, right?"

I lightly finger my Alicia hairdo and then, after a few seconds, pull it off completely, revealing the messy bun underneath.

Rolando doesn't look surprised. He simply nods, confirming his suspicions.

"You didn't . . . uh . . . tell anyone, did you?" I ask, suddenly feeling very anxious and a bit queasy at the thought of a grainy camera phone photograph of me showing up on *Access Hollywood* tonight. "Like your girlfriend? Or anyone at Don Juan's?"

"Nah," he says breezily. "I figured if you wanted people to know who you were, you would have said something."

I breathe a sigh of relief. "Thank you."

"So," he continues, "what *is* Lexington Larrabee doing working at a Don Juan's Tacos?"

"Well," I begin with a laugh, "how long have you got?"

"My mom is making enchiladas tonight," he tells me. "She makes the best enchiladas outside of Mexico. Why don't you come over for dinner?"

I glance down at my phone. Still no word from Luke on when he'll actually be here. Plus, an opportunity to put off seeing him for another few hours? That's pretty hard to resist.

I smile to myself when I think about him showing up here to find me gone. And then totally flipping out.

Well, well. Look who has the upper hand now.

I switch off my phone and place it back in my bag. "Sure," I reply with a shrug. "Why not?"

"Cool," he says, and cocks his thumb toward the bus stop on the corner. "Come on, you can ride home with me."

I glance anxiously in the direction his finger is pointing. "On the bus?"

He lets out a hearty laugh. "Oh yeah, I bet you've never even ridden public transportation before."

"Now that's not true," I correct him. "I rode the subway in Paris once when I was thirteen." I pause and then quickly amend. "Although it was to celebrate the new expansion of a subway line and the train was empty except for me, my father, and a bunch of French press."

Rolando starts to pull his sweatshirt back over his head. "Doesn't count."

"Yeah, I didn't think so."

He hands me the hoodie. "Here put this on." Then he flashes me a wink. "For a little extra camouflage."

I take it and slide my arms through the sleeves. It's tattered but smells like fabric softener. It feels incredibly smooth against my skin. Like nothing I've ever felt before. For some reason it reminds me of my mother. Or the little that I remember of her.

I guess this is what happens to clothes when you keep them longer than one season.

"C'mon, girl," Rolando says with a tug at my borrowed sleeve. "I'll show you *my* chauffeured transportation."

I laugh and place my wig back on my head and the hood of the sweatshirt over it. Rolando yanks down on the cords on either side, drawing the material tight against my head.

"Perfect," he says, grinning from ear to ear. "You'll blend right in."

HOW THE OTHER HALF LAUGHS

THE BUS IS PACKED. AND LIKE US, EVERYONE appears to have recently come off an eight-hour shift. Which doesn't exactly help in the odor department but I do my best to mask my displeasure. I don't want to offend Rolando, who clearly does this every day—based on the fluidity of his movements as he deposits bus fare for both of us and smoothly makes his way to the back, transferring his grip from handrail to handrail like a little kid on the monkey bars of a playground.

I attempt to emulate his technique but am decidedly less adept and end up knocking into about a dozen people as the bus lurches its way through the evening traffic.

Rolando finds two seats together in the back and we sit down. He chatters animatedly as the bus makes its way down the wide boulevard. There's something so innocently intriguing about Rolando. Like watching somebody jump on a bed. You can't help but want to laugh, toss off your shoes, and join in.

He has this infectious optimism about everything. Nothing seems to bother him. He tells me stories about growing up in the "armpit of Los Angeles," as he calls it, and starting community college but having to quit after only one semester to get the job at Don Juan's to help support his family because his dad had a heart attack and had to take time off from work. But when Rolando tells the story, instead of getting dark and whiny about his family's misfortune, he remains cheerful and carefree, as though he's simply recapping a dramatic episode of his favorite TV show.

It's amazing how he's able to do that.

Rolando is so easy to talk to. His energy relaxes me and somehow manages to quell the near constant flame that is always threatening to ignite in my chest. I find it effortless to open up to him. So when the conversation finally makes its way back to my week-long cameo at Don Juan's, I have no reservations about telling him everything. It all kind of spills out.

Rolando is a great listener. And the best part about it is, he's not being *paid* to do it. He doesn't work for my father. He's not on the official Larrabee family payroll. He simply wants to hear what I have to say. And when I talk, it actually seems like he genuinely *cares*.

"So these jobs," he says pensively, once I've finished talking, "do they have any meaning or are they just random?"

His question takes me by surprise. After all the griping and complaining I've done over the past few months, after all the ways I've tried to get out of them, I never even thought to ask that.

"I don't know," I finally admit. "I guess they're random. I mean, no one's told me any different."

"Hmm," Rolando murmurs, clearly unconvinced. "Does your dad usually do random things?"

Before the question is even out of his mouth, my head is shaking. "No way. Never."

"Then there's probably some kind of meaning to them. I doubt he just picked them out of a hat."

I shrug. "Not that it really matters to me. I'm still screwed for another thirty-seven weeks."

"You have to look on the bright side," he says playfully.

"And what would that be exactly?"

He flashes that adorable boyish grin of his that makes him look like he's five years old. "You got to meet me. Obviously!"

I laugh. "Oh right. How could I forget?"

Rolando lives with his parents in an apartment complex in Inglewood, which is about thirty minutes from the restaurant. We get off the bus a few blocks from his house and walk. The neighborhood is unsettling and the building he lives in is very old and rundown. Some of the windows have cracks in them that have been temporarily repaired with duct tape and the entire front wall is covered in graffiti. For a moment, I seriously think that this is some kind of joke. That he's messing with me because he knows I live in Bel Air and he wants to see my reaction to something like this. Because honestly, I can't imagine *anyone* living here. Except maybe the crackheads and murder suspects you see on those television crime shows.

Rolando, as if reading my mind, turns to me and says, "We used to share a two-bedroom house with four other families, so this is a huge improvement."

This is an improvement!?

I stare at him in utter disbelief but he just laughs and unlocks the front door of the building.

As he leads me through a neglected courtyard with landscaping that hasn't been attended to in decades and an empty pool caked with dried mud, I study his face carefully. I'm not quite sure what I'm looking for but whatever it is, it's not there. I guess I'm searching for some small traces of humiliation . . . or maybe even shame. You can't bring someone home to this and not feel the slightest tinge of embarrassment. Or at least scramble to make up some kind of excuse. Something like, *We're remodeling our mansion uptown and this is only temporary.*

The world I inhabit is full of cover-ups like that. Elaborate lies that shroud the ugly truth in fabricated beauty. Ornate disguises designed to elicit approval and acceptance.

But not here. Not Rolando. He looks like he could care less what I think of his family's humble dwelling.

"¡Mama! Papa!" he calls as he pushes open the door of his apartment with a shove of his shoulder and beckons me in behind him. *"¡Estoy a la casa!"*

I push back the hood of Rolando's sweatshirt and glance around the cramped apartment, taking note of the grungy brown shag carpeting, the peeling paint on the walls, and what looks like third- or maybe even fourth-hand furniture. But despite the evident lack of extravagance, there's something here that doesn't exist in my family's house. In *any* of our houses. Something dense and warm in the air—almost palpable. And it only takes me a few seconds to realize exactly what it is.

This place feels lived-in. And not only in the sense that people sleep in the beds and keep things in the dressers.

A tall and skinny middle-aged man rises from the couch and

walks over to us. He looks exactly how I imagine Rolando will look in twenty-five years. The same round face and bulging cheeks, the same but slightly larger nose, and dark almond-shaped eyes. They even have the same short haircut.

"*¡Hola!*" the man says in a husky but welcoming voice. "*¡Bienvenido a nuestra casa!*"

"*Papa,*" Rolando scolds, giving me an apologetic glance. "She doesn't speak Spanish."

But I step past Rolando and offer my hand to his father. "*Gracias, Señor Castaño. Estoy muy contento de estar aquí.*"

Rolando gives me a where-on-earth-did-that-come-from look while his father beams ecstatically in my direction and pulls me into a giant bear hug.

"*Hola, mi cariño,*" comes another voice as a short, heavyset woman scurries out of the kitchen with a spatula in her hand. Rolando kisses her forehead and introduces her as his mother.

"*¡Vengan!*" She beckons toward the dining table behind us. "Dinner is ready."

"I thought you spoke French," Rolando whispers as he holds a chair out for me.

"I was raised by a Mexican maid and an Argentinean butler," I explain, taking a seat.

He pushes in my chair. "Oh, right."

"I hope you're hungry," Roland's mom says as she buries the spatula deep into a giant platter of cheesy enchiladas. She carves out a humongous piece, sets it down on a plate, and hands it to me with a smile.

I laugh nervously and take the large helping, wondering how

I'm ever supposed to finish it. Good thing I'm still wearing my uniform with the elastic waistband.

After everyone has been served, I pick up my fork and take a cautious bite. I'm immediately bombarded by the most amazing burst of flavor—tangy spices mixed with rich, creamy cheese. It's by far one of the best things I've ever tasted. I chew slowly, savoring the taste, almost reluctant to swallow.

When I look up, I realize that no one else has started eating yet. They're all staring at me, waiting to see my reaction.

I blush and wipe my mouth with my napkin. "Rolando was right, Mrs. Castaño. These are the best enchiladas ever!"

The three of them break into matching grins and I can't help but notice how adorable they look with their wide eyes and contagious smiles. Everyone starts in on their own plates and I take another delectable bite.

The conversation flows easily as the Castaños share stories about their day and the people they encountered. Rolando raves about my top-notch score in Drive-Thru Guess Who and everyone cracks up at his animated retelling of my passionate encounter with the guillotine, complete with dramatic reenactment.

As I observe the interactions between Rolando and his family— the easy dialogue, the affectionate banter, the knowing glances that are exchanged between decade-long inside jokes—I realize how strange and unfamiliar it all is to me. Like I'm a zoologist observing some rare animal species in its natural habitat.

So *this* is what real families do.

They talk. Make each other laugh. Dole out warm smiles and tender looks as freely as the sun doles out light.

They sit together in one place. At one table. Sharing one meal. Without a photographer there to document it for the next issue of *Time* magazine.

And then, like a cold arctic wind, the reality of the situation hits me with an icy sting.

They're not the strange and unfamiliar ones. *I* am. I'm the one who doesn't fit in. I'm the one who no one can quite figure out.

My family is the rare animal species that everyone wants to observe in its natural habitat. That everyone wants to study and photograph and speculate about—its origins and the way its members interact with one another.

Well, *almost* everyone.

If Rolando forewarned his parents about who I am or who my father is, you wouldn't know it. They don't treat me like everyone else treats me. They don't ask about what kind of cars I drive or what it's like to be the daughter of one of the richest men in the world. Most new people I meet don't want to know about *me*. They want to know what I can do for *them*. Can I get their demo CD to the president of Capitol Records? Can I introduce them to the hottest new movie director in town? Or my personal favorite: Can I pass their résumé on to my father?

I find that one especially hilarious because it's not like my father would ever hire someone based on a referral that came from *me*.

Rolando's parents, on the other hand, behave as though I'm just another friend of the family. A welcome guest at their dinner table. And I've never felt more grateful to blend in.

I've never felt more normal.

"So"—Mr. Castaño turns the spotlight on me as his wife walks around the table pouring coffee into four mismatched cups—"How do you like working at Don Juan's?"

I sigh. "Well, let's just say I probably would have died if it weren't for your son, here. He has a knack for making prison feel like Disneyland."

Mrs. Castaño places the pot down on the table and rubs her son's head affectionately before returning to her seat and sipping her coffee. "Rolando was always a happy child," she boasts. "No matter what he was doing or where he was, he could keep himself entertained. When he was six—"

"Nuh-uh," Rolando interjects, extending his arm out in front of his mother as though he's attempting to halt her from flying through the windshield of a suddenly braking car. "I draw the line at childhood stories."

The table erupts with laughter and Mrs. Castaño presses her lips together tightly with a wry smile, obliging his request.

"How do you do it, though?" I inquire eagerly. "How do you show up there day after day and act like it's your dream job?"

"Ha!" he exclaims. "That is *so* not my dream job. Do you really think I *like* hawking ninety-nine-cent tacos every day? I hate it there! The only thing I want to do is coach NBA basketball."

"Really?" I ask, somewhat surprised. "That's what you want to do?"

Rolando nods earnestly. "Absolutely. It's been my dream since I was a kid. I've been coaching basketball from in front of my TV since I was five. And for the past three years I've been volunteer coaching in an intercity kids' league."

"He's very passionate about it," Mr. Castaño puts in proudly.

"One year for Christmas we got him one of those dry-erase boards and he sat and watched basketball nonstop for a week, drawing those Xs and Os and dotted lines all over the board. It was the best gift we ever got him."

I shake my head, baffled. "But you're always so upbeat when you're at Don Juan's," I say. "How can you be that way when you clearly want to be doing something else? How can you be so happy doing something you hate?"

"Happiness doesn't come from a job," Mrs. Castaño answers patiently, her thick Spanish accent turning the words into a poem. "Otherwise most of the world would be unhappy."

I want to counter with the argument that most of the world *is* unhappy. At least from what I've seen. But something compels me to keep quiet. To refrain from crashing the party with my cynicism.

"In Spanish we have an expression," Mr. Castaño elaborates. *"No hay mal que por bien no venga."*

"There is no bad," I translate slowly, "that doesn't come with good?"

"Sí," he replies, flashing me a strange look that I can't interpret. It takes a moment for me to realize what it is. And I only recognize it because I saw it a few minutes ago. When he looked at Rolando the same way.

It's pride.

Fatherly pride.

"It means," he continues, "there are always two sides to every-thing. Where there is bad, there is also good. I think in English they call it the gold lining."

"Silver," Rolando corrects.

"*Sí*, silver," he repeats. "Sometimes you have to look very hard to find this silver lining."

I have to smile at Mr. Castaño's little anecdote. The kindhearted tone of his voice. The way he describes it with such certainty. Such faith. It's endearing. In the same way Rolando's blind optimism about everything is endearing. But deep down, I find it hard to believe. Impossible, even. At least for me.

But a sudden disheartening realization brings me back to my cold, harsh reality.

Because the truth is, I can try to hide out in this simple, normal world where silver linings are a dime a dozen and happiness grows on trees. I can don a wig and a hand-me-down hoodie and pretend to fit in here. I can laugh with the other half and eat the local food and drink the supermarket coffee. But in the back of my mind, I know I'm only a visitor on this planet. I can't stay.

Eventually my kind will come looking for me. My world will catch up with me. Someone will knock on that front door and drag me back to where I came from.

To where I belong.

NO PLACE LIKE HOME

THE SUMMONING COMES IN THE FORM OF A phone call. Evidently when I didn't answer my cell, Luke found out from an eyewitness that I was last seen leaving the parking lot of Don Juan's with Rolando, tracked down his number from Javier, and called him instead.

After I've endured five minutes of Luke's angry rants and tried, for the sake of Rolando's family, not to let any of it show on my face, Luke finally hangs up. But not before warning me that he's coming to get me.

Not wanting him to barge in here and destroy this safe place that I've managed to create for myself, I say a fond farewell to Mr. and Mrs. Castaño, thank them profusely for the dinner and conversation, and opt to wait outside for my ride.

Rolando accompanies me, claiming that it's not safe for me to stand outside alone in this neighborhood. And as soon as I reach the curb and realize how much scarier this place is at night, I'm glad that he insisted.

"So, where do you go after the end of this week?" Rolando asks me, leaning casually against a streetlamp.

"I don't know. I'll have to check the list when I get home. But you can be sure it will suck. That seems to be the pre-requisite."

"Well," he says with a half smile, "I guess you'll have to figure out a way to make it *un*suck."

I shake my head. "That's your strength. Not mine. The rest of us just have to endure it."

"I don't know," he says thoughtfully. "I think you're gonna be okay. I have a lot of faith in you, girl."

I scoff at this. "You're probably the only one in the world who does."

He raises his eyebrows inquisitively.

"It's like this morning in the restaurant," I explain, tucking my hands into the pocket of my borrowed hoodie. "You were the only one who bet that I would make it longer than a day."

"And I won," he's quick to mention.

"That's not the point," I counter. "The point is my entire life has been like that. People betting against me. No one has ever ex-pected anything of me. Except failure. Sometimes it feels as though the whole world is waiting on the edge of their seat for my next screw-up. And my father is the worst of them all. I honestly think he set up this whole arrangement—this whole fifty-two-jobs thing—just to watch me fall on my face."

"Maybe," he admits, pushing himself from the streetlamp and walking over to me, "or maybe you've never succeeded because you *think* no one expects you to."

My eyebrows knit together as I try to follow his backward logic. "Huh?"

"I mean, maybe you've only been giving them what you think they want."

I shake my head adamantly. "No way. I would never knowingly *choose* to give my father what he wants."

"Exactly," he replies cryptically.

"Okay, Rolando. You're starting to get weird on me now."

"Sorry," he says with a soft laugh. Then his face turns somewhat serious again. "I'm just saying, instead of constantly living up to everyone's expectations, why not destroy them?"

"Destroy them?" I repeat with uncertainty.

He gives a small, unassuming shrug. "Yeah. If everyone expects you to fail, why not do exactly the opposite?"

"Succeed?" I take a shot in the dark.

"Not just succeed," he amends. "Blow them away. Shock the heck out of them. Be *awesome*."

A horn honks behind me and I look up to see Luke glaring at me through the windshield of his Honda Civic.

Rolando squints against the blinding headlights. "Boyfriend?" he guesses.

I roll my eyes. "Worse. Babysitter."

"I'm not even going to ask."

"Thanks for everything," I say.

"You got it, girl." He takes a step forward, opens his arms, and wraps me in a tight hug. I sink into him, feeling safe and warm there. Like he's an extension of his tiny apartment.

Luke honks again—this guy has *got* to think of a better way to get my attention—and I reluctantly pull away from Rolando's embrace and reach for the door handle. I stop when I realize I'm still wearing his sweatshirt. "Oh, here." I start to take it off.

"Don't worry about it," Rolando says. "You can give it back to me tomorrow. Or better yet, just keep it."

I hesitate but he insists. "You'll need it as part of your disguise if you ever want to come back here to visit."

"Well, I guess that's true. Thanks." I open the car door and drop into the passenger seat. "See you tomorrow at work!"

Rolando watches us pull away from the curb before turning back to his apartment building.

"New boyfriend?" Luke speculates snidely.

I can't help but laugh at his tone. It's not playful and fun like Rolando's was when he asked me the same question. It's more spiteful.

"No. Just a friend," I answer, buckling my seat belt. "I am allowed to make friends, aren't I? Or is that against the rules?"

Luke grunts and shakes his head, evidently opting out of the argument. "Just tell me next time you wanna go home with some guy."

I snicker at how ridiculous and overprotective he sounds. Like a jealous boyfriend. "Yeah," I say, rolling my eyes. "I'll be sure to do that."

The house is quiet and empty when I get home. Most of the staff have retired for the evening and Horatio has the night off. I stand in the middle of the entry hall and marvel at the stark difference between the home I just left and the one I stand in now. The one I supposedly call my own.

Like with all of our houses stashed around the globe, there's a hollow coldness that I never really noticed before—at least not consciously. An emptiness that's never really filled, even with a guest list of four hundred people.

I aimlessly wander through the various rooms of the first floor—the library, the billiard room, the salon. It doesn't take long for me to pinpoint what the Castaños' small, run-down apartment has that this fifteen-thousand-square-foot mansion in Bel Air doesn't.

It's not something you can buy in an expensive designer furniture boutique. It's not something you can hire an interior decorator to paint into the walls. It's not even something you can photograph and put on display in a home-and-garden magazine.

What the Castaños have made is a *home*. A place you return to not because of *what* is there waiting for you but because of *who*.

This is nothing but a pile of expensive bricks and imported fabrics.

And even though I'm grateful to have been able to catch just a fleeting glimpse of what I've missed out on my entire life, it also fills me with a sense of despair that runs deep. Deeper than I usually let anything go. I feel it sinking into me. Spreading out. I feel it being absorbed by my blood. Seeping into distant, back corners that are impossible to reach. Impossible to clean.

I feel cheated. Robbed. Like I got some kind of raw deal. And I'm not talking about the fifty-two jobs. I'm talking about my entire existence. Yes, I've been given everything I've ever wanted. I've been dressed in the most expensive clothes, slept in the most lavish hotels, eaten the most delectable foods since I was a baby, and yet I still feel like I got the short end of whatever stick is used to measure a life.

Numbly, I pour myself a drink from the bar in the library. I slosh the clear liquid around, listening to the familiar clink of the ice against the glass. But I don't drink it. I don't even bring it to my lips to taste. I abandon it on a table and head for the stairs.

With a sigh, I drag my tired body up the long, spiral staircase and down the hall to my bedroom. I slide the wig from my head, pull off Rolando's comfy black sweatshirt, slip on a pair of clean cotton pajamas, and wash the makeup from my face.

When I climb into bed and pull the covers up to my chin, I know that something has changed tonight. A switch has been flipped. A fuse has been lit.

And I know that, unlike so many other times in my life—so many other moments of bleakness—this time it won't be as easy to bury. It won't be as easy to suppress. I won't be able to pop a pill or down a drink and make it all fade into black.

But the most frightening thought of all, as I shut off the light and hug the pillow to my chest, is realizing that, this time, I'm not sure I want to.

CLICK <u>HERE</u> TO PLAY MESSAGE

Or read the free transcript from our automated speech-
to-text service below.

[BEGIN TRANSCRIPT]

Hey, Luke! Check it out! I'm recording this status report
from my cell phone using the new Video-Blaze mobile app.
Pretty cool, huh?

So here I am on the last day of my job at Morty's Flower
Shop. But I guess you can tell from this outdoor
ambience that I'm not actually *in* Morty's Flower Shop
right now. I'm out on a delivery run.

This is, by far, the coolest part of the job so I thought
I'd bring you along. You know, like, "live from the
scene."

If you look behind me you can see a house. But not just
any house. That's the house of Victoria Rivera and she's

about to find out that her husband is coming home from Iraq next week. How do I know this? Because he sent her flowers! And that's what he wanted written on the card. Isn't that sweet? And now I get to deliver them to her.

Oh crap. I left the flowers in the van. Hold on a second.

[Unidentified sound]

Okay, I'm back. With the flowers. See? Aren't they pretty? I made the arrangement myself. Turns out I have quite a knack for flower arranging. You can ask Morty himself. He even told me I could have a full-time job here when I'm done. How do you like that?

But seriously, this job has been really cool. You know what they say about shooting the messenger? Well, this is like the opposite of that. Check it out.

[Knocking sound]

Hello. Victoria Rivera? These are for you.

[Screaming sound]

I'm so glad you like them! Hey, can you do me a favor and look into the camera here and tell my friend Luke how much you like the flowers?

Oh my God, I love the flowers!!!

Thank you. And one more thing, would you mind telling him that I'm doing an *awesome* job being a florist?

Hi, Luke. This girl is awesome. The flowers are gorgeous.

Thanks!

Did you hear that, Luke? *Awesome.*

And speaking of awesome? Did you get a call from Phil, my supervisor at last week's job? He said he was going to call you in person to tell you how well I did. Who knew telemarketing was my thing? Did he tell you how many credit-protection packages I sold in one week? Phil swore it was some kind of company record. I guess I can be pretty persuasive when I want to be. Although I don't need to tell you that, right?

Seriously, though, you really should protect your credit card against fraud. There are a lot of dishonest people out there who would steal your identity in a heartbeat.

But I think my favorite part about working there was getting to talk to so many people on the phone. Sure, most people hang up and call you nasty things, but there are some really nice people out there too. One day I talked this sweet young woman out of marrying her emotionally abusive fiancé. That was kind of a highlight. I mean, imagine what her life would have been like if it weren't for me calling to sell her a credit-protection plan.

All right, so this is job #16. Job #15 was the telemarketing. What was before that? Oh, right. The car wash. I won't lie. That was pretty hard at first. But do you notice how tan I am? It's like I spent the week at the beach! That was definitely an unexpected plus from scrubbing cars all day. And check out these guns! Washing cars is like the best arm-toning exercise ever. Screw Pilates!

Okay, well, that's all for now. Consider yourself officially statused. I'm signing off.

Until next time.

[END TRANSCRIPT]

THE PURSUIT OF AWESOMENESS

AFTER PRESSING SEND ON LUKE'S LATEST VIDEO update, I start the engine of Morty's delivery van and head back to the flower shop. As anxious as I am to move on to the next job and keep plugging away, I'm actually kind of sad that this is my last day here. I really *did* have a good time.

Ever since I left Rolando's apartment a few weeks ago, I've been giving a lot of thought to what he said on the curb that night. About expectations.

And the more I thought about it, the more I realized he was right.

I've spent the last eighteen years living up to everyone's bottom-of-the-barrel expectations of me. For as long as I can remember people have thought of me as nothing but a failure. A spoiled-brat princess with no values and zero work ethic. And for as long as I can remember, I've been doing nothing but proving them right.

All this time I thought the only way to get back at my father for putting me through this hell was to sulk and throw temper tantrums and complain about how miserable I am. How unfortunate my lot in life is. How unfairly I've been treated.

But you know what? That's exactly what everyone expects me to do—my father, Bruce, even Luke. And that's probably because it's exactly what I've always done.

And where has it gotten me?

Nowhere.

I realized that if I truly do want to get back at my father I have to do exactly what Rolando said. I have to succeed with flying colors. For once in my life, I have to prove them *wrong*, rather than right.

I have to be *awesome*.

So that's exactly what I've been trying to do. And it turns out it's actually a lot easier than I thought. I'm better at some of these jobs than I would have ever imagined I could be. I guess I was so busy whining about doing them that I never gave myself the opportunity to figure out *how* to do them.

"I enjoyed your last status report," Luke says when he picks me up later that afternoon.

"Thanks," I say, smiling to myself. "I thought you might."

I buckle my seat belt and prepare myself for the drive but Luke doesn't move. He fidgets awkwardly with the end of his tie, looking like he wants to say something else but is having trouble getting it out.

"Is that all?" I prompt.

"Actually, no."

I turn and face him. "Okay. What? Is it about Morty? He hasn't called you yet with my final progress report because he's trying to fill a huge order for tomorrow. He said he'd call first thing in the morning."

"No, no," Luke says quickly. "It's not about work."

This makes me laugh. "Not about work? Since when do you *ever* not talk about work?"

"I know," he admits sheepishly.

"What's it about then?"

He contorts his mouth uncomfortably and looks away. "Actually it's about clothes."

"Clothes?" I spit back in disbelief. "You want to talk to me about *clothes*?"

Now he looks even more uncomfortable than before. "Well, remember the engagement party?"

"And you looked like you were showing up for a round of golf? Yeah."

"Exactly," he replies. "You told me the next time I needed help picking something out, I should call you."

My grin widens and I touch my hand to my heart. "Oh, Luke," I tease. "You want me to *dress* you? I'm so flattered."

His face starts to turn several shades of red. "Well . . . sort of . . . I mean, I have something in mind but . . ." He's all over the place now, barely even able to form a complete sentence. Very *un*Luke-like.

I decide to put him out of his misery. "Where and when are you going?" I ask authoritatively, stepping in and taking control of the situation.

He breathes a sigh of relief. "To a gallery opening. In Silver Lake. It's tonight."

"Who's the artist?"

"Some new kid from Brazil that everyone is talking about. My friend knows him and asked if I wanted to come."

"Okay," I sum up. "Silver Lake. Gallery opening. Hot new artist. I think I've got the picture."

"So what happens now?" Luke asks, looking awkward again.

"What do you think happens now? We go to Rodeo, of course!"

"Shouldn't we go to my apartment first so you can see what I already have?"

I shake my head and flash him a patronizing smile. It's nice to be on the other end of one for once. "Oh, Luke, Luke," I say condescendingly. "I can *guarantee* you don't have anything of use in your closet."

UNDERNEATH IT ALL

WHEN LUKE STEPS OUT OF THE DRESSING ROOM it's like he's a different person. The contrast is so startling, I almost feel inclined to peek my head around the curtain and check that he didn't leave the other version of himself in a lifeless heap in the corner.

He's wearing the vintage Diesel narrow-leg jeans I picked out for him along with the yellow graphic tee and white sports coat. Even though I'm the one who selected the outfit, I barely recognize him. In the more than three months that I've known him, I don't think I've ever seen him wear *anything* but a boring corporate suit. And that disaster he showed up in at my father's engagement party.

Right now he actually looks *normal.*

No. More than normal. He even looks kind of *hot.* I mean, the *clothes* look hot. On him.

I let out a low whistle and give him an encouraging nod. "Now *that's* much better." I spin my finger in the air, commanding him to twirl.

He gives me a bashful grin and does a full rotation.

I tilt my head to the side and study the outfit. "Actually," I say, my smile falling into a frown, "the T-shirt is wrong. Hold it right there."

I scamper back to the rack where we found the graphic tee. I locate a dark hunter-green version of the same one and bring it back to the dressing room. "Here," I say, sliding the shirt from the hanger, "try this one instead."

He shrugs off the jacket, lays it carefully to the side, and then starts to pull the yellow T-shirt up over his head.

"Uh . . . maybe you should . . ." I start to suggest that perhaps he should do that in the dressing room. That is, after all, the *name* of the room. But before I can get the full sentence out, the shirt is off and Luke's bare chest is staring me right in the face. And the sight of it dries up every last drop of saliva in my mouth.

Um, *hello*? Can someone say *ripped*? Where on earth did those pecs come from? And abs too? Don't tell me he's been hiding those under that stuffy suit this *entire* time. What a complete and utter waste!

And where does he find the time to tan? He looks like he's been spending the summer at the beach or something. Not cooped up in a tiny cubicle at my father's office. Or driving me to and from random job assignments.

I would tell myself to close my mouth but my brain is not really communicating with my body properly. Because if it were, I'd be able to command my eyes to look away. But that's *so* not happening.

"Lexi," I hear a voice say from far away. It takes me a few moments to realize it's Luke who's talking to me. I mean, I assume it's him. There's no one else around. But it's not like I'm going to risk glancing away from his chest just to check that his lips are moving.

"*Lexi,*" he repeats again. This time a bit louder. "The shirt?"

"Huh?" I blink and quickly realize that I'm still holding the green shirt that he's supposed to be trying on. I glance down at my hand and realize that the shirt is now totally crumpled from being clutched between my fingers.

"Oh," I say, suddenly unsure of what to do with my hands. "This one is wrinkled. I'll get you a new one."

"Where's that wrinkle-resistant clothing you suggested in your status report, huh?"

"Yeah," I call back with a nervous laugh as I stumble to the rack to fetch a fresh shirt.

When I return, I reluctantly hand it over and watch as he slides it over his body and replaces the white jacket.

He turns and faces the three-way mirror, pulling the lapels down.

"Better?" he asks.

No, I want to say. *It most certainly is* not *better.* But I manage to hide my disappointment with a forced smile and mumble, "Yeah, much better. That color makes your eyes pop."

He nods his approval into the mirror. "Okay, cool. I'll take it." Then he turns to me and grins. "Thanks. You're a rock star."

Luke returns to the dressing room to grab his suit and I wander up to the counter to check out a display of sunglasses. I pick out the perfect pair to complement his new outfit and place them on the counter. Luke reappears a few moments later, still in his outfit, and asks the salesgirl if he can wear the clothes out of the store.

"Of course!" she says with a bubbly little bounce as she grabs a pair of scissors and proceeds to cut the tags off so she can ring them up.

I slide the sunglasses forward. "He'll take these as well."

Luke raises one eyebrow at me. "Sunglasses?" he questions. "At night?"

"Trust me."

He holds up his hands. "You're the boss."

I laugh. "At least until Monday morning, right?"

Luke pulls out his wallet to pay for his new wares right as my cell phone beeps. I check the screen to find a text message from Morty, the owner of the flower shop.

"Oh," I say, somewhat surprised. "Morty just texted me. His evening driver didn't show up and he has a few more deliveries that need to be made. Would you mind dropping me back there? I can call Kingston for a ride home when I'm done."

Luke signs his credit card receipt. "Of course not. In fact, I'll go with you."

I give him a skeptical look. "To deliver flowers?"

He shrugs. "Sure, why not."

I nod toward his trendy ensemble. "What about your gallery opening?"

The salesgirl folds his suit and places it in a shopping bag. He takes it from her and glances at his watch. "I don't have to be there for another two hours. Besides, after that inspiring status report of yours today, how could I pass up an opportunity to see what all the fuss is about?"

"Well," I say with a lighthearted chuckle, "*those* are three words I never thought I'd hear in the same sentence."

Luke's forehead crumples. "What?"

"Inspiring status report."

DISCONNECTED

FOR THE NEXT HOUR AND A HALF LUKE AND I circle the west side, delivering delightful gifts to unsuspecting people. There's Beatrice in Beverly Hills whose husband is sorry about missing dinner the night before. Margaret in Santa Monica turned eighty and her grandson, who's away at college, sent a vase of beautiful white calla lilies (her favorite flower). The Carson family just moved into their gorgeous new home in Cheviot Hills and were welcomed to the neighborhood by the homeowners' association. And my favorite delivery of the night is twelve-year-old Nessa in Culver City who received a dozen red roses from a secret admirer. Seeing that girl's face light up when she read the card was like seeing the Rockefeller Center Christmas tree light up in November.

I watch Luke's reactions carefully throughout the evening. I can tell he's completely enjoying himself. There's really no way *not* to enjoy a job like this. The look on someone's face when they open their front door and see you standing there with that bouquet of flowers in your hand is an instant mood shifter.

Like a drug.

And it has to be because Luke and I have never gone this long without saying something nasty to each other. In fact, we spend most of the evening laughing. Only a mood-altering substance could do something like that—turn mortal enemies into giggling allies.

When all the orders have been delivered, apart from one whose recipient wasn't home, we climb into the cab of Morty's van and head back to the flower shop.

"I want to tell you something," Luke says as I turn onto Washington Boulevard and head toward the freeway, "but I'm afraid it's going to come out wrong."

I give him a sideways glance. "Luke, I just saw you shirtless. Spit it out."

He laughs. "Okay." He takes a breath. "I wanted to say that I'm proud of you."

I give him a strange look. "For what?"

"For learning how to make the most of what you're doing. When we first started working together, you were exactly how I expected you to be."

"And how exactly did you expect me to be?" I ask coyly.

He teeters his head from side to side. "You know . . . spoiled, ungrateful, bitchy . . ."

"The usual?" I confirm with a smirk.

He laughs. "Yeah, I guess. I mean when your father told me what he wanted me to do—that he wanted me to be your . . . well, let's face it, *babysitter*, I was completely skeptical about the whole thing. But I wanted to work for your father so badly that I agreed. I honestly didn't know how I'd be able to put up with you for a whole year. After everything I'd read about you in the tabloids and seen on TV, I was sure I'd quit after one week. Or at least *you* would."

"Thanks, Luke," I say mockingly. "I'm flattered really."

"But," he says, holding up one finger, "you've genuinely surprised me in the last few weeks. It's like you've managed to find the fun in what you're being asked to do. The silver lining or something."

I think about Rolando's father and what he said over dinner about this very subject and I can't stop the grin from spreading across my face. "Or something."

"Anyway, I'm impressed. That's all."

My grin widens. "Well, thanks, Luke," I reply playfully, pulling into the parking lot of Morty's and killing the engine. I turn to face him. "You've impressed me too."

He flashes me a curious look. "Oh really, how so?"

"Well, for one, I never expected you to have abs like that."

He busts out laughing. The van is dark inside so I can't exactly see the color of his face but I'm pretty sure it's turned a bright shade of crimson again.

"And," I continue, "you've certainly gone above and beyond the call of duty tonight."

"In what way?"

I gesture to the inside of the van. "I don't think delivering flowers with me on a Friday night is part of your job description."

He laughs again. This time it's softer. More subdued. I've never noticed the way his eyes crinkle when he smiles. It's actually kind of sexy. He leans forward slightly, just close enough that I feel his energy pulling me in.

"There are probably a lot of things I've done over the past few months that aren't in the job description," he jokes.

But his smile fades as soon as his eyes lock on mine. He's only a few feet away from me but suddenly it feels like miles too far. For some reason I find myself willing him with my mind to scoot closer.

"And does that bother you?" I ask softly. "Doing things that aren't in your job description?"

"I guess that depends on what they are," he breathes. Barely a whisper.

The words draw me in and I feel the space between us closing. I'm not really sure what's happening right now. It's as though my mind has once again detached from my body. Just like it did back outside the dressing room. Like whatever wire connects my brain to the rest of me has suddenly snapped and there's nothing but empty static filling my head.

But for some unexplained reason, I find myself welcoming the white noise. Appreciating the inability to think. Because if my brain were to suddenly start working again, I know it would tell me that whatever is happening right now is wrong. Very, very wrong.

And at this exact moment I'm not sure that's something I want to hear.

Luke's lips are inches away from mine. I allow my eyes to slowly drift closed. Through the narrowing gap in my vision, I see his do the same. And right before the blissful darkness surrounds me, a shrill beeping sound snaps me awake.

I blink and shake my head, returning blearily to reality.

What is that noise?

When I'm fully aware of everything around me again I notice Luke pulling his cell phone out of his pocket. "Sorry," he says hoarsely before clearing his throat. "That's my calendar reminder." He glances at the screen. "Oh, darn! I'm totally late for the gallery opening. My friend is waiting for me. She said she would meet me out front. How long will it take to get to Silver Lake from here?"

But I don't answer his question. I barely even hear it. I'm too wrapped up in a certain pronoun. *"She?"* I ask in disbelief, and then immediately wish I had kept my mouth shut because my inflection came out totally wrong. Now it's my turn to clear my throat. "I mean," I continue, trying to infuse aloofness into my voice, "I didn't realize it was a date."

Luke shifts uncomfortably in his seat, rubbing his palms against his new jeans. "Oh, did I not mention that?"

I shake my head.

"Oh. Sorry. I thought I did. I mean, it's not *really* a date. Kind of. Actually, I'm not quite sure what it is. I met her on campus last week and it's, you know, sort of *unknown* at this point . . ."

He's rambling now and I really need to stop him. For both our sakes. Mostly mine though. "Totally," I respond hastily. "I mean, whatever it is . . . it's none of my business. You should definitely go so you're not . . . late."

"Is that okay?" he asks, scrunching up his face.

"Of course it's okay!" I trill eagerly. "It's more than okay! I mean, I'm happy for you that you're . . . you know, dating. Or whatever."

Okay, I warn myself. *That's enough. Time to be quiet.*

Luke chuckles nervously. "I meant is it okay if I leave? You can call someone, right?"

"Oh, of course," I chirp. "I'll call Kingston. He'll be here in a jiffy."

A jiffy?

Oh God, I'm acting like such a spazz right now. And every word out of my mouth is only making it worse. I need to get out of here. I need *him* to get out of here.

I grapple for the handle and kick out the door, slamming it closed behind me. Luke steps out of the passenger side, seemingly less hurried. "What about that last delivery?" he asks, nodding toward the back of the van.

"Oh, don't worry about it," I assure him, running around to the back, pulling the door open, and unstrapping the bouquet from its harness. "I'll throw it away. You can just get on your way."

"You're going to throw it away?" He looks like a lost puppy when he says this.

"Yeah. That's usually what they do if they can't be delivered. They'll make a fresh one tomorrow and try again. Otherwise they'd be dead by the time we delivered them."

Luke looks at me and then at the ground. "Well," he begins hesitantly, "do you mind if I take them?"

I stare down at the flowers in my hand. "What for?" I ask lamely. But as soon as the question is out of my mouth the answer has already struck me.

He wants to take them to his date.

"Oh!" I say, slapping my forehead with my free hand. "Of

course!" I thrust the flowers at him. He manages to catch the bouquet before it falls to the ground. "They're all yours."

"Thanks."

"No problem."

Then I watch him pluck one of the pink roses from the bunch and hold it out to me. "Here," he says.

I reach out cautiously and accept it. "What's this for?"

He smiles. It instantly brightens me from the inside out. "I really did mean what I said. I think you're doing a great job. Keep it up."

"Right," I say weakly, feeling my shoulders drop and the light dim. "Thanks."

THE FAMILY MAN

I HAVE NO *IDEA* WHAT THAT WAS ABOUT BACK there.

So what if Luke is going on a date? Why should I care in the slightest? I shouldn't. So I don't. I won't.

I just think he should have mentioned that up front. You know, when he first asked me for help picking out something to wear. That kind of detail is important in clothing selection. If I had known I was dressing him for a date I might have picked out something different. Maybe slightly less sexy.

But only because you shouldn't be overly sexy on a first date. You should dress sexy to *get* dates but then you're supposed to tone it down a bit. You know, play hard to get. Leave them wanting more. Everyone knows that. It's like the number one rule of dating.

Kingston arrives twenty minutes after Luke leaves. I bypass the back door of the car and join him in the front. He looks surprised by my choice in seating but doesn't question it.

I'm not sure I'm in the mood to sit back there in the dark by myself. Even if Kingston and I don't talk the entire way home, simply having him there next to me makes me feel safer somehow. Less secluded.

There's a car I don't recognize parked in the driveway when we get home. I'm not sure who (or what) I expect to find when I walk through the front door but as soon as I lay eyes on the person who's waiting for me, I admit I'm not terribly surprised to see her.

"I've been trying to get hold of you for weeks, Lexington!" Caroline stands in the middle of the foyer with one hand on her hip and the other holding a large stack of paperwork.

"Lovely to see you again, Caroline," I grumble as I walk past her into the kitchen. I set the pink rose Luke gave me on the counter and grab a bottle of water from the refrigerator.

Her heels clack against the marble floors as she tags along behind me. "I've left messages and sent *numerous* e-mails."

"Really?" I say with fake surprise as I unscrew the cap and take a large gulp. "I didn't get them. Maybe I should check my spam folder."

I turn and head for the back stairs but Caroline is on my heels faster than a fly on food. "Don't walk away from me, Lexi. I've planned an appearance for you, Rêve, and your father next week at the opening of the new Miley Cyrus movie. It's supposed to be the family film of the year and you're going. No ifs, ands, or buts."

"I'm sorry, I'm busy next week," I say dismissively, starting up the stairs.

She follows me. "Well, you're going to have to get *un*busy because this is very important. Your father needs the publicity. There's a big merger in the works and if he's going to get the support he needs from the stockholders who will be voting on it, he's going to have to boost his public image. He's been coming off a bit too unapproachable in the media lately. Uncaring. I'm launching a whole new publicity initiative to make him appear more affable. Like a family man. And I need your assistance."

I can't help but cackle with laughter as I sweep through my bedroom door. "Can you even *hear* yourself? You want him to *appear* like a family man. You want him to *pretend* to be likable. And you want *me* to pretend that it's working. Don't you see that's all we are? A bunch of people running around pretending to like each other. Pretending to get along. It's ridiculous."

Seething through her clenched teeth, Caroline yanks a magazine from the stack in her arms—the latest issue of *Forbes*—and shoves it toward me. My father's face is on the cover under a large, bold headline that reads: RICHARD LARRABEE: SUPERHERO OR VILLAIN?

I have to turn back around so that she can't see the smirk that's creeping across my mouth. Finally someone is questioning this superstar image my father has managed to hold on to all these years. *Finally* someone is starting to see things from *my* point of view. I might actually start reading *Forbes*.

"Do you see this?" she asks, tapping abrasively at the headline. "Do you see that question mark? It represents doubt. And doubt is not good for business. I was not hired to elicit doubt. I was hired to elicit confidence."

I take another sip of water. "Yeah, well, looks like you've got your work cut out for you."

Caroline sighs. "Why do you have to make everything so difficult, Lexi? All I'm asking for is a smidgen of your time. An hour, tops. Is it so much to ask that you put on a cute outfit, smile for the cameras, and give your father a quick hug on the red carpet? Seriously. It's not as though I'm asking you to do manual labor here."

I turn back to face her. "You're right," I concede, and I see her shoulders drop with relief. But I'm not done. I'm only getting warmed up. "It's *not* manual labor. Manual labor is what I've been doing nonstop for the past four months. I've worked myself to the bone for that man and he deserves every single drop of bad press that he gets. In fact, I hope tomorrow the newsstand is *lined* with headlines like that. And I'll tell you, I'd much rather be scooping up horse poop in a stall than dishing it out on a red carpet with *him*. You wanna know why my father has to *pretend* to be a family man? Because we're not a family! We haven't been one for twelve years and I'm sick and tired of pretending otherwise. I've seen what a family is—what they do for each other—and this is not it. So you can count me out from now on. I'm not going."

Then I slam my bedroom door in her face and call out, "My apologies to Miley Cyrus!"

CLICK <u>HERE</u> TO PLAY MESSAGE

Or read the free transcript from our automated speech-
to-text service below.

[BEGIN TRANSCRIPT]

Hey, Lexi. It's me. Luke. So it turns out I have this
built-in camera on my laptop and this is the first time
I'm actually using it. Can you believe that? Yeah, you
probably can.

Well, anyway, here I am. I thought maybe I'd send *you* a
video message for a change. You know, shake things up a
bit. Not that things need to be shaken up or anything.
I mean, things are perfectly fine as is. There's really
nothing wrong with the way things have been. Or are, for
that matter. It was just a figure of—

You know what, I'm rambling. I just wanted to send you
a quick message to tell you thank you again for helping
me with the whole wardrobe situation tonight. I guess

we both went above and beyond our job descriptions, right?

[Laughter]

Well, anyway. Thank you. I had so much fun tonight and I owe that to you.

So. That's all. I better go. I have an accounting exam to study for. I guess I'll see you on Monday morning. I hope you have a great weekend.

Did I say that already? No. I didn't.

Okay, then. Bye.

[Unidentified sound]

Now I just have to figure out how to turn this thing off.

[END TRANSCRIPT]

I SEE DEAD PEOPLE

I WATCH LUKE'S VIDEO MESSAGE THREE TIMES ON Saturday morning. It makes me laugh the way he looks so nervous and uncomfortable in front of the camera. It's actually kind of adorable.

But mostly I keep rewinding it because I can't figure out what he meant when he said *I had so much fun tonight and I owe that to you.*

Did he mean he had fun delivering flowers with me and that's why he owes me? Or he had so much fun on his date and he owes me because I helped him get ready for it? Why do men have to be so freaking elusive? Why can't they just say whatever the heck they're thinking and stop hiding their emotions behind vague statements that are impossible to decipher?

Whatever. It's not like it even matters what he meant anyway.

I shut my laptop and head downstairs into the kitchen for breakfast. The chef has prepared my favorite: eggs Benedict with vegetarian Canadian bacon. I grab the plate and head for my usual seat at the kitchen counter to start devouring it.

Horatio hates when I eat at the counter. He prefers that I eat in the dining room, which is why he sets a place for me there every morning. A subtle hint. But I rarely acknowledge it. Ever since Cooper shipped off to the Peace Corps it's usually only me in the house for breakfast and it's not like I'm going to sit at that giant table for twelve all by myself.

It's depressing.

Plus, I like sitting at the counter because then I can watch the flat screen TV that's mounted in the kitchen. There's no TV in the dining room. It's un–feng shui.

But today as I grab a fork and knife from the silverware drawer, I notice that Horatio has put out a place setting for me at the kitchen counter. Complete with place mat, expertly folded cloth napkin, and utensils. And right above it, he's positioned a slim crystal vase filled with a single pink rose.

I immediately recognize it as the rose Luke plucked from the bouquet last night. I must have left it on the kitchen counter when I got home.

Although Horatio's gesture touches me, I can't help but wonder what became of the rest of the roses in that bouquet. Whose kitchen table are they sitting on right now? What was their recipient's reaction upon receiving them? Did they elicit a hug? A kiss? *More* than a kiss?

No. Certainly not.

Luke doesn't strike me as the kind of guy who does things like that on a first date. He's too . . . I don't know . . . square.

But despite my convictions, I still find myself whipping out my cell phone and double-checking the time stamp on the video message he sent last night: 10:10 p.m. That's only two hours after he left Morty's Flower Shop.

"Ha!" I say aloud, causing Chef Clement to turn around from his prep station and shoot me a funny look.

I bury my face in my phone, hiding my involuntary smile behind the screen.

Two whole hours, huh?

That date of his must have been a real doozy.

I dip my angled eyeliner brush in a cup of water and then drag it carefully across the surface of the dark brown eye shadow palette open in front of me, covering the tip with a generous amount of pigment.

"Okay, Mrs. Schmerty," I command pleasantly, "close your eyes."

With a steady hand, I paint a long, dotted row across Mrs. Schmerty's upper eyelid. Then I grab a nearby Q-tip, wet it, and use it to smudge the dashes into a solid, smoky line.

I lean back to admire my handiwork.

Not bad. Not bad at all.

I grab a handheld mirror from the tray of supplies next to me and hold it up. "What do you think, Mrs. Schmerty? Don't you look gorgeous? I love the way that sumptuous green shade complements your skin tone."

Mrs. Schmerty doesn't respond. Nor does she open her eyes to look at her reflection.

Not that I was really expecting her to. After all, she *is* dead.

Today is my third day as an assistant at Lancaster and Sons Funeral Home in Manhattan Beach. And although I wasn't exactly thrilled at the thought of working with a bunch of dead people for the entire week, I have to admit, it's not *that* bad. When I arrived, Mr. Lancaster was thrilled to hear that I had makeup-application skills since his previous makeup artist had recently quit, and so far he's seemed nothing but pleased with my artwork.

And yes, it did take a few days for me to get used to the fact that the faces I'm applying makeup to will never actually see or appreciate what I'm doing for them, but I'm over it for the most part now.

Plus, I've found that talking to the dead people as though they were alive helps a lot.

"Yes, I agree," I tell Mrs. Schmerty with a nod. "More lip gloss is definitely in order."

I grab the tube of Chanel gloss that I picked up yesterday and deftly apply a second coat to her lips.

I lean back once again to assess the outcome. Then I nod. "Much better."

I give myself a small pat on the back. I've undoubtedly shown some massive improvement since first arriving here on Monday morning. Mrs. Schmerty is by far my best work yet. In fact, I'm so full of pride that I suddenly get this uncontrollable urge to share it with someone. Someone who will appreciate it.

And honestly I can only think of one person who fits that description.

I take out my cell phone and launch the video camera. I hold the phone out in front of me, center my face in the frame, and press the record button.

"Hi, Luke," I say brightly. "Okay, I know it's only the middle of the week so obviously this is not like an official status report or anything, but I really wanted to show you what I did today.

"As you know, I'm here at Lancaster and Sons Funeral Home

working as an assistant. And you know this obviously because you dropped me off this morning. Oh by the way, can you burn a copy of that CD you were listening to in the car? What was that? Like some kind of new-age motivational stuff?

"Anyway! Today Mr. Lancaster asked me to do makeup on Mrs. Schmerty. I just finished and you simply have to see how great she looks."

I turn the camera around and zoom in on Mrs. Schmerty's face.

"Ta-da!" I exclaim. "Isn't she lovely? Eighty-seven years old and she's never looked better."

I spin the phone back toward me. "I picked out the colors and everything," I add proudly. "Of course the funeral home doesn't exactly invest in the best quality makeup so I had to do a little shopping run on their behalf. But trust me, now they're fully stocked on all the latest fall colors.

"Okay," I conclude. "That's it. Just thought I'd share. Hope you're having fun at the office. See you tonight."

I punch at the record button once again and start to upload the message to Video-Blaze.com. But when it asks me if I really want to send, something stops me from instantly clicking okay like I normally do. This time, I actually have to think about the question.

Do I really want to send this?

And then that question starts a whole avalanche of subsequent questions and concerns.

Did I sound a bit too excited in that message?

Maybe I should rerecord it and take it down a notch.

I don't want Luke to think I'm that excited about working with corpses.

What if he thinks I'm some kind of necrophiliac?

Maybe I should just delete the whole thing.

"Ugh! Stop!" I finally command myself aloud, shaking my head clear. I turn to Mrs. Schmerty. "What do you think, Mrs. Schmerty?"

I pause and wait. "You're right." I confirm with a tight nod of my head. "I should just send it and stop obsessing."

I click okay on the phone and return it to my bag.

"I'm not sure what that was about," I respond to Mrs. Schmerty's unasked question.

"No!" I exclaim, aghast, shooting her a derisive look. "That's not it at all! He's not even that cute. I mean, like in a normal way. He's an *intern*."

Mrs. Schmerty appears to be frowning at me. As though she doesn't believe a word I'm saying.

"Well, I'm sorry you feel that way," I respond snidely. "But for your information, a ripped body is not my only criteria for a relationship."

I roll my eyes and glance away. "Well, I don't care what my criteria has been in the past. Okay?"

Getting tired of this argument (and the slightest bit freaked out), I pull the sheet back over Mrs. Schmerty's face, silencing her for now.

Then, a few moments later, I feel bad for covering her up and pull the sheet back once again, taking one last look at my handiwork. She really does look nice. As creepy as it can be working here, I must admit there's something very rewarding about it. It's pretty cool knowing that you're helping create a lasting memory of these people. This is the final time their friends and family are ever going to see them. It's kind of satisfying to think that you're contributing to that in a positive way.

I don't have a last memory of my mother. At least not one I can directly pinpoint and say, "Yes, that's the last time I saw her." The wake was closed casket because of the severity of her accident. But now, having worked here only a few days, I wish I could have had one last moment with her. Something to hang on to. To look back upon.

All I have is a hodgepodge of scattered memories and testimonials about my mother's character that don't seem to add up. And I'm starting to wonder if they ever will.

A WAKE

THE WAKE FOR MRS. SCHMERTY TAKES PLACE ON
Friday afternoon, my final day working at the funeral home. I help
Mr. Lancaster with the last-minute preparations and then I stand
off to the side as dozens of grievers approach the casket, murmur
quiet prayers, and find a seat. I watch them curiously, taking in
the way each person mourns in a different way. Some cry full out,
wearing their grief on their sleeves for everyone to see. Others dab
politely at their eyes with monogrammed handkerchiefs and I can't
tell if they're really crying or just want people to believe they are.
And then there's a select few—maybe two or three—who completely shut down. Check out. Their bodies are on autopilot. They
walk. They nod. They make small conversations with their neigh-
bors but there's nothing behind any of it.

They're just numb.

It takes a few moments for the realization to hit me. For me to
comprehend why that particular look is so unnervingly familiar.

It's because I've seen it before. The distant eyes. The far-off gaze.
The hardened features.

It's immortalized in a portrait that's currently hanging above a fireplace in my house.

It's the permanent expression my father has been wearing for as long as I can remember. I've always thought there was something missing from his eyes. But watching these people as they sit stone-faced and hollow in their chairs, listening to the pastor speak but not really hearing anything he says, I realize it's not something that's been *missing* from my father's eyes. But rather something that's been *blocking* them.

Almost like a shield. A glass wall. A fortress.

I think back to my favorite picture. The one I found on the Internet from *Better Homes and Gardens*. I think about the man in that photograph, smiling with his wife as their only daughter takes her first steps into an unknown world. In that photo my father is exposed. He's open. He's *there*.

In every picture since, he's somewhere else.

The moment I get home that evening, I head straight for the library to validate my new theory. It only takes a second—a single glance—to confirm that I'm right.

My father has been mourning my mother since the day she died.

He's never stopped.

The weight of this realization causes my knees to buckle. I drop into a nearby armchair, hugging my legs to my chest, and burying my forehead into my knees.

I stay like that well into the night, drifting in and out of sleep, until finally, around two a.m., I stand up and drag my tired body out of the library.

But instead of heading for the stairs, I take a right and find myself striding directly to the closed door at the end of the hall. My father's personal study. I try the handle. As I suspected, it's locked. I shake it with frustration, knowing there's got to be something behind that door—a reason to keep it locked year round—but it doesn't budge.

Exhaling loudly, I spin on my heels and march into the servants' quarters. I knock on Horatio's door. Softly at first, then with growing persistence until he finally opens it. He's tying a red robe around his T-shirt and boxers and rubbing sleep from the corners of his eyes.

"*¿Qué pasa?*" he grumbles, clearly too tired to speak English.

"Where's the key to my father's office?"

He shrugs. "*No se.* Probably with your father."

"Isn't it tradition for the butler to have a master key that unlocks every room in the house?"

"Not this butler," he replies dismissively.

I sigh and attempt a more direct approach. "I need to know what my mother was like."

"*Ah sí,*" he says diligently with a smile. "*Muy bonita.* So wonderful. Loving. Maternal."

I roll my eyes at the standard response that's nearly word for word what I've been hearing my entire life. Like some kind of subtle indoctrination that I never noticed until now. "No," I tell him. "I need to know what she was *really* like."

Horatio instantly looks at the ground. "I don't understand," he mutters unconvincingly.

"Cooper said she used to go away a lot. Where did she go?"

He shrugs but still won't meet my eyes. "Cruises. Mrs. Larrabee loved to go on cruises. They were relaxing. Raising five children was very stressful."

"And she was on one of these cruises before she died?"

"*Sí,*" he says, nodding adamantly, as though he's just remembered this detail. "*Exacto.*"

"I think you're lying," I challenge. "I think there's something you're not telling me."

Horatio appears visibly uncomfortable now. I glare at him, trying to make eye contact so that I can extract some piece of information from his rapidly dilating pupils. But he won't let me.

I pause to take my internal temperature. It's boiling hot. I inhale deeply and wait a moment until it's simmered to a normal 98.6. Or close enough to it. Then I drop my voice to slightly above a whisper and reach down deeper than I've ever reached. To a place where manipulation cannot survive. Where spoiled temper tantrums cannot be heard. And the only tool left to use is my raw humanity.

"Please, Horatio," I implore. "They've been lying to me my entire life. I just want to know who my mother really was. Don't you think I deserve at least that?"

His eyes close but only for a moment. And in that instant I truly believe that I've gotten through to him. That he's suddenly morphed into a new person. No longer a butler. No longer a servant. But maybe, possibly, a real friend.

But the second passes. Time ticks tenaciously on. His eyes open once again and I realize miserably that nothing has changed. He's the same person he's always been. The same person I've known my entire life.

An employee of the Larrabee family.

A keeper of Larrabee secrets.

"It's late," Horatio finally says with an exaggerated yawn. "I'm tired. Can we talk about this in the morning?"

My shoulders fall in defeat. "Fine," I tell him. "But I'm *going* to get to the bottom of this. I'm going to find out the truth. With or without your help."

Despite the fact that Horatio is the one standing in front of me when I declare this solemn vow, as soon as the words leave my mouth, I recognize that the person I'm really declaring it to is me.

And as sick to my stomach as it makes me feel, I have a sinking suspicion I know where I have to go next.

I'm going to have to talk to my father.

LET THERE NOT BE LIGHT

COME MONDAY MORNING I'M A FRAZZLED MESS. I spent the entire weekend having phantom conversations with a man I hardly know. And let me tell you, having an imaginary dialogue with a stranger is virtually impossible.

On the way to my new job assignment, Luke asks me what's wrong but I just kind of mumble something that sounds like *Nuffing*, and continue to zone out in space.

I have no idea what I'm going to say to my father. Not to mention the challenge of actually getting him into a room for more than five minutes. He's not the type of guy you can simply call up and invite to sushi. Especially with that big merger that everyone has been talking about lately.

"Luke," I interrupt my silence, trying to make my voice sound light and natural, "where's my father these days?"

"He's here in LA," he tells me. "He's been in meetings for the past few weeks trying to iron out the last-minute details of the merger."

I nod, like I'm truly interested. "Oh, right. What's the status with that, anyway? Is it almost over?"

Luke looks pleasantly surprised that I'm finally taking an interest in my father's business affairs. "Well," he begins eagerly, "they're getting down to the nitty-gritty now. The French company we're merging with—LaFleur Media—has been a little difficult but they seem to finally be in the clear. Of course, the shareholders still have to vote on it. That will happen later this week but . . ."

He proceeds to blather on about the details. Apparently news of the impending deal has been all over CNBC and everyone at work is superexcited about it because it's supposed to significantly increase Larrabee Media's market share in Europe.

Or at least this is how much I'm able to absorb through my current half-conscious state. I try, for the sake of being polite, to sound at least somewhat interested as Luke talks, throwing in random *mmm hmms* and *oh, reallys*, hoping that they happen to land in appropriate parts of his speech. But I assume I'm not doing a very good job at it because Luke finally stops talking, laughs, and says, "Sorry, I guess you didn't need *all* that information. I'll shut up now."

I open my mouth to protest and apologize but then I notice the car has stopped and we've arrived at our destination. I'm actually grateful for the distraction this job promises to bring. My thoughts have been getting very difficult to live with lately.

This week I'm working for a catering company. As a member of their wait staff. I have to wear this completely unflattering tuxedo vest and bow tie but after a few hours of training I realize that the work itself is not that bad. And it turns out I'm actually kind of good at it. I guess all those catered affairs I've attended over the course of my life are coming in handy.

But there's a very solid line between being a guest at an event and being a member of the help, and the biggest challenge in this job is, of course, getting used to being on the other side of that line. You know, like passing around the trays instead of eating off them. Filling the champagne glasses instead of drinking from them. Picking up the dirty plates instead of dirtying them.

Once my training session is complete, we start loading up the van to head off to the location of my first event. It's a private party at a huge mansion in Palos Verdes Estates.

This week, my alias is Heidi, a sweet and innocent blonde with long pigtails.

Kate, the owner of the catering company, starts me off on tray duty, handing me a large, silver platter of cucumber cups filled with tuna seviche and sending me out of the kitchen into the living room.

Just like they taught me in training, I keep my head down and my mouth shut and make my way through the first floor of the house, silently offering my wares to the sea of elegantly dressed guests.

The party reminds me of the kinds of events we often throw at my own house. With bartenders and tray passers and an orchestra in the backyard. It's high society at its best. And the most ironic part of all—the most ironic part of this whole experience—is not that I'm now the one working the event, but the fact that not one single person here recognizes me. And that's probably because not one single person here has looked at me long enough to give themselves the chance to recognize me.

I don't get second glances. I barely even get first glances. I might as well be a piece of furniture with a tray attached for the amount of attention people pay me.

Don't get me wrong, it's not like I *want* to be noticed. I most certainly don't. But even after nearly five months, it still boggles my brain.

I pass through the living room, out the back doors, and onto a large terrace where a group of business men are standing in a circle, swirling red wine around in large goblets.

There's a man with horn-rimmed glasses in the center who seems to be doing most of the talking. I think this is his house because I saw him talking to Kate earlier about where to set everything up. Based on the scope of this party and the way he's dressed, I assume he must be a rich business man.

It's not until I approach the circle that I realize he's speaking in French. I proffer my tray and a stack of napkins. A few of the men treat themselves to an appetizer without even glancing in my direction. They all have their eyes glued intently on the man in the center who's speaking animatedly.

Since my French vocabulary is usually limited to talking about food and fashion and celebrities I'm only able to pick up bits and pieces of the conversation. Something about making a secret arrangement to evict an annoying chef.

Evict a chef?

Whatever. I think I'll stick to passing out appetizers.

I clear the rest of my tray and return to the kitchen for a refill.

But Kate apparently has other plans for me. "Heidi, I think we've got everything covered here." She nods at her assistant, who is carrying a stack of dirty baking sheets out the servant's entrance.

"Why don't you ride back to the office with Marshall and help him close up."

"Okay." I shrug and set the tray down on the counter before following Marshall out the back door.

Kate's catering headquarters is only five miles away and once we get there Marshall asks if I wouldn't mind emptying all the trash cans in the kitchen.

"Sure," I reply, and grab an overflowing bag from the bin near the prep station. Fumbling to keep the contents from spilling, I cinch up the top, hoist it over my shoulder, and head outside.

As soon as I reach the street, the bag bursts open and the trash scatters everywhere. I curse under my breath and bend down to start scooping it up. It smells revolting and I try to breathe out of my mouth as I pick up items one at a time and toss them into the Dumpster.

I'm halfway through the mess when I hear a voice call, "Lexington!"

I know I shouldn't look up because tonight my name isn't Lexington—it's Heidi and people named Heidi don't usually answer to the name Lexington. But my reflexes are apparently quicker than my brain and I raise my head just in time to see the first blinding flash.

It's followed by a second and then a third, until I'm completely surrounded by a blaze of flickering lightbulbs.

"Lexi!" a voice calls from somewhere behind the pulsating glow. "Lexi! Over here! Look over here!"

My eyes struggle to see through the wall of light as my mind struggles to make sense of the chaos.

What are they doing here? I'm not at a club. I'm not at a premiere. I am at a catering office. Why are the paparazzi here?

"Lexi," comes another voice, and out of the confusion steps a woman with a microphone. She's followed closely behind by a man with a camera hoisted onto his shoulder. She thrusts the microphone—which I can now see has the familiar *E! News* logo on it—into my face and asks, "Tell us about what you're doing here."

"Uh," I stammer dazedly, blinking against the bright flashes.

And then suddenly another microphone is in front of me. "Lexi. Is it true you're working for this catering company?"

"Huh?"

"Lexi!" A third reporter nearly knocks me over as he shoves his way into my space. "How do you feel about your father's decision to make you work for an entire year to gain access to your trust fund?"

The gears of my brain suddenly click into place. *"What?"* I bellow in return.

The *E! News* woman shoves the man aside and fights to regain her spot right in front of me. "Lexi," she asks, "out of all the jobs he's made you do, which one has been the most difficult?"

I can hear my heart hammering in my chest. My breathing quickens. I stare into the growing mass of cameras and reporters and news vans. Three just pulled up and I can see people running toward me, equipment being lugged behind them.

I try to back away but walk smack into a wall of people. I'm completely surrounded now.

The questions keep coming. The bulbs keep flashing. A hand

reaches out and pulls the wig from my head. I reach for it but it's lost in the sea of commotion.

Fortunately my instincts kick in. Countless years of dodging the press and running from mob scenes like this. I bow my head, crouch low, and slither through the crowd until I'm back in the safe confines of the catering company's kitchen.

Well, *safe* meaning that they can't come in here. They can't follow me. They're not allowed on private property.

But certainly not safe in the larger sense of the word. In the larger sense of my life. My reputation. My anonymity.

I fall against the large stainless steel sink, panting heavily, forcing reluctant air in and out of my lungs, silently willing my heart to keep beating even though it's threatening to stall.

Twenty weeks in and it's over. It's all over. I don't know how it happened but it has.

They've found me.

DRIVE-THRU CONFESSION BOOTH

FOR NEARLY FIVE MONTHS NOW, LEXINGTON Larrabee, the famed daughter of billionaire entrepreneur Richard Larrabee, has been performing various low-wage jobs across southern California in what some have been describing as a 'life-rehabilitation program,' designed and implemented by Richard Larrabee himself. The details of the arrangement are still not entirely clear but we do know that Lexington will be forced to perform a different job every week for a year if she wants to receive access to her trust fund, which experts have estimated to be valued at approximately twenty-five million dollars. Although unconfirmed by official spokespeople of the Larrabee family, it is believed that Richard Larrabee's decision to enroll his infamously troubled daughter in this unique program came immediately after she crashed her car into a convenience store on Sunset Boulevard, approximately four and a half months ago.

"Our list is not yet complete, but so far our research has revealed that Lexington has worked as a maid, a catering server, a crossing guard, a dishwasher, a telemarketer, and a car wash attendant, among other things.

"The news of this unusual yet intriguing arrangement was brought to the attention of the press by an anonymous tip. Both Lexington Larrabee and Richard Larrabee have declined to comment but today in the studio we have a child-development psychologist here to talk about . . ."

I switch off the TV and collapse onto my bed. I can't watch any more footage of myself in that heinous catering uniform, scooping garbage up off the street. It's humiliating.

And those experts they keep interviewing are driving me insane. Child-development psychologists. Teen-drinking-abuse specialists. Doctors. Shrinks. Sociologists. It's like they put out some kind of call to action. Anyone who has an opinion about Lexington Larrabee's life, stop by the studio and we'll put you on the air.

They all say the same thing too. They sing my father's praises and then proceed to bash me. Hooray for Richard Larrabee for taking a proactive, responsible approach to his daughter's well-being. If only all parents paid that much attention to the needs of their struggling teen children, our world would be a better place.

Blah. Blah. Blah.

What they fail to mention is that beyond orchestrating this little endeavor, my father hasn't been involved in the slightest. In fact, he's so *un*involved that he actually had to hire an official liaison to pay attention to me on his behalf. Because he was too busy and important to do it himself.

And where's my credit for actually manning up and doing the jobs? I'm the one out there busting my butt every week at fast-food restaurants and fish markets and dairy farms, I'm the one doing all the work. But do I get any of the glory? Of course not. *That* goes to my father. The working-class hero. The man of the people. I'm just the spoiled-brat princess who screwed up enough to get herself into this predicament. I'm the ungrateful rich heiress who deserves to be taught a lesson.

The house is like a federal-disaster area. The phone has been ringing off the hook, Horatio had to disconnect the doorbell, and the news vans are once again lining the streets. I haven't been able to leave since I got home last night.

And worst of all, I don't have a clue who did this to me.

Anonymous tip? Yeah right!

There's a traitor in our midst. And I am determined to find out who it is.

And kill them.

At first I suspected Luke. But after I cussed him out on the phone for about an hour last night, he finally convinced me that it wasn't him. That he would never betray my father's trust like that. And he's right. He wouldn't. He's too much of a butt kisser to do something like that.

Then I suspected Bruce but he denied it too, spouting off some mumbo jumbo about attorney-client privilege and how he could go to jail and lose his license if he were ever to divulge my father's secrets to the press.

I know it wasn't Jia or T. They would never double-cross me like that. All the staff had to sign confidentiality agreements the day they were hired. And my brothers are far too wrapped up in their own lives to even bother with something like this.

So who does that leave?

That's pretty much everyone who knows.

I sit up on my bed and stare into my empty room. There's a knock on the door and Carmen comes in with a basket of folded laundry. Wordlessly, she disappears into my closet to start putting stuff away.

I continue to rack my brain, trying to figure out who could possibly have done this.

"Miss Lexington. Where you want me put this?" Carmen's voice pulls my focus upward and my eyes are drawn directly to the item draped over her arm. A ragged old black hoodie.

A gift from a friend. A very dear friend. A friend who knew who I was but strangely enough wanted nothing from me.

Could that have been because he knew he could get *more* somewhere else? Somewhere like *Us Weekly* or *Tattle* magazine?

My mind is reeling as I numbly rise to my feet, walk over to where Carmen is standing, and pull the item into my hands.

Once I have hold of it, I immediately yank it over my head and draw the strings tight under my chin.

"Kingston!" I call as I bound down the stairs.

He's there by the time I reach the bottom step. "Yes, Miss Larrabee."

"I need your car."

He nods politely. "Of course, miss. Would you like to drive the Range Rover? Or perhaps the Jaguar?"

"No." I grab his arm. "I need your *personal* car."

"But," he says, "Miss Larrabee. I drive a Ford Focus. My car—"

"Is perfect," I interrupt. "I also need you to drive me to the end of the street."

He looks like he's about to argue. I squeeze his arm and stare fiercely into his eyes. "Of course, miss," he finally agrees.

I duck behind the front seat and Kingston covers me with a beach towel he finds in his trunk. He drives me through the crowd of press, who clearly think nothing of his car, and stops at the end of my street.

"Thank you," I tell him sincerely as I hop out of the back and get in behind the wheel. "I really appreciate this. And sorry to make you walk back."

He offers me a tender smile. "That's okay, Miss Larrabee. I drive around all day. I could use the exercise."

I close the door and take off toward Sunset.

Thirty minutes later, I screech into the drive-thru of the Don Juan's Tacos, roll down the window, and wait.

"Welcome to Don Juan's. This is Rolando. How may I help you today?"

I lean out the open window, getting as close to the built-in microphone as I can, and scream, "You can tell me why you be-trayed me, you jerk!"

There's an awkward pause and then he tries again. "Hello?"

"I know it was you!" I yell, leaning to the point where I'm in danger of falling right out of the car. "I know you were the anony-mous source who tipped off the press about me!"

"Lexi?" he ventures a guess after another bout of silence.

"Duh!" I scream back.

"Lexi, what are you talking about?"

I sigh. I'm losing my patience for his little innocent act. After all, it was that stupid act that made me trust him to begin with. What an idiot I was!

"The press!" I shout. "You told the press that Lexington Larrabee was working undercover at Don Juan's Tacos and fifty-one other places. You totally outed me!"

"Lexi," he says warningly. "I think you just outed yourself."

"What?"

"Did you forget that everyone here wears a headset? The entire staff can hear you right now."

Crap.

Well, not that it matters anyway. I'm already exposed. They're going to see it on the news if they haven't already.

"Why don't you drive around back and I'll come out and talk to you," Rolando suggests.

I lower myself into the car. "Fine."

But Rolando isn't the only person who shows up. The entire staff pours out the door, all stumbling on top of one another to get a look. I can hear their curious murmurings from inside the car. Jenna is shrieking into her cell phone. "I totally knew it was her! I mean, I thought she looked like her, but it really *was* her!"

Rolando taps on the glass of the passenger-side window and I lean over and unlock the door. He gets in and we sit in silence for a few moments. I'm much calmer now. The anger has mostly burned off, leaving behind only bitter sorrow.

"I trusted you," I seethe, trying to keep my voice from breaking. "I thought you were my friend. Why did you do it?"

"I didn't," he says quietly.

"I don't believe you!" I snap back.

"Lexi, why would I do that?"

I throw my hands up in the air, flustered. "I don't know! Money! Publicity! Fame!"

"Well, anyone who gives an anonymous tip is not looking for fame."

"Fine. Money then."

He gestures at his salsa-stained mustard-colored shirt. "Would I still be working here if I had sold your story for money?"

I consider this. He's got a point.

I sigh and slouch in my seat. I guess I'm back at square one. "If not you, then who?" I whisper.

"I don't know," Rolando says unhelpfully. "I would consider who has the most to gain from exposing you."

"That's the point. I have no idea!"

"Well, who's getting the most out of your exposure?"

I groan. "Certainly not me. My life is ruined. My father's the only one who actually comes out looking good from . . ." My voice trails off and then, "Oh my God!" I shriek. "My father! The upcoming merger. He needs the shareholders to vote on it. He needs to build confidence. This is a total image booster for him."

Rolando doesn't seem to be following. "So, your father tipped off the press himself?"

I laugh at this as I rebuckle my seat belt. "Of course not," I tell him. "My father doesn't do anything himself. He hires people."

He looks skeptical. "So he hired someone just to call in an anonymous tip?"

"He didn't have to," I clarify. "She already works for him."

THE TIN MAN

LEXI!" CAROLINE TRILLS IN HER NASAL FRENCH
accent the moment her assistant patches me through to her cell.
"I'm glad you called. I was just on my way to your father's office for
a strategy meeting. There's so much to discuss after this exciting
new development! I'm going to suggest to him that we move up the
wedding to capitalize on all this positive press. Which reminds me.
We have to get you into a fitting for your maid of honor dress
ASAP. Shall I have Brent get Vera's assistant on the phone and
schedule something for you for tomorrow?"

"Cut the crap, Caroline," I growl into the phone. "I know it was
you who tipped off the press."

She lets out a little squeak, which I think is supposed to repre-
sent her shock at such an outrageous accusation. "Lexi, *chérie*, I'm
not sure what you're talking about."

I don't buy her act for a second. "That was low. Even for you.
Do you realize my entire life is ruined? All for the benefit of
some stupid merger."

"Lexi," she begins in a patronizing tone, "don't you see? This
news helps everyone."

"How?" I snap back. "How does this help everyone? How does exposing my secret to the world help everyone?"

"When this merger goes through, Larrabee Media profits will skyrocket. Do you know what profits are?"

I roll my eyes. "Of course I know what profits are."

"Well," she continues airily, "then you must know that Larrabee Media profits are what fund your lifestyle. They pay for your cars and your clothes and your yachts and everything else." She sighs, sounding mighty pleased with herself. "This merger is the most important thing to happen to Larrabee Media in a decade. I had to come up with something that would ensure the shareholders' confidence in your father as a leader. And this was a perfect solution. You should feel honored that you're able to contribute to the company's success. Pay off some of that publicity debt you've been racking up over the years."

"And my father agreed to this?" I ask, feeling unwanted tears start to well up in my eyes. I quickly blink them away. But the knot forming in my stomach refuses to budge.

She makes a condescending *tsk tsk* sound with her teeth. "Your *father* wants what's best for the company. As should you."

So that's it. My father sold me out for his business. Just like that. Because his *publicist* convinced him it was a smart business move.

But then again, should I really be that surprised? He's been doing the same thing for years. To everyone in this family. My father's company has always come first. And it always will.

I can't *believe* I actually felt sorry for him. Even for a second. I thought maybe, possibly, somewhere deep down, there was at least some *minuscule* splinter of a sensitive bone in his body. The hiding place for all the pain and grief he's been carrying around since my mother's death.

But I can see now that was only a pipe dream.

Why is it that every time I start to feel the slightest bit of something for my father—an inkling of possible sympathy—he always manages to disappoint me? Without even being in the same room.

It's a special talent he seems to have.

And to think I actually considered trying to talk to him. Did I honestly think I could sit down with Richard Larrabee and engage in some kind of sentimental father/daughter heart-to-heart?

I should have recognized the epic flaw in that logic to begin with.

It would require my father to actually *have* a heart.

"Plus," Caroline continues, oblivious to my growing desolation, "you've been living off that bad-girl image for way too long. It was time for a makeover. For you and your father. Now the world will *sympathize* with you. Instead of despising you. And your father comes off looking like a responsible, compassionate parent."

"Right," I say, dejected. "A *family* man. Just like you wanted."

"Exactly," she agrees enthusiastically, seemingly pleased that I appear to be coming around. "And so far, it's working. The media *loves* his proactive approach to raising a teenage daughter. They're calling it a 'life-rehabilitation program.'"

"I know," I mutter.

"Trust me," she encourages. "This is all for the best. You'll see. And if you want me to schedule a press conference for you to publicly express your gratitude to your father, that would *really* help."

I feel defeated. Conquered. Done. I have no more fight left in me. I'm just this pitiful one-woman army trying to do battle against a commander who has the world at his fingertips. And a trained army ready to spring into action at a moment's notice.

With odds like that what's the point in fighting?

Eventually you have to surrender.

And for me, eventually is now.

I don't respond to Caroline, I just hang up the phone without another word. It rings less than thirty seconds later, Caroline evidently believing that the call was simply dropped. I press ignore and drive the rest of the way home in silence. No radio. No cell phone. Nothing.

I stare at the little white dashes on the road in front of me and allow them to hypnotize me.

I steer the small Ford Focus through the sea of press, ignoring the bulb flashes that blind me through the windshield, and park in the garage. I sludge into the house, hand the keys back to Kingston, and offer him a muted, dreary thank-you. I can feel his eyes following me as I start for the stairs. I'm ready to crawl into bed, pull the covers over my head, and never surface again. Except, of course, to do my father's bidding and act like the brainless puppet that I am.

I am a prisoner of war now. I have no choices. I have no rights. I have no freedom. I am to survive in this lavish jail cell until the day I die. There is no escape for me.

I guess it was foolish of me ever to think that there was.

I'm a Larrabee after all.

For better and especially for worse. And I guess I'm just going to have to get used to it.

FLY AWAY WITH ME

THERE'S A KNOCK ON MY BEDROOM DOOR AN hour later and Horatio announces that I have a visitor downstairs. "I've placed him in the salon," he says, as though my guest were simply a package that's been delivered or some other inanimate object.

"I don't want to see anyone," I tell him.

"He's insisting that he see you."

With a sigh, I grudgingly climb out of bed and push brusquely past Horatio into the hallway.

"Also," Horatio adds, suddenly sounding even more formal than usual, "I found that *thing* you were looking for."

I turn to look at him. "What *thing*?"

Without a word, he reaches into the pocket of his jacket and removes a small brass key, holding it up for me to get a close look, and then places it gently on the table next to the chaise longue with a soft clink.

The master key. The one that opens every room in the house. Even rooms that have remained locked for as long as I can remember.

I bite my lip to hold back the emotion that threatens to escape. "Thank you," I tell him softly.

He replies with his traditional bow and then motions ceremoniously toward the stairs. "Your visitor," he states, as though the last five seconds never happened.

There are a few faces I expect to see when I step into the salon a few moments later. A reporter sent by Caroline to do some kind of exclusive interview. Possibly Bruce here to talk about some legal matter. Maybe even Luke, since I'm scheduled to be at a catering job downtown in two hours. Not that I'm in any condition to go.

But the one person I never expected to see—ever again, let alone sitting in the salon waiting for me—is Mendi.

As soon as I enter the room, he's up out of his seat, rising to greet me in a way that only well-educated sons of money know how to do.

He floats toward me—all cool and confident—and takes my hand and kisses it. But it's not cheesy when he does it. It's never been cheesy. That's the thing about Mendi. Everything he does and says, no matter how hokey it might look on someone else, is always smooth. Like melted milk chocolate running through a fountain.

He can strut into an ultra-hot Hollywood nightclub one day and act like a regular celebrity bad boy and then stride through the salon of a multimillion-dollar Bel Air mansion the next and effortlessly transition into a man of culture and poise. The perfect embodiment of European society.

"I came as soon as I read about it online," he tells me, his sweet, melodic accent instantly lulling me into a familiar trance. A spellbound state in which I'm fully alert and yet fully his at the same time. It's a spell I've learned can only be broken if you can find the strength to physically leave the room. Because once you're in his presence, it's all over.

"Thanks," I find myself saying weakly. Weak, not in that my voice has no energy left in it, but in that my body has no will to fight his magnetism. Nor the tears that are welling up in my eyes.

They start to fall. Hard and heavy. Like they're made of more than just salty water. The weighty material of broken hope and shattered illusions.

Besides Horatio, Mendi is the only person I've ever allowed to see me cry. Well, at least since I was old enough to know that crying in front of someone is the equivalent of packing up your power in a box, tying it with a bow, and handing it over.

And let's face it. I've never had power when it comes to Mendi.

As he watches me weep in front of him, shedding my emotional boundaries faster than clothes in a game of strip poker, his face fills up with concern. It's genuine and compassionate. It always has been. Mendi can be a lot of things—irrational, unstable, insensitive— but inauthentic has never been one of them.

He pulls me into his chest and I go willingly, allowing my tears to be absorbed in the thick fabric of his shirt. He strokes my hair and the side of my face, practically singing as he whispers, "It's okay, my darling. Shhh. It's going to be fine."

When I'm all cried out, he holds me at arm's length, lowers his head so that he can look directly into my eyes, and asks, "Why didn't you call me?"

I sniffle and rub my wet cheeks as I look back at him with a confused expression.

"When your father took away your trust fund and left you with nothing," he clarifies. "Why didn't you call me? You know I would have taken care of you."

I turn my head to the side, averting my eyes. "I know," I admit. "But we were broken up. We said terrible things to each other that night in the club. Before the crash. And then you never called again. That's how I knew it was truly over."

He bows his head, looking ashamed. "I wanted to call," he says softly. "But your friends warned me not to."

My eyes widen in surprise. "They did?"

He nods. "After you ran out of the club that night, they insisted that I let you go. That if I ever wanted to give you a chance at being happy, I'd forget about you. They said the three of you were going away for the summer and they didn't need our drama following them to Europe."

I'm so touched thinking about Jia and T sticking up for me like that. Looking out for me. Like friends are supposed to.

"They told me you'd be better off without me," he continues. "And for a while I believed them. But now I'm not so sure."

"What do you mean?"

He cups my face in his large, warm hands and holds my gaze captive. "I'm saying enough is enough. We belong together."

I can feel my knees start to shake under the weight of his words.

"What about Serena Henson? I thought you two were an item now."

He scrunches his face in revulsion and shakes his head. "Oh God, she was such a waste of space."

I want to smile. But it's as though my face has forgotten how.

"Come with me." His command is direct. Simple. Full of promise.

"Where?"

He releases my face and gestures to the world around him. "Anywhere! You don't belong here milking cows and frying grease and God knows what else. You're too good for that. I can give you the life you deserve, Lexi. The life you've been raised for. We can go today. Anywhere you want."

My thoughts immediately float to the south of France. To the photograph of the villa that my friends sent me. The thought that I could be there with them—in only a matter of hours—makes me feel weightless. Free.

"Can we go to the French Riviera?"

He laughs. It's jovial and effortless. "Of course! I'll call the hangar now." He whips out his cell phone and starts dialing. I listen as he gives his name, is put directly through to the right people, and books a flight to Marseilles in a matter of seconds.

I almost forgot how easy it is. How easy it *could* be. How easy it used to be for me too.

And the pang of longing in my stomach tells me that I've missed it. That ease. That uncomplicatedness. That buoyant, carefree existence.

He presses a button on his phone and returns it to his pocket. "The jet is ready whenever we are." He takes my hands in his and holds them close to his face. I can feel his warm breath on my fingertips. "You don't need your father. Or your trust fund. Or any of it. Let me take you away from all this."

Then he tugs my hands toward him, wraps them around the back of his neck, and kisses me. It's exactly like I remembered. The same hunger. The same passion. The same spark that ignites my senses and makes me feel alive.

I didn't even realize I was dead.

When he pulls away he leaves behind a large, beaming grin that lights up my entire face. He brings his lips to my forehead and presses against it gently.

I unlock my fingers from the back of his neck and press my slightly swollen lips together, savoring the lingering taste of him . . . and all the ways he promises to fix everything that's wrong with my life. "Just give me a few minutes to pack."

EXIT STRATEGY

MENDI SITS ON MY BED, PLAYING TUG-OF-WAR with Holly and an old sock while I hastily throw items into a suitcase. For some reason I feel frazzled. Frenetic.

Mendi notices and catches hold of my arm as I'm dumping a heap of dresses into my bag. "Relax, Lex," he tells me—no, with Mendi it's always more like an *order*. "The plane is not going to leave without us."

"I know," I say, taking a deep breath, but it does little to slow me down or quiet my quivering nerves.

I race back to my closet and pull out my bathing-suit drawer. I have no idea which ones to take so I just grab all of them and run them to the suitcase.

Mendi laughs as he watches the growing pile of mangled clothes. "I don't think your entire closet is going to fit in there. You know we can always go shopping in France."

I laugh nervously and then head over to my desk and shut my laptop down. When I lift it up, I find a mangled piece of paper underneath. I reach for the paper, knowing exactly what it is even before I've completely unfolded it.

The list.

52 Reasons to Hate My Father.

Although, based on the numerous lines of crossed-out text, I only got to number twenty. Not even halfway through. I skim the thirty-two remaining jobs, running my finger down the page, taking a brief moment to imagine the experiences I'll never have. A toll-booth operator, a waitress, a newspaper delivery girl, a rent collector, a fruit picker, a movie theatre usher . . . all the way down to the very last one. Number 52. Working in the copy room of the *Santa Monica Mirror*—a local newspaper.

The copy room of a local newspaper? That was my father's first job. His first step toward becoming the billionaire he is today.

That can't be a coincidence.

A bark breaks me from my thoughts and I glance over at Holly who's managed to rip the sock out of Mendi's hand and is now completing her victory prance around the bed.

Mendi laughs and lunges forward for a rematch.

I give my head a shake, toss the list into the trash can, and get back to packing, hastily stuffing my laptop into its pink Prada carrying case and adding it to the collection of luggage on the bed. Then I dash into the bathroom to start filling my train case.

I'm not sure why I'm in such a hurry. Maybe it's because this whole day feels like a dream and if we don't leave right this very minute—or as close to it as possible—something or *someone* is going to wake me up.

Someone is going to try to stop me.

And just as Mendi is lugging the last of my suitcases down the stairs, that someone walks through the front door.

"Going somewhere?" he asks, looking perplexedly from Mendi to my luggage to me.

"Luke," I say simply. Because I'm not sure what else to say. Where else to begin. "I was going to call you."

"From where?" he asks, once again glaring at Mendi and then looking back to me.

I trudge down the last few steps and meet him in the foyer. "I think we both know this is over."

Apparently Luke doesn't know. "What are you talking about? I'm here to take you to your next catering job. It starts in an hour."

Mendi sets my suitcase down at the foot of the stairs and stalks up next to me, putting a hand on my lower back. "Lexington won't be working any more low-wage jobs for her father. It's demeaning and beneath her."

Luke gives him a dubious look but doesn't respond. Instead he addresses me. "You can't quit. You know what happens if you quit."

"I know," I say softly, unable to meet his gaze.

"You won't be able to come back here," he warns. "Your father will cut you off."

"She doesn't need her father." Mendi steps menacingly forward. "She has me now."

"I wasn't talking to you," Luke growls, sidestepping Mendi so that he can focus back on me. "Lexi, don't do this!"

"It's done, Luke," I say morosely. "I'm exposed. The entire world knows. They're not going to leave me alone. They're going to follow me to every single job, every single week, for the rest of the year. They're going to turn it into some kind of media circus!"

"That doesn't matter," Luke insists. "What matters is that you were starting to get the hang of it. You were taking it seriously. You were earning people's respect." He drops his head and lowers his voice. "Like mine."

"I'm sorry," is all I can say.

"So what," he continues sarcastically, "you're just going to throw it all away and run back to your spoiled, indulgent life like nothing ever happened?"

"Hey!" Mendi steps between us again. "You have no right to talk to her like that."

But Luke is undeterred. He walks past Mendi and gets right in my face. His nose inches away from mine. "I have a right to point out what a huge mistake you're making." His eyes burn into mine as he takes hold of my wrist. "I've seen what you're capable of— I've seen what you can do—and it's worth something, Lexi. *You're* worth something. You're more than just a frivolous, shallow party girl. If you go with him you'll only be running from one crutch to another. Instead of learning how to stand on your own."

"Oh, like you care," I mutter.

"I do care," Luke insists.

"The only thing you care about is my father and his quarterly stock report. You don't want me to leave because then it'll make you look bad in front of him. You don't give a crap about me."

"That's not true," he counters. "I admit it hasn't been easy dealing with you. You're no picnic, Lexi. In fact, you're everything I hate about upper-class America. Everything that I have to work my butt off for, you were handed on a silver platter. And you took it all for granted.

"But I agreed to do this because I believed in what your father was trying to do. He was trying to help you. To show you that there's more to life than partying and shopping."

I yank my arm free and shove against his shoulders. "Don't talk about things you don't understand," I roar. "You think just because your father left, and you grew up with no money, and have to work your way through a psychology degree that you know everything about me and my life? You don't know anything! You don't even realize what a hypocrite you are!"

"I'm a hypocrite?" he fires back.

"Yes!" I thunder. "You can't idolize my father and hate me in the same sentence. Don't you know how contradictory that is? I am who I am *because* of my father. He *made* me this way. Everything you worship about him—his work ethic, his obsession with his job, his detachment from emotions—I'm a product of all that. Do you really want to know what it was like growing up here?" I've lowered my voice but the intensity is still there. "I'll tell you. It was learning to play pool from the butler and soccer from the gardeners and poker from the chauffeur. Because there was never anyone else around to entertain you. It was coming home from school and showing off your artwork to the maid. It was spending Christmases with the nanny and birthdays with whatever girl was hired to dress up like a Disney princess and knock on your door with an armful of presents. You're not the only one who grew up without a father, you know? But at least you didn't have to spend your life wondering when he would walk through the door and how long he would stay. You didn't have to lie in bed at night, counting the number of words he said to you on his latest phone call from Japan, and then celebrating quietly to yourself when it was a whopping three more than the last time."

Luke has lowered his gaze. His breathing seems smoother. Less ragged than it was a few minutes ago. But mine feels like a tornado. I pull up on the handle of my suitcase and start pulling it toward the door, pausing long enough for one final glance in Luke's direction. "You should be grateful your father left and never came back."

DEFYING GRAVITY

SOMETHING TO READ?" THE FLIGHT ATTENDANT'S
chipper voice interrupts my thoughts, and I tear my gaze away from
the window to see that she's holding a tray with several magazines
splayed out across the surface like playing cards.

I smile graciously at her as I scan the selection. Underneath the
latest issue of *Glamour* I can see half of my father's face peeking
out. With curiosity, I push *Glamour* aside and study the cover
of this month's *Fortune*. Of course it's a cover story about my
father's upcoming merger. The headline reads: NEXT STOP: GLOBAL
DOMINATION. Then, in smaller letters underneath his photo: *An
exclusive interview with Richard Larrabee on his humble beginnings,
bumpy romances, and the upcoming merger that will make him
king.*

I reach for the magazine but Mendi's hand swoops in right before I make contact and snatches it out from under me. "She doesn't
need to read that," he tells the flight attendant. "It will only upset
her." Then he plucks this week's issue of *Tattle* from the tray and
hands it to me.

I murmur a small thank-you and start flipping through, rather uninterestedly. Although I am grateful I'm not on the cover yet. That will be next week when I'll be far, far away from here.

I glance somewhat contemptuously over at Mendi, who's been jabbering nonstop into his cell phone and has barely said two words to me since we left the house. I'd forgotten about that small yet annoying trait of his. With Mendi, you're everything—the earth, the moon, *and* the stars—until his phone rings. Then you're but a speck of meteor dust floating around a lonely universe, waiting for the gravitational pull of some planet or sun to reel you in and make you part of something significant.

The pilot's voice comes over the speaker, informing us that there's another jet on the runway that's unable to take off due to mechanical issues so we're going to have to wait here, at the hangar, until it's been towed away.

I close my magazine and stare out the window, forcing myself to picture azure seas, giant villas, and glamorous masked balls. Holly, who's been snuggled between me and the edge of the seat, stirs slightly and I reach down to scratch behind her ears.

I've decided not to call Jia and T to tell them about my imminent arrival. It'll be much better as a surprise. That way they won't have time to get mad at me for showing up with Mendi. I know they're not going to approve. But hopefully they'll be so ecstatic to see me they'll be able to overlook that detail. Besides, if he's the one bringing me there—springing me from my father-made jail— then they can't be too upset. Right?

Plus, I don't even know if we're officially back together. I mean we kissed. And we're going to Europe together. And we plan on *staying* in Europe together, but what does that really mean?

Then, of course, there's the other problem. The one I've been trying to ignore since we left the house—but obviously I'm failing miserably.

Luke.

Why does his face keep popping into my mind every time I let my thoughts wander for even a second?

Why do I feel like I'm betraying him simply by being here?

Almost as though we were together or something. I mean, not in *that* way obviously. We've never even kissed. Unless you count that huge mistake in the club, which I certainly don't. But in some other way. Some strange way that I've never experienced before.

It's like we were both a part of something. We had this common goal. And yes, neither one of us particularly enjoyed each other's company but we were still in it together. And no matter how bad things got—how many toilets I had to scrub, how many dishes I had to wash, how many graves I had to dig—Luke was always there. He was the one constant that could be counted on through the whole nightmare.

He was willing to go the distance. He was willing to stick with it and see the entire thing to the end. And I gave up. I abandoned it. I left him hanging. Without even a real explanation.

I look over to Mendi, who's finally finished his call and is now e-mailing someone from his phone.

"Mendi?" I ask.

He barely looks up. "Yeah."

"How is this going to work?"

"Hmm?"

"I mean, with *us*," I clarify.

He finally sets his phone down in his lap and pulls me deep into his gaze, into the center of the universe again. "Well, we're together now, aren't we?"

"Are we?" I ask back, and marvel at how calm and collected I sound. I don't think I've ever been this rational when talking to Mendi about our relationship. Normally this type of "defining" conversation is accompanied by screaming and pacing and throwing stuff. *Lots* of stuff. Last time we got back together I broke an heirloom that had been in his family since the French Revolution.

But not today. Not right now. For some reason I feel in control.

"Of course we are," Mendi says, taking my hand and bringing it to his lips.

I shiver from his touch. "But how is it going to work when we get to Europe? I mean, I have nothing now. No money. No houses. No cars. Nothing."

He smiles tenderly at me, tugging gently at my hands until our faces are inches apart. Then he kisses me long and deeply and I nearly lose track of time and space. Are we on a plane? Are we still on the ground? Or did the runway finally clear and now we're in the air? I certainly feel like I'm flying.

"You don't have to worry about any of that," Mendi says when he pulls away, leaving me breathless and heavy once again. "I'll take care of you." He touches my nose with the tip of his finger. "As long as we're together, you don't have to worry about anything."

There's something in the way he says it that causes me to pause and stare at him inquisitively. Although his tone is just as soft and tender as it always is when he's talking to me, the words feel cold and callous. Like they are typed on a piece of paper—in a boring black font—not tumbling forth from the mouth of the guy I'm supposed to be falling back in love with.

Then, as if my mind is separate from the rest of my body, I hear myself say, "And if we're not together?"

Mendi laughs at me, implying that I'm being ridiculous again. "But we *are* together," he points out. "Just as it should be."

"But we break up," I point out. "All the time. We've been breaking up and getting back together for the last two years."

Again, my rationality and ability to think and process information pertaining to the facts of our relationship is mind-boggling.

"Well, then let's not do that," Mendi says, as though it's the easiest, most straightforward answer in the world. As though the tumultuous nature of our relationship has been a simple choice and we've been continually choosing wrong. How silly of us.

I can't help but feel the emotion creeping in. However, it's not the usual emotion that comes with this conversation. It's a new one. One that can only be described as frustration with Mendi for not taking this conversation as seriously as I am. For not seeing how important this detail is.

But then it suddenly dawns on me. Of course he doesn't see it. It's not important to *him*. If we break up, it's not *he* who will be in danger of becoming a vagabond, a street vagrant, another statistic in Europe's already sky-high unemployment rate. It's not *he* who's leaving behind his entire family and everyone who has been a part of his life since the day he was born.

If we break up, he'll be totally fine.

But then again, I'm not sure why I'm surprised. That's the way it's always been. He wasn't the one who crashed his Mercedes into a convenience store. He wasn't the one found passed out on the floor of a gas station bathroom. Because regardless of whether we're together or not, Mendi is always fine. I'm the one who falls apart.

I'm the one who always finds myself emotionally (or in this case literally) homeless.

"But what if we do break up?" I ask, hating the desperation that's starting to seep into my voice. "What will become of me?"

He shrugs and goes back to his BlackBerry. My fifteen minutes are officially up. "I don't know," he admits. "I guess you'll go back home. Or stay in Europe. Whatever it is you do when we're not together."

"But I can't!" I scream, causing the flight attendant to peek at us from behind her curtain to make sure I'm okay. I instinctively lower my voice. But not by much. "Don't you get that? I can't go back. I'm totally cut off! I have *nothing*, Mendi. Do you even understand what nothing is?"

As soon as I've asked the question I know what the answer is. Of course he doesn't understand what nothing is. The same way *I* didn't understand what it was five months ago, either. It's not a word in our vocabulary. But I understand it now. I've seen it every place I've worked in the past twenty weeks. I've seen what it does to people. How it motivates them. Even me.

"Well, I guess that settles it," Mendi says distractedly, tapping away on his phone. "You better not leave me, then."

Although he laughs when he says this, I know it's not a joke. It's the truth. I better not leave him if I want to eat. I better not leave him if I want to survive. I better not leave him if I want to live the life I've grown accustomed to. If I want to have what I've always had.

I better not leave him if I want money.

And in that instant, I realize what this really is. What I'm really doing here.

This isn't a conversation about our relationship.

It's a business negotiation.

The intercom squawks to life and the pilot's voice comes over the speakers. "Sorry about the delay, Mr. Milos. It looks like the runway has been cleared and we're ready for departure. So I'm going to ask you and Miss Larrabee to buckle your seat belts now for takeoff."

I glance over at Mendi as he switches off his BlackBerry, buckles his seat belt, and stretches his long toned legs out in front of him, resting his head back, and closing his eyes. As I stare at him, looking so peaceful and untroubled and perfectly content to fly across the world with me at the drop of a hat, I know the pilot is not actually asking me to buckle my seat belt. He's asking if I really want to do this. If this is really where I want to be. *Is this how you want to spend the rest of your life, Miss Larrabee? At the whim of someone else's unpredictable and possibly even* nonexistent *emotions? Because if you buckle that seat belt, if I take this plane into the air, that's it. There's no turning back.*

He's offering me an ultimatum. Speak now or forever hold your peace.

And when have I *ever* been known to hold my peace?

I tuck Holly under my arm and leap up from the seat, stepping over Mendi's outstretched legs to get to the aisle. "I'm sorry," I say. "I can't do this."

Mendi opens his eyes and looks up at me in surprise. "What?"

I reach into the overhead bin and pull down my laptop. "I have to go." Then I call to the flight attendant, "Excuse me? Can you tell the pilot that I need to get off the plane?"

I can see Mendi's visible struggle to stay patient with me. It's a look I know too well. The last time I saw it was fifteen minutes before I drove my Mercedes through the window of a convenience store.

"Baby," he says, standing up and taking my hand, "sit down. You're being dramatic. Look, let's fly to Europe and see how it goes. You can't live your life worrying about what will happen next. You have to just close your eyes and let go."

I pull my hand free and use it to touch his face. I rest my palm on his cheek and absorb his heat for the last time. "I'm sorry, Mendi," I say softly. "But I'd rather live my life with my eyes open."

Then I reach down and swipe the *Fortune* magazine from his lap and walk off the plane.

THE OTHER LIST

MENDI DOESN'T FOLLOW ME. NOT THAT HE EVER has. But for the first time in our dramatic two-year relationship, I'm grateful. The man working the front desk at the hangar asks if I need transportation. He motions to the long black limousine that Mendi and I arrived in and tells me that Mr. Milos's driver will be happy to take me wherever I need to go. I shake my head and ask if he can just call me a cab.

He appears surprised by my request but doesn't argue. He places a quick call and then informs me that my taxi will be here in ten minutes.

Left with nothing to do and about three vacations' worth of baggage, I have no choice but to squat down on the top of one of my suitcases and wait.

I open the magazine in my hand and flip to the cover story about my father. I'm not sure why I'm so interested, but something compels me to look.

The article consists of three pages and there's a whole introduction about the upcoming merger with LaFleur Media. It goes on about how powerful Larrabee Media is going to be once the two

companies are combined and about how my father will be present-
ing the merger to the shareholders to vote on.

Basically the same stuff Luke told me yesterday.

Jeez, was that only yesterday?

It feels like months ago. It's amazing how much can happen in
a single day. I've been exposed to the press, sold out by my father,
swept off my feet by Mendi, shunned by Luke, and now abandoned
on an airport runway. Although to be fair, that last one was by
choice.

And now I don't know what I'm going to do.

Go back to work, I suppose. Finish my fifty-two-week-job
sentence, collect my check, and get the heck out of here.

I start to flip the page of the magazine but a photograph catches
my eye and I stop.

It's of a man with a broad face, a long nose, salt-and-pepper
hair, and horn-rimmed glasses. It's one of those corporate promotional photos with the dull background. Essentially the grown-up
version of those horrible portraits they make you take back in elementary school.

But I honestly could care less about what *kind* of photo it is. I'm
more concerned by the person in it.

I *know* him.

But how?

I read the photo caption: *Pascal LaFleur, founder and CEO of
LaFleur Media.*

Oh, right. He's the guy they're negotiating the big merger with.
Basically the French version of my father. That must be why he
looks so familiar.

But the longer I study his face, the more unconvinced I become.

Why would *I* recognize the guy my father is conducting business with? It's not as though I keep tabs on these things. That's Luke's domain. Did Luke show me a picture of him once? I don't think so. Or maybe I saw him on the news or something? Luke said the story has been running on CNBC for weeks.

I snort at the thought.

Me watch CNBC? Sure. Sounds *just* like me.

Well, maybe Horatio was watching it in the kitchen and I walked in and caught a glimpse of this guy's face.

No, something in my head protests. *That's not it.*

I know him from somewhere else. I've seen him in *person* before. Recently. I can almost hear the sound of his voice.

And for some reason, I remember him talking about evicting a chef . . .

Yes! That's right!

He was the host of the party I worked the night before. He was the one I overheard speaking French to a group of people while I was passing around hors d'oeuvres. Before I was photographed by every media outlet on the planet while scooping trash off the sidewalk.

I shudder at the memory and quickly turn the page to try to smother it.

But even as I continue reading the rest of the article, that man's face lingers in my mind. Something feels very wrong here. My instincts are telling me there's something off about the whole situation.

I flip back to LaFleur's photograph and stare intently at it, trying to figure out what I'm missing. If he really *is* a French version of my father, then I have every reason to be distrustful of him.

But unfortunately, I have no idea why. So I turn the page once again and keep reading.

My eyes skim the remainder of the text until I get to the part about my father starting out his career in the copy room of a small newspaper in Fresno and going on to build his empire. I stop and gape at the page. What interests me at this moment is not what's written in the article—I've already heard that particular story a million times—but the sidebar that appears *next* to the article. This one happens to be a list.

A list of successful people who have started at the very bottom. Just like my father.

And my eyes can't devour it fast enough.

Michael Dell, the founder and CEO of Dell, started out washing dishes in a Chinese restaurant before going on to start one of the biggest computer companies in the world. Warren Buffett worked in a grocery store before becoming a world-famous billionaire entrepreneur. Barack Obama and Madonna both worked in fast food. Walt Disney started out as a paperboy. Rod Stewart was a gravedigger. Jerry Seinfeld was a telemarketer. Donald Trump was a rent collector.

I nearly fall off my suitcase.

The list reads exactly like the one that's now sitting at the bottom of my trash can.

The 52-reasons-to-hate-my-father list.

The seemingly random jobs I've been forced to do over the past few months have not been random at all. They've been carefully selected. Because of the people that once started out in them. Successful, influential people who have managed to climb their way to the top from those very jobs.

I sit in the middle of the empty airport tarmac, completely flabbergasted. And then something echoes in my brain.

"For once in your life, Lex, can't you just trust that someone else might know what's good for you? That your father might have your best interests at heart?"

No. I couldn't believe that. At least not at the time Bruce Spiegelmann first uttered those words to me on that fateful day in his office. But now I'm starting to wonder if I could. If maybe my father does have some kind of redeemable quality about him. And if maybe this list is the proof.

Well, even if it is, I know it's not enough.

I need more. And I think I know where I can find it.

ON THE SAFE SIDE

THE DOOR TO MY FATHER'S STUDY OPENS WITH an eerie creak. The way doors tend to in scary movies. I place the master key Horatio gave me into the pocket of my jeans and hesitantly step inside. I haven't been in this room since I was a child. And even then I was terrified of setting foot in it. Because it meant seeing my father. Talking to him. Interacting with him. And that was always a petrifying notion.

For as long as the Larrabee family has owned this house, there's only ever been one reason to enter this room and that's because my father was in it. And for the last ten or so years of my life, whenever my father was in the house, I've learned how to make myself scarce.

But one thing I never did—I'd never *dare* to do—was come in here alone.

For starters, the room itself has a certain menacing quality to it. The dark wood, the tall bookcases, the low light seeping in from between the thick branches that shade the windows. It's more like a hidden cavern than an office. Even the Van Gogh hanging on the wall—a portrait of a forlorn man sitting next to a dying flower—is known to be one of his darkest paintings.

Most people like bright rooms with lots of natural light and color and cheerfulness. But not my father. In fact, I wouldn't be surprised if he specifically chose this room because it *wasn't* all those things. And I have to say, the baleful ambience suits him perfectly.

I grapple for the light switch on the wall. It turns on a single dim lamp on the desk, making the murky shadows contort into odd, shapeless creatures that I swear are watching me. Wondering what this uninvited stranger is doing roaming around their hidden lair. I take a deep breath and remind myself that I'm being silly. It's just a room. Like any other room in this house.

The fact that the only memories I have of this place are of my father sitting at that desk and staring down at me intimidatingly is irrelevant.

He's not here now. And that's what matters.

I shake my head to clear it and get to work searching. Careful not to leave any evidence of my visit, I start with bookshelves and cabinets and then move on to drawers. But the problem is, I'm not even sure what I'm looking for. Something exonerating. Something to prove that my father isn't a monster. That there's more to the story.

To be honest, at this point I'd settle for an old shoe box filled with photographs of my mother. *Real* photographs. Ones that used to occupy frames and decorate mantels. The kind of pictures taken by amateur photographers with cheap disposable cameras. Not the kind that require lighting setups and a crew of ten people.

Maybe if I could just see her as she truly was—not as the publicists wanted her to be—then I would feel better.

But after thirty minutes of tearing the place apart and putting it all back together to cover my tracks, I'm still no closer to any answers.

I've searched every cupboard, drawer, shelf, filing cabinet, nook, and cranny there is and I've found nothing of interest. If my father is keeping any information about my mother—or anything that might change my opinion of him—it's not in here.

I turn toward the Van Gogh painting on the wall and observe the sad man's face and the wilting flower on the table in front of him. His desolate expression mirrors my own.

Maybe he's been looking for something as well. Something he can't seem to find.

I step closer to the painting and suddenly notice a detail about it that I didn't see before. For some strange reason, it doesn't appear to be flush with the wall. It looks like there's a tiny gap between the frame and the paneling behind it.

Then again, I think to myself, taking another step forward, *maybe the sad man's not looking for something. Maybe he's* hiding *something.*

I walk around my father's desk and press my cheek to the wall, closing one eye in an effort to peer behind the painting.

Just as I suspected, there's something back there.

Ever so carefully, I grab the base of the frame and lift it but the painting doesn't budge. After a moment of contemplation, I decide to try another tactic. I pull the painting toward me. It starts to move, swinging open from right to left like a doorway.

Behind it, embedded in the wall, is a rectangular metal safe with a combination lock.

My heart gallops inside my chest in excitement.

This is it. This is what I've been looking for. It *has* to be.

The only problem now is getting it open.

I try every combination of numbers I can think of: my father's birthday, my mother's birthday, RJ's birthday, even my *own* birthday, but none of them work. I Google the date my father's company went public and try that. No dice.

I rack my brain for other clues. A combination that would make sense for my father. Something that has *meaning* to him. But, of course, I come up short. The man is a zombie. *Nothing* has meaning to him.

But then I think back to the portrait hanging over the fireplace in the next room. The empty look in my father's eyes. The same look I saw on those grieving people at the funeral home.

I swivel the Van Gogh painting back around so that I can scrutinize the face of the man guarding the safe. I study the way he's leaning into his hand, his mouth drawn into a hopeless frown. He too is mourning something.

I return my focus to the safe and slowly dial the following numbers in order: 01-27-00.

The date of my mother's death.

The lock clicks open.

I pull the heavy metal door toward me. Inside I find countless stacks of cash in various currencies. Probably totaling more than ten million dollars. I bypass the money and instead reach for the dark wooden box sitting at the back of the safe.

I place it on my father's desk and lower myself into the chair. Slowly, I unhook the metal clasp and lift the lid. Photographs of all shapes and sizes are contained within. Every memory of my mother that my father hid away. Wedding photos, honeymoon pictures, snapshots, candids, Polaroids, even a strip of photographs from one of those cheesy booths you find in arcades. My mom is every age in these pictures. Baby to teenager. Child to adult. Her smile is radiant. Her eyes are warm. Her face is flushed with color.

One photo in particular stands out. It's a small, wallet-sized picture. I assume it must be a school photo. She appears to be about my age. So I'm guessing she was in high school when it was taken.

I sit paralyzed as I stare into it, taking in the shape of her face. Every curve, every point, every line. Her clothes might be dated. Her hairstyle might be ripped from the eighties. But one thing is for certain.

It's like looking into a mirror.

We're practically identical.

My paralysis finally lifts and I place the school photo aside and continue sifting through the rest of the pictures, until I finally come to the bottom of the box. But the last item I find is not a photograph. It's a plain white piece of paper.

I flip it over and, with a hard swallow, glance at the top of the page.

OFFICIAL CORONER'S REPORT FOR ELIZABETH LARRABEE

A coroner's report?

Why would my father lock up something like this? My mother died in a car accident. Her BMW was crushed by a giant eighteen-wheeler. It says so right here in the cause-of-death section. What more is there to know?

But as I glance farther down the page, I quickly come to realize that there is, in fact, a *lot* more to know. More than I was ever meant to find out.

I come to the line describing the alcohol level in my mother's bloodstream at the time of her death and my eyes stop dead in their tracks. There's no need to read any farther. All of my questions have suddenly been answered. In a mind-numbing, blood-boiling, breath-stealing flash.

My mother died with a blood-alcohol concentration of 0.28. More than three times the legal limit.

With the document clutched tightly in my hand, I bolt out of the office and call for Kingston. He appears in the foyer a moment later.

"Yes, Miss Larrabee?" he prompts.

"I need a ride. Right now."

He nods obligingly. "I'll pull the car around front."

I should have done this a long time ago. There's only one person, besides my father, who knows all the secrets of this family. And it's been his job to protect them.

"Where to?" Kingston asks as I climb into the backseat of the limo.

"Take me to see the Lieutenant."

LIKE MOTHER, LIKE DAUGHTER

BY DEFINITION, A LIEUTENANT IS SOMEONE WHO assists the captain in all matters pertaining to the successful running of a ship. In the Larrabee family, these duties include distributing trust-fund checks, administering wills, and managing the aftermath of drunk-driving accidents caused by delinquent teenage daughters, among other things.

In our family, these responsibilities are handled by the one and only Bruce Spiegelmann, who looks up from a stack of paperwork on his desk and flashes me a smile when I step into his office and close the door behind me.

"Lexi," he says, rising to his feet to greet me. "What a pleasant surprise. What brings you down here?"

I don't waste any time with small talk. I simply lower myself into the chair across from him and get right to the point. "I'm here to talk about my mother."

There's a flash of something unrecognizable on Bruce's face. I have an inkling he knew this day would come. It was only a matter of time.

"Your mother was a wonderful woman," he says patiently.

"Yeah, yeah," I hear myself intone. "Maternal, supportive, loving, all those things, right?"

He chuckles lightly but I know it's a cover for something else because I hear the anxiety in his voice. I see the discomfort in the way he shifts in his chair. And I know what it means when he starts to gnaw on the inside of his cheek.

"I guess everyone failed to mention that she also had a drinking problem."

Bruce freezes and gives me a long, hard stare. I pull the coroner's report from my bag and slide it across the table to him. Bruce takes one look at it, closes his eyes, and pinches the bridge of his nose with his thumb and forefinger.

"She died in a drunk-driving accident. And *she* was the drunk one!" My voice rises as I struggle to keep my temper in check. "Don't you think I had a right to know that?!"

"Yes," he replies softly. "I do."

I shake my head in confusion and lean forward. "Excuse me?"

"I've been telling your father the same thing for years. That you have a right to know. All of you do. But this was his call. And as his lawyer, I can't—"

"So it's true?" I interject impatiently. "She was an alcoholic?" I hear myself asking and the conviction in my voice surprises me. It's as though I'm speaking a truth I've known all along.

"Your mother," Bruce tries, "was a very complicated woman. She had trouble with—"

"Just answer the question."

Bruce shoots me a heavy look, as though asking if I really want to know. If I really want to open Pandora's box. Because everyone knows, once it's opened, it can't be closed again. I return his gaze with determination, letting him know, without uttering a word, that I'm not afraid. That I came here for the whole truth, and nothing but the truth, and I'm not leaving until I get it.

He exhales loudly, his breath signaling his surrender. But I need to hear the word. And he knows it. "Yes," he finally says.

"The cruises she used to go on?" I prompt.

He struggles. Hesitates. And then, "Your father tried so many times to get her help. But nothing worked. She was in and out of rehab your entire childhood. The moment she would get back, your father would leave on a business trip and she would relapse again."

I let this sink in. As much as I hate hearing it, it seems to fit. It feels comfortable. Not in that it brings me physical comfort (quite the opposite actually), but in knowing that it's the truth. *Finally* the truth. Now I can breathe.

"Why did he insist on lying about it?" I ask. "Why not tell us the truth about her? Did he think we couldn't handle it?"

Bruce shakes his head. "It wasn't that. He was trying to *protect* you. He was so pained by her sickness and he didn't want you and your brothers to have to go through that same agony. He thought if he could hide the truth from you and convince you she was someone else, you'd be better off."

Suddenly it makes perfect sense. In one crushing instant everything is clear. This is why he insists on marrying people he doesn't love. This is why he thinks you're better off keeping everyone at arm's length. If you don't let anyone in, no one can hurt you. If you never love anyone, no one can die and take a part of you with them.

And then I'm struck with an unsettling thought.

But I almost did *die.*

Nearly five months ago. In a car crash. A car crash that started this whole thing. The fifty-two jobs. The life-rehabilitation program.

I sit frozen in shock. I can't move any part of my body. Which means I can't reach up to catch the tears that are spilling forth. Bruce plucks a tissue from a box on his desk and hands it over but I don't take it.

After a few more blurry seconds, I find my tongue. "That's why he did this," I conclude. "That's why I'm spending a year working these jobs."

Because if each one of those jobs eventually led to wealth and success for someone else, you would think at least *one* of them would work for me.

Bruce nods. "I wanted to tell you, Lex. I swear I did. Your father blames himself. For all of it. Including her death."

"But it clearly wasn't his fault!" I argue.

"Try telling him that." Bruce removes his glasses and rubs his eyes. "He's been haunted by it ever since. He thought if only he had caught the problem earlier, he could have stopped it before it got bad. But he didn't."

"And then I crashed my car into a convenience store." I finish the thought.

Bruce nods. "And he wasn't about to make the same mistake twice."

*   *   *

I leave Bruce's office feeling numb. I've been bombarded. There's so much new information to sift through, I don't even know where to start. Or what to do with it once I've finished.

A few lousy words and a single sheet of paper and suddenly my entire life is turned upside down.

All this time I thought my father was out to get me. When really it was the other way around. He didn't hate me. He wasn't trying to torture me or set me up to fail. He was trying to *save* me.

And if that's the case, then there's only one thing for me to do now.

I'm going to have to save him right back.

I yank out my cell phone and dial Luke's number.

Skipping the formalities, I bellow into the phone, "We have to talk. Meet me at the Nest in twenty minutes."

FAKE FRIENDS

I THOUGHT YOU WERE LEAVING," LUKE SAYS
grumpily as soon as Horatio leads him into the library. I'm already
knee-deep in my preparations, sitting on the floor with my laptop
open and contracts and printouts spread out around me.

"I changed my mind," I say simply.

"What do you want?" Luke asks, crossing his arms over his chest.

"Your help."

He looks taken aback. "*My* help?"

I nod. "Yes."

"Why?"

"Because you're the only one I can trust right now."

He thinks about this for a moment and then, after seeming to
decide it's a good enough reason for him, joins me on the floor in
the center of the room. "What's going on?"

Excitedly, I turn the *Fortune* magazine around so that he can
see the page it's open to. "See this guy?" I ask him, pointing to the
picture that inspired this whole crazy plan.

He nods. "Sure. It's Pascal LaFleur. The CEO of LaFleur
Media."

"Well," I say importantly, "he's also a liar."

Luke blinks. "Excuse me?"

"I saw him at the party I was working. I served him a tuna-seviche cucumber cup!"

Luke's eyes widen with disbelief. "And that makes him a liar?"

I wave my hand. "Listen," I tell him urgently, "he was speaking to this group of people." I search through the scattered paperwork around me until I locate a photograph that I printed from the Internet. It shows ten people standing behind a large conference table. I've already circled three of their faces in red marker.

"These people," I say, pointing to the circled heads. "And he was speaking to them in French."

"Well, he *is* French," Luke points out.

"I *know*," I say, growing impatient. "Just *listen*. He said something about a plan to evict the chef."

Luke looks at me as though I've clearly cracked.

I ignore him. "I didn't think anything of it because I was like, what? Evict the chef? Whatever, crazy Frenchman."

"Is this going somewhere?" Luke interrupts.

I grit my teeth and try to hold on to my dwindling patience. "Yes!" I take a deep breath and continue. "But it wasn't until I saw his face in this magazine that I realized I misunderstood him. You see, my French is pretty much limited to talking about fashion and food and celebrity gossip."

"Really?" Luke jokes. "You don't say."

I slap him with the piece of paper in my hand. "Anyway, I totally forgot that *le chef* doesn't mean 'the chef.' It's a *faux ami*!"

"A what?"

I sigh. "A *faux ami*. It means a false or fake friend. A word that you think would be the same in French and English because it sounds the same in both languages, but it's not. Like *librairie*. It doesn't mean library. It means bookstore. Or *napkin*. You would think it means napkin but it's actually a French word for sanitary pad."

"Okay, okay!" Luke says, putting up a hand to stop me. "I get it. So if *chef* doesn't mean chef, what does it mean?"

I inhale deeply and hold his gaze. "It basically means CEO."

It takes Luke a moment to catch up with my frantic thought process and when he does, I see his expression start to shift. "Evict the CEO?"

I nod eagerly. *"Expulser,"* I explain. "That's the word he used. It means to evict. But I looked it up and it also means to expel. To oust. To cast out."

Luke doesn't say anything. He doesn't have to. The look on his face says everything.

"So I started reading about the upcoming merger," I continue, nodding at all the paperwork around me. "I even found a few corporate e-mails about it in my spam folder."

He cocks an inquisitive eyebrow at me.

"It's a long story," I reply, with a hasty wave. "Anyway, after reading all this stuff, I discovered that once the merger is complete, the plan is for my father to be the CEO of the new entity and this Pascal guy to serve under him. But if you take into account the five new board members that are coming in from LaFleur Media, you would actually only need three additional votes to gain a majority."

I tap again at the three circled heads in the photograph. "*These* three votes."

Luke regards me in sheer astonishment. I have no idea if it's the information itself that's so shocking or the fact that *I'm* the one who discovered it. Perhaps a little of both.

"I don't believe it," Luke says finally, after finding his voice again. "LaFleur's going behind your father's back to control the whole company?"

I nod. "Apparently *he's* the *faux ami* here." Then I spell it out in even simpler terms. "If this deal goes through, my father is out of a job."

I SPY

LUKE IS IMMEDIATELY UP IN ARMS. HE JUMPS TO his feet and starts pacing. "So we call your dad and warn him not to recommend the merger to the shareholders tomorrow," he thinks aloud.

But I immediately shake my head. "Won't work."

"Why not?"

"He won't believe me! He'll talk to Caroline and think I'm trying to sabotage him after they exposed me to the press."

"Wait, what?" Luke stops pacing and stares down at me. "Your *father* was the one who tipped off the press?"

"I told you my family was complicated."

He ponders this for a moment and then seems to be content to store it away for further reflection later. "Okay, fine, then *I'll* tell him."

I shoot him a dubious look. "What will you say?"

"I'll just tell him he can't trust LaFleur and not to make the recommendation. If the stockholders don't vote it through, your father's job is safe."

"Sure," I say sarcastically. "My father is going to call off a billion-dollar business deal because his twenty-year-old *intern* has a hunch."

He knows I'm right and that's why he breaks my gaze and continues pacing.

"We need proof," I tell him. Although I'm sure he doesn't need to be told. He has to have come to this conclusion himself by now. "My father will only respond to hard evidence."

Luke throws up his hands. "How the heck are we supposed to get proof? And in only a matter of hours? The vote is tomorrow morning!"

"Don't worry," I tell him calmly, scooping up the paperwork around me. I pull everything into my arms and stand up. "I have a plan."

Grabbing Luke by the elbow, I lead him upstairs, into my room, and close the door behind us.

He glances uneasily around before taking a seat on my chaise longue. Holly yips and jumps up next to him. He cautiously pets her head. Like he's afraid he's going to break her. "Uh . . . nice room," he says awkwardly.

"Thanks." I disappear into the closet and start peeling off my clothes.

"So what is this big plan of yours?" he calls anxiously.

There's a knock on the door and I hear Horatio come in. "What's this?" Luke asks him.

"A request from Miss Larrabee," Horatio replies cryptically and bows out of the room.

I poke my head out of the closet to see that Luke is holding a small, unmarked cardboard box, struggling to get the top open.

"What's this?" He repeats the question to me as he finally manages to remove the lid. Then he reaches into the box and pulls out a black headset with a microphone attached and a tiny earpiece. He holds each item in one hand and stares at them questioningly.

I draw my head back into the closet and scour through the back shelves, behind all my evening gowns, until I find the dress I'm looking for. "It's our spy gear!" I say excitedly as I pull the frock over my head and push my arms through the sleeves. The fabric feels familiarly uncomfortable and I cringe slightly at the memory of wearing this hideous thing.

God, it feels like *forever* ago!

And staring down at the blue-and-white pinstripes and white collar, I realize how much has changed since this whole thing began. I feel like an entirely different person from the girl who first donned this outfit more than four months ago.

"Our *what*?" Luke's voice questions skeptically.

I pull the dress taut and slide my feet into my shoes. "LaFleur is renting a house in Palos Verdes," I call back. "It's where the party was last night. I noticed an office on the first floor. He's got to have something in there that proves he's in cahoots with those board members. So I'm going to sneak into the house and find it."

"You're going to do WHAT?" Although I can't see his face, I can tell from his panicked tone that he's starting to doubt the efficacy of my plan.

"Relax," I say, rummaging through my box of wigs until I find the perfect one. The tag calls it *Nikki*. It's a dark chocolate-brown, asymmetrical, chin-length cut. I tie my hair up in a rubber band, tilt forward, and squeeze the wig onto my head. "I'm going in disguise."

"Huh?"

With all the elements of my costume now in place, I make a grand, sweeping entrance back into the bedroom and sink into a little curtsey.

He looks me up and down in confusion, taking in every inch of my ensemble. "Is that your Majestic Maids uniform?"

I nod. "Uh-huh. I'm going as the maid." I strut over to him, grab the small earpiece from his hand, and wedge it into my ear canal. "You're going to wait outside with this"—I tap on the headset in his other hand—"and tell me what I'm supposed to be looking for."

He shoots to his feet and starts backing away from me like I have some kind of infectious disease called insanity. "No way," he vows. "That's breaking and entering. You'll be recognized. We'll totally get busted."

"I'm not going to be recognized in *this*." I gesture to my outfit.

"Um, hello!" he says, dumbfounded. "You're Lexington *Larrabee*. The *daughter* of the man who's brokering this deal. You can't just walk into LaFleur's house and expect to go unnoticed."

I step toward Luke and place a reassuring hand on his cheek. "Oh, Luke," I say in a sympathetic voice, "you're forgetting one of the most important lessons I've learned throughout this whole journey."

"What's that?" he says, eyeing me suspiciously.

I flash him a wry smile. "No one notices the help."

ESPIONAGE 101

I PIN THE TINY MICROPHONE BROOCH TO THE lapel of my uniform and whisper, "Testing, one two three. Can you hear me?" A surge of giddy electricity jolts through me. This is too cool.

After a soft crackle, I hear Luke's voice come through my earpiece. "Yes, I can hear you."

"Okay," I say, taking a deep breath. "Here goes nothing."

I hoist myself up onto the low-hanging branch of the tree then push to my feet. I grab hold of the balcony railing to steady myself and toss my legs over. Once I'm on the other side, I lean over and give Luke a thumbs-up. I can see him watching through the windshield of his car parked down the street.

I quietly push on the sliding glass door and squeeze through. I find myself in what appears to be an unused guest room. I open the door to the hallway and tiptoe toward the stairs, leaning over the banister to see if there's anyone in view on the first floor.

The coast is clear so I start down the stairs, trying to keep my footsteps as silent as possible. I recognize the large entryway and salon—after all, I was just here—and silently make my way to the study.

The door is closed. I knock gently and when there's no answer I twist the handle and enter, shutting the door softly behind me.

"Okay, I'm in," I whisper, leaning my head toward my brooch.

"What do you see?" Luke asks through my earpiece.

I hurry over to the desk and start riffling through paperwork. "I don't know," I tell him. "It looks like reports of some kind. Lots of charts. *Revenue projection*," I read from the top of the page in my hand.

"No," Luke replies decisively. "Those are probably stock reports. You need to find some kind of contract, a written agreement, between LaFleur and those three board members. Something that outlines their promise to vote him in as CEO when the deal goes through."

I put that page down, exhale loudly, and start sifting through more paperwork.

"It's probably not going to be right there on his desk," Luke suggests.

I nod. "You're right," I whisper, and start pulling open drawers. But there's nothing even remotely similar to what Luke described.

Then I reach the bottom drawer of the desk. It's locked. I tug on the handle, trying to yank it open but it won't budge. And I can't very well take the whole desk back out the window with me.

This has to be it, though. Why bother locking a drawer unless it has stuff in it that you don't want people to find?

I just need a freaking key! But that could be anywhere. Including *on* LaFleur himself. And as far as I know, he's probably with my father at his office right now. At least I hope that's where he is right now. Although anywhere but in the house would suffice.

"Dang it!" I swear.

"What's wrong?" Luke responds, sounding panicked.

"There's a locked drawer. It has to be in there. But I can't get in it."

"Can you pick the lock?" he asks.

"Listen to Mr. Goody Two-shoes now," I jest. "Encouraging me to pick locks."

"What can I say? You must be a bad influence on me."

"Or a good one."

He laughs. "So, can you pick it?"

"No!" I cry back. "I don't know how to pick a lock. Do you?"

"What do *you* think?"

"You mean they don't teach you that in college?" I ask snootily.

"I must have been sick that day."

"Wait," I say, getting an idea. I glance down at my uniform. The last time I was wearing this thing, I couldn't figure out how to turn on a vacuum cleaner. Or even how to use one. But I figured that out, didn't I?

I hastily pull my cell phone out of the pocket and open up YouTube. I type in *How to pick a lock* and get about a hundred results. The first one, however, has three million views and a four-and-a-half-star rating so I figure it's probably my best bet.

I select it, turn the volume down low, and press play, scouring the desk for the two paper clips the video says I'll need. Watching the woman in the video closely, I unbend the first paper clip and then tweak the end to create a small hook. Then I completely straighten the second paper clip, kneel down, and insert it in the bottom of the lock, turning it clockwise. Following the step-by-step directions in the video, I slowly slide the hooked paper clip on top and feel around for something called *the pins*.

I grunt in frustration as I struggle to pop each pin but after a few minutes of trying, I don't think I've even gotten one.

"What are you doing?" Luke's voice comes through my headset, causing me to lose my concentration.

I sigh. "Trying to pick this stupid lock. Hold on."

I take another deep breath, lean in closer, and try again. My hook finally makes contact with the first pin and I'm able to push it upward. I hear a tiny click. "It's working!" I whisper excitedly.

I follow suit with the second one, then the third, turning the bottom paper clip slightly as I go until the last pin pops and the lock turns all the way to the right. I pull on the drawer handle. It opens.

There's only one thing inside. An unmarked manila folder. Eagerly, I pick it up and flip it open.

"Agreement to elect Pascal LaFleur to the position of CEO of the new Larrabee Media Corporation." I read the top line of the first page aloud.

"That's it!" Luke squeals so loudly into the headset, it nearly bruises my eardrum. "Is it signed?"

I flip to the last page and find four signatures. The first three I recognize as the names of the board members from the photograph I printed from the Internet and the final signature belongs to Pascal LaFleur himself.

"Yes!"

"Okay," Luke says authoritatively. "Now get the heck out of there."

With a huge grin, I fold up the documents and stick them down the front of my uniform. I return the empty manila folder to the drawer and push it closed with the side of my leg. I start back to the door but just as I reach for the handle, it begins to turn, seemingly on its own.

I gasp and search for a place to hide but there's no time. The door opens and in walks the man of the hour himself. Pascal LaFleur.

Our eyes meet for a brief moment and as soon as I'm capable of reacting, I cast my head downward, breaking our stare.

I sink into a shallow curtsey. "Hello, Mr. LaFleur," I say, trying my best to remember and imitate Katarzyna's distinct Polish accent. "Welcome home."

He stands there glaring at me for a moment, and then glances suspiciously around the room. I keep my head down, avoiding eye contact, trying to quiet my breathing. I pray that he can't hear the way my heart is thumping in my chest.

"Holy crap!" Luke says in my ear. "He's there? I didn't even see his car pull into the garage. What are you going to do?"

I want to whisper back that screaming into my ear is *not* helping but obviously that's out of the question.

"What are you doing in here?" he says, his French accent harsh and nasal.

I plaster a clueless expression onto my face and motion to the room. "I was to clean the room."

What I wouldn't give to have a feather duster in my hand right now. Or even a bottle of all-purpose cleaner. I really hope he doesn't realize how hard it is to clean a room empty-handed.

He continues to stare down at me, his eyes burning into the top of my head.

Please believe me, I implore silently. *Please.*

"I told the maid service I didn't want anyone in here," he finally says, and I feel my lungs exhale.

"I'm so sorry," I offer, scooting past him to get through the door. "Is my first day, sir. I will not make same mistake twice."

He lets me pass but his eyes follow vigilantly as I hurry down the hallway toward the salon. I make a show of fluffing the couch cushions in the salon until I see him disappear behind his office door.

Then I tiptoe through the entry hall, quietly slip out the front door, and make a mad dash to Luke's car, praying that Monsieur LaFleur doesn't notice the empty manila folder in the bottom desk drawer or the two straightened paper clips on the floor until we're long gone.

UNWRITTEN

IT'S DARK BY THE TIME WE ARRIVE AT MY FATHER'S
offices downtown. Luke parks the car and moves to unbuckle his
seat belt but my hand lands atop his. He peers up at me with a
curious expression.

"Do you mind waiting in the car?" I ask him. "I need to do this
alone."

He nods but doesn't move his hand. It stays securely underneath
mine. "Sure."

"You're positive he'll see it before he goes to the shareholders'
meeting?" I ask him.

"Yes," Luke assures me. "If you leave it on his desk, I'll make
certain he sees it as soon as he gets to work in the morning."

I bite my lip. "Okay, good."

I give Luke's hand a quick squeeze, then clasp the documents
in my arms, and swing the car door open. I hurry across the parking garage to the elevator.

I use Luke's key card to open the door to the reception area and
again to open the door to my father's office.

I locate a notepad bearing the Larrabee Media logo and rip a sheet from the top. I scribble a quick message urging my father to read these documents carefully before making his final decision about the merger. Then I paper clip the note to the stack of documents I stole from LaFleur's office and place them on the desk, right on top of his keyboard, where he's sure to see them when he comes in the next morning.

And now it's time to leave.

The only problem is, my feet won't move. I'm frozen here, my eyes glued to the evidence I risked everything to obtain.

My father has sacrificed so many things for this company. Including time with his family. His wife. Me. He even sold me out to the press just for the benefit of this merger.

He was never around. He was always away on business. Sometimes it felt as though Larrabee Media was always his true love, his true passion, and the rest of us were just abandoned hobbies. Half-finished model airplanes left to gather dust in the garage.

So why am I so eager to save something like that? Why am I rushing to make sure he doesn't lose control of it?

What on earth am I thinking?

Ever since I saw that picture of LaFleur in the magazine and figured out his plan, I've been on some mad rampage to be a hero and save the day. To take down the bad guys and rescue the damsel in distress (in this case, my father's job).

I never even stopped long enough to consider what would happen if I *didn't* show him these documents. If I just quietly slid them back down the front of my uniform and pretended none of this ever happened. If I allowed tomorrow's shareholder vote to continue as planned.

I know exactly what would happen. My father would recommend the merger, the stockholders would vote it through, and immediately after the contracts were signed, the board would vote to have him removed.

My father would be out of a job. And not just any job—the job that kept him from being my father. The job that prevented me from having any real relationship with Richard Larrabee.

If my father is too blind to see that this company has ruined our family, then maybe someone needs to show him. To hit him over the head with it. And maybe that someone should be me.

I slowly reach down and clutch the papers in my hand, marveling at how much heavier they suddenly feel now that they've been given so much weight.

Tomorrow it could all be over.

Maybe *this* is supposed to be the silver lining of this whole thing. These fifty-two jobs that my father has forced upon me. Maybe the good buried deep beneath all the rubble and chaos of the bad is this realization. That I can get my father back. Simply by withholding this information from him. I can destroy the one thing that has kept him from me. From all of us.

If I had never taken on this seemingly endless series of low-wage jobs, I never would have overheard that conversation between LaFleur and his cohorts. Maybe this was some grand scheme set up by the universe in an effort to show me the way out. To show me the light at the end of the tunnel.

And now all I have to do is walk toward it.

But as desperately as I'd like to believe that, something about it feels amiss. It's too deceptive to be a message from the universe.

Aren't universal transmissions supposed to be pure and uncor-
rupted?

Keeping this information from my father just so that I can have
him to myself is nothing more than glorified manipulation. I should
know. It's been a skill of mine for many years.

On the other hand, maybe this is the universe's way of proving
to me that I still *want* there to be a light at the end of the tunnel.
That I still care enough to look for one. That I haven't given up yet.

Maybe the real silver lining is realizing that although I might
have fifty-two reasons to hate my father, I really need only one reason to love him.

And maybe that reason isn't spelled out on a list. Or written in
a book. Or featured in a magazine article. Maybe it's a reason that
can't be published. A deleted chapter from my life story. Or better
still, a chapter that hasn't even been written yet.

And I know exactly what I want that chapter to say. How I
want to be remembered.

As the girl who saved her father's job despite all the reasons he
gave her not to.

Because that's what families do.

THOUGHTLESS

LUKE PULLS INTO THE DRIVEWAY OF MY HOUSE and kills the engine. "Can I walk you to your door?" he asks, and it makes me smile.

I don't think anyone's ever asked me that question before. It feels so old-fashioned and sweet. But then again, Luke is pretty much both of those things. I just never noticed it before. I was too busy focusing on his faults. Faults that suddenly I can't even remember anymore.

"Sure," I say, and step out of the car.

We walk in silence. The only sound is our footsteps on the pavement. The stillness is making me anxious. I want to say something to him but for the first time since we met, I'm speechless around him.

All I know is that I wish the distance from the driveway to the front door were one hundred times longer because we arrive way too quickly and I find myself wanting to ask him to stay.

I reach for the doorknob but stop when I feel his warm fingers land on top of mine. "Wait," he says, gently prying my hand away and holding it loosely in his own. "There's something I've been wanting to do."

I look up and meet his gaze. His hazel eyes seem to sparkle against the floodlights that glow from the landscaping. "Okay," I say hesitantly.

He sighs and glances away. "I just haven't been able to do it."

"Why?" I ask.

His gaze returns to mine and a small smile creeps across his lips. "Because I'm pretty certain it's not in my job description."

"Well," I say, pretending to glance at an invisible watch, "it's way past business hours. Maybe you should just do it."

His eyes crinkle as his smile broadens. It's beyond adorable. "I don't know," he begins. "Things are complicated."

"Complicated?" I repeat playfully.

"Well, this thing I've been wanting to do, it's not exactly appropriate for two people who are working together and might *continue* to work together. It might make things awkward."

I nod, feigning deep contemplation. "Mmm hmm. I see. That *is* a problem."

"On the other hand"—Luke pulls my hand upward and rests it against his chest—"someone once told me that I think about things too much. And that I should learn how to just let go. Throw caution to the wind."

"That person sounds very wise," I remark, doing little to hide the grin that's surfacing.

"She can be," he muses.

"Well, you want to know what I think?" I ask.

But I never do get an answer. Nor am I able to finish my thought because his hands are suddenly on my cheeks. They guide my face right to his. Our lips come together. He kisses me, softly at first, intensifying with each passing second. And although I'm getting drunk off his smell, his taste, his touch, for some reason I can't seem to let my mind go. Something doesn't feel right. It's not me who's kissing him back. It's someone else. And I can't do it like this. I can't be anyone else anymore.

"Wait," I say, pressing against his chest and pulling away.

His face shrouds with concern. "What's wrong?" he asks, slightly breathless.

I pull off my wig, yank the rubber band out of my hair, and shake my head violently. I keep shaking and shaking until slowly but surely I start to feel like myself again. Until it's only me standing next to him. No one else.

"Okay," I say with a sigh. "Now can you do that again?"

He smiles and leans into me. I close my eyes. This time, when our lips meet, I melt into him. All of my fire and fever become his. And all of his patience and sincerity become mine.

For months we were at war. Sworn enemies. Separated by one man. One king. I suppose it only makes sense that the very thing that divided us is now bringing us together.

Because apart we might be as different as night and day, black and white, right and wrong, but together we create two sides of a whole. Together we balance.

RETURN TO SENDER

THE NEXT MORNING I'M GLUED TO THE TELEVISION screen in the kitchen. Luke assured me nothing would happen until the shareholders' meeting at eleven but that doesn't stop me from waking up at the crack of dawn and turning on CNBC. Now I know why I've never watched this network before. It's nothing but boring business news and people droning on and on about stock prices. I think I must be getting hypnotized by that annoying little scrolling ticker tape at the bottom of the screen because I can't even bring myself to change the channel.

Horatio tries to get me to eat something, laying out an assortment of breakfast items, but I refuse all of them. I'm *way* too nervous to eat. My stomach feels like it's on a spin cycle. Anything I swallow down is just going to come right back up.

Finally, at eleven o'clock the anchorman announces that he's interrupting their usual broadcast to bring us special footage from the Larrabee Media shareholders' meeting, where Richard Larrabee is scheduled to present an important business decision that is expected to dramatically impact the future of the company.

I sit in my pajamas at the kitchen counter, leaning so far forward my butt is nearly falling off the stool. I can see Horatio giving me strange looks out of the corner of his eye as he goes about making his weekly grocery shopping list.

The scene changes and the screen now shows a giant meeting room with hundreds of people sitting in chairs and my father positioned behind a podium at the front.

This is it!

"Thank you, everyone, for being here," he begins. "We are here today to talk about a very important matter that you've probably been reading about lately. A possible merger between Larrabee Media and the prominent and successful French corporation LaFleur Media."

I notice Pascal LaFleur standing off to his right. I can't help but snarl at him. My father, on the other hand, gives him a small, knowing nod and LaFleur returns the subtle gesture.

I'm actually somewhat surprised to witness my father's usual stiff and impassive demeanor. I guess I kind of thought that after reading my note and the evidence attached to it, he would look a little more, I don't know, outraged? Incensed? I mean, he was seriously double-crossed by people he trusted and he looks exactly like he always does. Calm and collected. And, most important, ready to get down to business.

But I suppose that's a testament to his superior business skills. That he's able to look so calm and unaffected in the face of such betrayal.

He must be preparing for something really good. I can just imagine it. In a few minutes, he'll turn to LaFleur, reveal the truth about this two-timing sleazebag, and then really let him have it.

I can feel my heartbeat accelerate in anticipation.

"I'm here today to voice my official recommendation for this promising business venture," my father says.

Wait, what?

I grab for the remote and press the instant replay button.

"I'm here today to voice my official recommendation for this promising business venture," he says again before continuing. "I firmly believe that a merger with LaFleur is the best course of action for Larrabee Media and its investors and I trust that you'll heed my recommendation and vote in favor of this endeavor. Thank you."

I watch in total shock as he steps down from the podium and makes his way off camera.

What is he doing?

Did he not get the note? Did it fall through the cracks of his desk and now it's sitting idle on the floor? Darn it! I knew I should have waited until this morning and handed it to him in person!

Or what if he got it and simply ignored it? What if he thought it was just me playing around, trying to pull another one of my stunts. Or worse yet, what if he saw my name on the note and then threw the whole thing in the trash, assuming that if it came from me, it wasn't even worth looking at?

Oh, God. I feel sick to my stomach.

I grapple for my cell phone, nearly dropping it twice before I can steady my fingers long enough to dial Luke's number.

"What's going on?" I ask desperately the moment he answers.

"I don't know," he admits. "I'm not sure. He walked right out of the meeting and didn't even wait around to hear the outcome of the vote. I tried to talk to him as he was leaving but he just stalked off."

"Did he see my note? Did he read the documents?"

His voice sounds a million miles away. "I don't know, Lex."

I hang up the phone and start pacing the kitchen. Eventually, though, the room starts to make me feel claustrophobic so I move outside. I walk the garden frantically until there's sweat dripping down my face and my bare feet are stained green.

I need to go talk to him. It's the only choice. Maybe it's not too late. Maybe I can still convince him to call off the deal.

I race inside the house and up the stairs. I throw on a pair of ripped jeans and Rolando's black hoodie. For some reason it gives me an extra ounce of courage. And I could use all the courage I can get right now.

I hurry down the stairs and call for Kingston.

"He's not here," Horatio informs me after the third shout at the top of my lungs.

"Well, where *is* he?" I implore. "You know what—never mind, I'll drive myself."

I spin toward the entrance to the garage just as the front door opens and my father strolls into the foyer.

I've been listening to my father's entrances (and exits) for eighteen years. You might even say I'm some kind of expert on them. A scholar of sorts. If his comings and goings were a class offered at a university, I would be the resident professor.

Which is how I'm immediately able to catch the subtle difference in the way he enters the room now. For some reason, there's more patience in his gait. Longer time between footsteps. A deeper resonance in the rhythm of his stride.

"Dad!" I finally find my voice, but it's a cracked and battered version of what it used to be. "Didn't you read my note? And the documents I left on your desk?"

"I did," my father replies, his tone even and measured. "And I chose to ignore them."

I knew it. He doesn't trust me. He thinks I'm playing games. But I'm *not*. For the first time in my life I'm 100 percent sincere.

"Lexi," he states calmly, despite my visibly frayed nerves, "I think we should talk."

"No!" I call out in desperation. "There's no time. You have to get back to the office. You have to talk to LaFleur. He's trying to steal your job!"

"Lexi," my father says again, this time more forcefully. That familiar authority suddenly back in his tone. He motions toward the salon. "Sit down so I can explain."

I know that tone well enough to know that it's not worth arguing with because you'll never win. You'll just spin your wheels like a truck stuck in the mud until you run out of gas.

So with a sigh, I walk into the salon, checking repeatedly over my shoulder to make sure my father is still following me. That he hasn't mysteriously disappeared out the front door without a word, like the ghost that he's always been in this house.

I perch hesitantly on the edge of the couch but my father chooses to stand. Actually, he chooses to *pace*.

He takes long, uneven strides across the room, rubbing his fingers continuously along the surface of his chin.

I stare in bemusement at this strange, unusual behavior, trying to make sense of it. It takes me a few moments to realize what exactly it is. And when I do, I nearly slide off the edge of the couch.

My father is *nervous*.

"Bruce told me that you came to see him," he says.

Comprehension settles into my mind. So *that's* what this is about? He's pissed off because Bruce betrayed his secret?

"Dad," I'm quick to argue, "you can't be mad at Bruce for that. I figured it out on my own."

"I'm not mad," my father responds rapidly. Then he actually breaks into laughter. I can't remember the last time I heard him laugh. Well, when there were no TV cameras around to document it and transmit it to the world.

The laughter fit ends just as abruptly as it began. And instantly my father's face is serious again.

"Bruce was right all along," he decides. "I should have told you the truth about your mother. I was wrong to keep it from you."

This admission causes me to fall very silent. And very still.

I was wrong?

Did I just hear that correctly?

As if reading my mind and answering my question directly, he goes on. "I've made a lot of mistakes in my life, Lexi. Some more consequential than others. But I've learned how to live with those mistakes. I take full responsibility for them."

I can't keep my mouth closed. It drops open on its own accord.

Where is all of this coming from?

I'm tempted to glance around me for a camera crew or reporter.

Because the only time my father *ever* comes off this personable is when he knows he's being filmed.

"But the biggest mistake I ever made," he continues, "my life's biggest regret was not getting your mother the help she needed."

My head starts to shake. "Dad," I implore. "That wasn't your fault. Bruce told me the whole story. You tried to get her help. You sent her to rehab. There was nothing more—"

But he lifts a hand in the air to interrupt me. "Please allow me to finish."

I shut up. But only because I'm afraid if I don't, whatever more he's about to say will be lost forever. Who knows when will be the next time my father will decide to open up? Maybe it's like one of those freakish planetary alignments that only happens once every five billion years. So you better get your butt outside and watch the sky.

"I did send her to rehab," my father admits. "Many of them. The best of the best. But it's since dawned on me that *that* wasn't the help she really needed."

My face lines with confusion.

"You have to understand, Lexi," he continues. "I came from nothing. My family grew up without anything. My father was a bum who could never keep a job. I swore to myself that would never be me. I thought the best way to be a good husband and father was to work. And so I did. All the time. And the more I worked, the worse your mother got. It never even occurred to me at the time that what she really needed was a husband who came home every night."

He stops pacing and finally joins me on the couch. But I can't bring myself to look at him. So I look at the floor.

"After she died, my reasons for staying away changed. It became more of a survival mechanism. I blamed myself for her death and the guilt was so overwhelming that I couldn't even bear to look my children in the eye. You especially, Lexington."

My head whips up and I turn to face him. *"Me?"* I repeat in disbelief. "Why?"

My father's eyes soften in a way I've never seen before. Like two pale blue puddles left over after a rainstorm.

"You look more like her every day," he muses quietly. "You have no idea how hard it's been to look at you knowing that I took your mother from you."

"No you didn't," I argue, but my voice gets caught in my burning throat and I'm forced to leave my protest at that.

"Ever since your accident a few months ago," he explains, "I've been thinking a lot about work and the company and what it's all worth in the end. I can't have any more regrets in my life. I can't lose you the same way I lost her." He pauses a moment to loosen his tie and suck in a breath. "Which is why I turned in my resignation today."

It takes me a few seconds to fully understand what he's just said. And once I do, I'm out of my seat like a rocket. "You did *what?*"

"I resigned as CEO of Larrabee Media. Effective immediately. I've stepped down. Pascal LaFleur will take my place as head of the company."

"But w-w-why would you do that?" I stammer. "After everything I went through to *save* your job."

He smiles. It's a delicate, subtle smile but it reaches all the way to his tired eyes, giving them a tiny spark of life. "That's *why* I did it."

I shoot him a baffled look.

My father explains. "Every decision I've made for this family has been a selfish one. Self-serving and rooted in my own interests. And so I could never completely fault you for your countless selfish acts growing up. Because I knew you learned them directly from me.

"But what you did for me and my company was so completely *un*selfish, I knew there was no way you could have learned that from me. That was something you taught yourself." He pauses and takes a deep breath. "And something *I* could certainly learn from."

"So what?" I ask, still trying to wrap my head around this new information. "You're just . . . done? With work? You're retiring?"

"Not exactly," he replies. "I'll be serving in more of an adviser role for the company. But it will cut back on my hours significantly and I'll have much more free time."

"To do *what*?" I ask.

He glances around the room, as though he's seeing it for the first time. "Well, *this* for starters."

Perplexed, I follow his gaze but find no answers.

"Talk to my children," he explains. "Spend time with them. Be *here*."

And now suddenly I'm seeing the room for the first time as well. The whole house, really. I try to imagine what it will be like with my father living under the same roof, walking through the same hallways, sleeping in a room two doors away. But to be honest, I just can't picture it. It's too foreign a concept. A language I can't understand, let alone speak.

But then again, it took several years of living in France for me to learn how to speak French. It took an entire childhood of growing up with Horatio for me to understand Spanish. New languages are not something you can pick up overnight. They take time. Patience. The willingness to change the way you think about what you already know.

And for the first time in eighteen years, that willingness is something my father and I appear to have in common.

Slowly, I lower myself back onto the couch. This time, however, I don't aim for the seat on the extreme other end—as far away from my father as I can get. But I don't dare take the seat directly next to him, either. Instead, I choose a space somewhere in the middle. Halfway between who I've been and who I hope to become.

Because this isn't some happy-ending movie where I fall into my father's arms as joyful music swells. And this isn't some sappy TV special intended to garner support for my father's latest business endeavor.

This is real life.

And in real life, nothing changes in the blink of an eye.

But you have to start somewhere.

"There's something I still don't understand," I begin thoughtfully, settling into my new seat.

My father turns to me, his eyes inviting, his expression open. "What's that?"

"If this whole fifty-two-jobs thing really was about helping me, why did you expose me to the press?"

My father's eyes darken and he lowers his head. "I didn't," he replies quietly.

"Yes, you did," I hear myself arguing. "Caroline told me you—"

"Caroline has been let go."

"What?" I choke out. "As in *fired*?"

"Yes. She pitched me her idea to drop an anonymous tip to the press a week ago and I told her no. I wouldn't approve it. But apparently she disagreed with my decision and was convinced I would change my mind once I saw how well it worked. So she went behind my back and did it anyway. And I fired her."

"But," I protest, struggling to piece all the details of the last twenty-four hours together in my mind, "I spoke with her today. She was on the way to your office for some kind of strategy meeting."

"That's what I had my assistant tell her," my father clarifies. "Otherwise she probably wouldn't have shown up."

I can just imagine Caroline's smug face as she sauntered into my father's office earlier today. So pleased with her diligent work effort. Thinking she was going to get a pat on the back, maybe even a raise, and instead she got the boot.

It makes me snicker quietly. And I can't hide the glorious smile that's taking over my face as I process this.

Caroline. Fired. Gone.

My father. On my side. Sticking up for me.

It's almost too difficult to believe.

"Speaking of those jobs," my father says, reaching into his jacket pocket and retrieving a slim white envelope, "I wanted to give this to you. I had Bruce prepare it this morning."

Curiously I take it, flip up the flap, and pull out the contents, staring numbly at the small, rectangular piece of paper in my hands.

A piece of paper worth twenty-five million dollars.

It's exactly how I always imagined my trust fund check to look. My name typed out in thick black ink. My father's infamous signature scribbled along the bottom right corner. And of course that long string of beautiful, crisp, round zeros.

I glance up at him in bewilderment. "But I still have thirty-two and a half jobs left."

My father chuckles endearingly. "Oh, I think you've earned this by now," he says.

I look back down at the check in my hands, feeling the smooth paper between my fingertips.

I've dreamed of this moment for as long as I can remember. For as long as I've understood the meaning of the term *trust fund*. And in every single one of those dreams, this simple sheet of paper was always the source of all my joy, all my happiness, all my sense of freedom. I pictured receiving an envelope just like this one, turning it around, lifting the flap, and drawing out the gorgeous document in slow motion. I pictured holding it in my hands, caressing it, running my fingertips across the surface, marveling at how beautiful it was, how significant it felt, how much promise it contained.

But never once, in any of those dreams, did I ever imagine myself shaking my head, replacing the check in the envelope, and handing it back to the person who gave it to me.

Never once did I see myself *returning* it.

Yet that's exactly what I find myself doing now.

"No," I tell my father. "I *haven't* earned it. At least not yet."

He glances inquisitively down at the returned gift. "Of course you have. You've exceeded all my expectations."

"While that may be," I say with a shrug, "I haven't yet exceeded mine."

I reach out and tap my finger against the back of the envelope. "Would you mind hanging on to that for me for another thirty-two and a half weeks?"

"Well, of course," he starts to say, regarding me with great fascination. "But I'm not sure I understand."

I smile affectionately at my dad. "You may have figured out what you want to do with your life, but I still don't have a clue. If I took that money now, I wouldn't have the first idea of what to do with it." I breathe out a long, happy sigh. "I think I'm going to need the full fifty-two weeks to figure it out."

I rise to my feet and stretch my arms above my head. "Now if you'll excuse me," I say politely, "I have to get ready for work."

CLICK <u>HERE</u> TO PLAY MESSAGE

Or read the free transcript from our automated speech-to-text service below.

[BEGIN TRANSCRIPT]

Hey, Lukey! It's me! Your favorite spoiled heiress.

Well, this is a very sad day because it's officially my last status report to you. I think we made the right decision though, don't you? I mean, it's not exactly *appropriate* for you to be my liaison when you're also my . . . well, *liaison*. If you catch my drift.

Plus, now that I'm the one choosing to finish the remaining jobs, I guess I don't need a babysitter anymore, huh? So at least you don't have to worry about my dad hiring some new, even hotter college intern to take your place. Right?

Just kidding! Calm down. Don't get all bent out of shape.

But seriously, I'm going to miss leaving you these little video messages. Maybe I'll have to keep sending them anyway. You know, just for fun. Although I realize, since I'll no longer be required to talk about work, I guess I'm going to have to come up with . . . *other* content to include.

Hmm. Very interesting notion. More on that soon.

And speaking of other content. Totally excited about dinner tonight! Don't worry. My friends are going to *love* you! Ever since they got back from Europe a few days ago, all they can talk about is meeting you. But just to warn you, be prepared for some serious drilling. After some disastrous past relationships (we won't name any names), they tend to be a tad overprotective of me. But I'm not worried. I know they're going to adore you. Just like I do.

And after dinner, we're totally having a rematch at Clue. I can't believe you beat me yesterday . . . again. Colonel Mustard in the observatory with the rope. Bah. Lucky guess! It's really not a fair match, though. I mean you having like *years* of experience at this and me being a total rookie. Whatever. Tonight, Miss Scarlet and I are going to take you down.

Oh! Speaking of hot chicks in red. I can't believe I

completely forgot to tell you! Did you hear the news? It was *all* over Twitter this morning. Remember Rêve, my father's fiancée? Well, she totally ran off with Pascal LaFleur! Can you believe that?

Well, actually, I can. They totally deserve each other.

My father seems pretty fine about it. Although I'm not surprised. It's not like he ever really liked her. Plus, I think he's too busy getting ready for his trip to visit Cooper in Africa next week to even notice he just got dumped. But keep an eye on him around the office for me, will ya? You know, just in case.

[Unidentified sound]

Ooh, that's my phone. Hold on, I've been expecting this call.

Hello? Yes, hi. Thanks for calling me back. I got your number from Jia Jones. You know, Devin Jones's daughter? Well, I heard you were looking for a coach's assistant and I think I have the perfect candidate for you. Can I e-mail you his contact information?

Awesome! I really appreciate it. I'll get it right out to you. Thanks so much! Bye!

Okay, I'm back. Sorry about that. That was the head coach of the LA Lakers. Jia's dad used to play for them. I'm working on getting my friend Rolando a new job. Fingers crossed it works out for him!

So anyway, I guess this is it. The end of the road. Or the beginning, depending on how you look at it. Did you ever think, when we first met, that it would end like this?

Come on, be honest. When you saw me in that flapper dress throwing up all over Bruce, you totally fell head over heels for me, didn't you? I know you looked at me and my crooked wig and clown-face makeup and thought, *I'm going to get that girl, if it's the last thing I do.*

Well, congrats, Luke Carver. You've succeeded. I'm yours . . . officially.

And that's the final report on my status.

[END TRANSCRIPT]

ACKNOWLEDGMENTS

These are the 52 reasons I'm able to do what I love every single day:

1. My parents, Michael and Laura Brody, who continue to offer support, love, advice, laughter, and sometimes even line edits.

2. Charlie, my partner (in business, travel, crime, adventure, and, most of all . . . life).

3. Terra, my talented and stylish li'l sis, who gets paid to dress people but who dresses me just for the challenge.

4. Janine O'Malley, my perfect editor, who builds me up and talks me down (from metaphorical ledges).

5. Bill Contardi, my brilliant agent, who is responsible for everything cool that happens to me and who finally got a BlackBerry.

6. Simon Boughton, who is one awesome bloke and whom I'm grateful to have on my team.

7. Elizabeth Kerins, who is the publicist of the year, and a blast to hang out with.

8. The Fink family (George, Vicki, Jennifer, and Addison), who are the coolest Texans I know.

9. Jazz, Bula, Caesar, and Baby, who can make me smile even during my lowest of lows.

10. Pete Moody, who let me take a crash course at his very efficiently run fast-food restaurant.

11. Sandra, who gave me that crash course.

12. Jane Startz and Kane Lee, who are giving Lexi a shot at the big screen.

13. Elizabeth Fithian.

14. Ksenia Winnicki.

15. Joy Dallanegra-Sanger.

16. Kathryn Hurley.

17. Jessica Zimmerman.

18. Jon Yaged.

19. Eileen Lawrence.

20. Dan Farley.

21. Jean Feiwel.

22. Jim Morris (a.k.a. "Tagline Jim"), for his brilliant mastery of words.

23. Nikki Hart, who can spin straw into gold. At least on paper.

24. Marianne Merola, who rocks the foreign rights.

25. Ella Gaumer, who is the busiest person I know and yet always manages to find time.

26. Christina Diaz, without whom my world would stop turning and my Web sites would be sad, empty pages, lost in cyberspace.

27. Brittany Carlson, who lets me be her "buddy."

28. Leslie, Billy, and Landon Euell, who are my family away from family.

29. Brad Gottfred, who is talented and amazing and all-around awesome (and not just because he bought me an iPad . . . although that helps).

30. José and Pepe, who corrected my Spanish.

31. Noémie Demol, who corrected my French.

32. Taylor Coliee, who is a superstar and a gorgeous human being and should never ever forget it.

33. Jason Fitzpatrick, who makes everything look good and who puts up with misbehaving ruffles.

34. All the talented actors of the *My Life Undecided* book trailer (Troy Osterberg, Kellan Rhude, Riley Chambers, Emily Skinner, Jennefer Ludwigsen, Hoyt Richards, Kendra Landeen, Reagan Drown, Cesar Manzanera, Rob Thelusma, Jessica Bennett, Cindy Vela, Madisen Hill, Gina Cecutti, and Megan Yelaney), who are rock stars of all ages.

35. All the amazing crew of the *My Life Undecided* book trailer (Jason Fitzpatrick, Holly Clark, Terra Brody, Monica Giselle, Adrian Ranieri, Jason Bell, Charlie Fink, and Clark Muller).

36. The voices and musical talent of Savannah Outen, Josh Golden, and Gerald Brunskill, who make me want to quit writing and learn to play the guitar.

37. Dean Bennett, who always welcomes me to his campus.

38. Thatcher Peterson and Matt Moran at Company 3 in Santa Monica.

39. Sunny Kruschwitz and Kathy Alfeld, who introduced me to my first love: the French language.

40. Bob Simpson, who inspired "Mr. Simpson."

41. Jade Corn and Cori Ashley, who are champions of children's books.

42. All the bookstores around the world who continue to put my books on the shelf.

43. All the book bloggers who have featured my books on their wonderful sites.

44. Viviane Cordeiro.
45. Hilit Meir.
46. Claire Kidman.
47. Melissa Fairley.
48. Tsui-lun Liu.
49. Mark Stankevich.
50. Jeff Levin.
51. Steve Glodney.
52. You. The reader of books. Thank you on behalf of all my characters (Jennifer, Maddy, Brooklyn, and now Lexi). It's you who make them real. It's you who give them life.

THE 52 REASON$ TO HATE MY FATHER HEIRESS STYLE GUIDE

BEAUTY AND FASHION TIPS ON HOW TO LOOK LIKE AN HEIRESS

(for much less than a million-dollar trust fund!)

From Heiress Lexington Larrabee's personal makeup artist and wardrobe stylist!

BEAUTY TIPS

. . . .

Provided by Anna Bratton Makeup Artistry, a Hollywood makeup artist who styled Heiress Lexington Larrabee in the 52 REASONS TO HATE MY FATHER book trailer!

1) MILLION-DOLLAR LASHES

To achieve longer, more luxurious lashes, apply a small amount of Vaseline on the top of your lashes and brush through with a clean mascara wand before bedtime. As this acts as a moisturizer, you should see healthy, more lush lashes within a few days to a week. Vaseline is also great to moisturize cracked hands, elbows, heels, and lips!

2) "VIP" SKIN

For softer skin and treating breakouts, generously apply egg yolk (closer to room temperature is best) to a freshly washed face and let it set for 5-7 minutes. When you start to see it dry and crack, you'll know it's ready to wash off with a warm washcloth.

3) JET-SETTING GLAM GIRL

For an instant "photo-ready" look on the go, use a tinted moisturizer with SPF, lip balm, mascara, and you're done! I like Laura Mercier's Tinted Moisturizer or Aveeno's Positively Radiant Moisturizer (as long as you do not overapply, as it can get splotchy). You can find great lip balm and gloss everywhere from Burt's Bees to Stila. For heiress-worthy lashes, try Maybelline's Define-A-Lash and Bare Escentuals Buxom mascara.

4) DRAMA QUEEN EYES

Dramatize your look with a bold eyeliner. I prefer MUD's cake liner for long-lasting wear. Experiment with different shapes from thin, natural lines to a striking "cat eye." Great trick: Hold a pencil from the corner of your nose to the outside of your eyebrow to use as a guideline for your cat eye.

5) RED CARPET CHEAT SHEET

Time to get creative with your makeup drawer! The right colors can be used for anything. Eye shadow can be used as bronzer and cheek highlight. Blush can be used to alter lip color. And light lip gloss can be used as a dewy eye shadow (as long as you avoid lip plumping and minty balms).

FASHION TIPS

Provided by Terra Brody, a Hollywood wardrobe designer who has worked in the costume department of hit shows like ABC's Private Practice and Charlie's Angels, the Disney Channel's Pair of Kings, and Showtime's Weeds, as well as on the music video for Miley Cyrus's "Who Owns My Heart." In addition, Terra styled Heiress Lexington Larrabee in the 52 REASONS TO HATE MY FATHER book trailer.

WANNA DRESS LIKE AN HEIRESS WITHOUT THE USE OF A PLATINUM CARD? FOLLOW WARDROBE STYLIST TERRA'S TIPS FOR GETTING GLAM!

G IS FOR GUTSY

Heiresses are all about making brave fashion statements! Don't be afraid to mix fabrics in the same look. Denim on velvet, silk on chiffon, or linen on leather are some of my favorites. Also, combining different patterns in one ensemble (try a striped skirt with a plaid top) will make your outfit "pop!"

L IS FOR LAYERS

Playing with layers can give your look the red carpet flare you've been craving! Try layering a pair of knee-high socks over tights or leggings, vests over body suits, dresses over button-down shirts, or a mini over your favorite pair of jeans to make them feel new again. I personally love layering two belts over the same outfit!

A IS FOR ACCESSORIZE

When it comes to accessories, all fashionistas know the golden rule: More isn't always better. If you're complementing a simple outfit (like a basic black dress), feel free to use bigger accent pieces that make a statement, like an oversized bangle in a popping shade, a bejeweled collar necklace, or bright-colored shoes. But if your outfit is already bursting with colors or patterns, minimize your accessories so you don't overpower the look. I like to complement "busy" outfits with one-toned jewelry (in gold, silver, or black) or a modest thin bracelet.

M IS FOR MIX AND MATCH

Variety is the spice of the heiress life! Have fun with clothes and accessories from all different price points and time periods. I always say no outfit is complete without something vintage, something thrift store, something label, and something from H&M. Put it all together for a look that is sure to have the paparazzi bulbs flashing!

GOFISH

JESSICA BRODY

© Brian Braff

What did you want to be when you grew up?
Believe it or not, I wanted to be an author. Actually, I wanted to be an author who owned her own publishing company. I guess one out of two's not bad.

When did you realize you wanted to be a writer?
In the second grade. I had a book report assignment that was supposed to be one paragraph long and I turned in four pages. I remember how impressed the teacher was (she went around the whole school telling all the other teachers about it) and I remember thinking, "What's she going on about? That was easy!" That was my first clue that writing came naturally to me. And I've wanted to be a writer ever since.

What's your first childhood memory?
You know, people always tell me about their first childhood memories and it baffles me because I think, "How do you *know* that's your first memory?" I have a lot of memories from when I was little but I have no idea which one came first. They're all kind of jumbled in my mind. But *one* of those earlier memories was when I was three and my best friend chose someone *else*

to sit next to her during her birthday party at school. I was *reeee-ally* upset. Not to mention, totally betrayed! But I'm pretty much over it now. We're still friends today. And every once in a while I give her a hard time about it.

What's your most embarrassing childhood memory?
Okay, *this* one I can answer. I was three. My mom had just picked me up from preschool and we were walking down the long driveway to the street. I was skipping, not really paying much attention, and I grabbed my mom's hand and said, "Mommy! Can we go for ice cream?" Then I looked up and realized that it was *not* my mom whose hand I was holding. It was some *other* mom. I was mortified. I can *still* feel the humiliation. The woman thought it was adorable. I wanted to climb under a rock.

As a young person, who did you look up to most?
I think I'll have to say my grandfather. I used to spend every other weekend at his house. I totally idolized him. Funny story. When I was young, I was extremely shy. Especially around new people. My grandfather would introduce me to his friends and I would hide behind his legs and refuse to say a thing. He would ask me, "Cat got your tongue?" Then one day, I told him I thought he was the "smartest man in the world." And I did! Although I often said that about my dad as well. So my grandfather jokingly asked me, "Who do you think is smarter, me or your dad?" And I got really quiet and murmured, "Cat got my tongue."

What was your worst subject in school?
PE. Oh, gosh, how I hated PE. I've never been very athletic. I used to hide behind the handball courts during PE and pray that the teacher wouldn't find me (she always did). Then in sixth grade we had to run "the mile." It was my least favorite day EVER! I think I have the slowest mile in my elementary school's history. It was

like 22 minutes. I pretty much walked (or more like lolly-gagged) the entire way! I've always thought I should get a plaque or something, honoring my achievement, but I've yet to see it.

What was your best subject in school?

Math. I *looooved* math. It appealed to me because there was always a right answer to every problem. And if I tried hard enough, and studied long enough, I would find it. My rewards would directly pay off. English, on the other hand, was too abstract and subjective. You could read and read and analyze and analyze and the answer was still always "up for discussion." I hated the uncertainty of that. Which is probably why I try to outline my novels with as much detail as possible before starting to write. To eliminate uncertainty. But with writing, uncertainty is unavoidable. Characters often have minds of their own. So I'm learning to be more flexible. And if I ever need a dose of certainty, I can always get out my old math textbooks and do a few problem sets.

What was your first job?

My parents owned a restaurant when I was a teenager so I always worked there—waiting tables, bussing tables, washing dishes, cooking—I pretty much did everything! But I would have to say that *technically* my first job was selling stationary when I was nine years old. I made over a hundred dollars in profit! Of course, my biggest customer was my grandfather. I think he bought one of everything.

How did you celebrate publishing your first book?

Pretty much with my mouth hanging open and my eyes all gaga. I was in a state of total disbelief. But once I came around to actually believing that I had sold my first novel (as opposed to thinking it was all a sick joke), I'm fairly certain there was a lot of screaming, dancing around the living room . . . and then more screaming.

Where do you write your books?

I can tell you where I *don't* write my books and that's in my office. It's so strange. I have this whole big, nice office all to myself and I *cannot* write in there. I think because there's so much else to do. I get too distracted. I've learned that I have to leave the house and go somewhere to get any writing done. So I usually go to a coffee shop or café. But it's really weird, I have to trick myself into writing by bringing my laptop and *not* my power cord. So I have 3-4 hours of battery life to get my daily word quota complete. It keeps me focused and prevents me from fooling around on the Internet and other such time-wasters. I also have to listen to white noise soundtracks on my headphones. It drowns out all the commotion of the coffee shop. I know, I know. I'm totally weird. But hey! I'm a writer! It's expected.

Where do you find inspiration for your writing?

Everywhere! I'm an observer. I watch people. But not in the creepy stalker way.

But seriously, if you look closely, there are characters and stories everywhere. The trick is to take the real-life stories you hear and experience and exaggerate them times ten. That's what makes for interesting fiction.

What inspired you to write *52 Reasons to Hate My Father*?

My inspiration always comes from the most random of places! With this book, I was sitting in my car, watching a meter maid write a parking ticket and I thought, "Wouldn't it be cool to be a meter maid? But only for a week." Then I started to brainstorm all the other jobs I'd like to do for only one week. I started to get really excited about the prospect of spending an entire year trying out different jobs before I realized that I didn't actually have time to do any of these jobs because I had books to write! So I thought, "No problem, I'll just create a book character who does it instead and live vicariously through her." So I sat down to think of what kind of character would have the most to learn from this experience (and who would be the funniest character to do it) and the answer was immediate: a spoiled heiress who has *never* had to work a day in her life! And Lexington Larrabee was born.

If you had twenty-five million dollars, what is the first thing you would do with it?

Although I'd love to sound like one of those really upstanding people who says, "Give some to charity!" first off, I don't think that would be accurate. The first thing I would do was book a cruise around the world (which I've always wanted to do!), *then* I would give a big portion to charity. Probably a charity that was dedicated to putting an end to puppy mills. This is an issue very near and dear to my heart.

Have you ever had one of Lexi's fifty-two jobs? Which one? How did it go?

I've actually had quite a few of her jobs! I've cleaned horse corrals, washed dishes at a restaurant, worked as a catering server, and in researching this book, I went "undercover" at a fast-food restaurant to train as a new employee for a day. That was really fun! My favorite part was working the drive-thru. That futuristic, *Star Trek* headset was too cool! I've never actually worked for a maid service, but sometimes, I feel like cleaning my own house is just as bad.

If you had to pick one of Lexi's jobs to do for the rest of your life, which one would you pick?

Ooh! Fun question! I'm going to say "working at a flower shop." I really do feel like that would be a rewarding job. Being able to deliver people good news every day. It's the reason I put it exactly where it is in the story.

How are you similar to Lexi?

Well, we're both about to receive 25 million dollar–trust fund checks. HA! Don't I wish!? Lexi and I are very different. Which is why she was so much fun for me to write. It was like being able to live in an heiress' shoes for half a year! However, I think one way we are similar is that we both hate feeling abandoned by people. But we both put on brave faces to hide it. Oh, and we both love dogs!

Who was your favorite character besides Lexi to write about?

I'm going to have to say Horatio, the butler. I know he's not the most fun character in the book, but he was interesting to me as the author. He really does love Lexi, but he's also always the consummate professional. He's constantly torn between fulfilling his duty to the family as an employee, and his duty to Lexi as kind of a father figure, and that made for a fun dynamic in his personality. It was entertaining for me to be able to hide his affection for her in little subtle actions that some people may miss.

When you finish a book, who reads it first?

Two people actually: my dad and my husband. They're my first editors. Then after I've gotten their stamps of approval, it goes to my agent and my editor. My dad has been reading my manuscripts since I was seven years old. And trust me, there have been *many*. More non-published than published. That's serious dedication.

Are you a morning person or a night owl?
Three years ago, I would have laughed and said night owl, of course. But it's so strange, ever since I turned thirty, I've switched! I'm a complete morning person now. I used to think morning people were crazy! I totally made fun of anyone who went to bed before eleven at night. Now I'm one of those people!

Go ahead . . . make fun. I deserve it.

What's your idea of the best meal ever?
Sushi and afternoon tea sandwiches. My two favorite things in the world.

Hmmm . . . I'm kind of hungry all of a sudden. Is anyone else hungry?

Which do you like better: cats or dogs?
Definitely dogs. Although I've known some pretty awesome cats in my life. Mickey and Samya, I'm talking about you!

What do you value most in your friends?
Their ability to think outside the box and do their own thing. All too often, we do things and make decisions without knowing why. Without questioning the "norm." I love how my friends have all blazed their own trails.

Where do you go for peace and quiet?
What's that?

Okay, okay. I usually go to get a massage. I do my best brainstorming on the massage table, actually. I think because it's the one place where my mind can be still long enough to come up with solutions.

What makes you laugh out loud?

My husband's imitations. He takes boring, inanimate objects (like bookends and coffee mugs) and gives them little voices and personalities. Some of them even have accents. It's hilarious.

Who is your favorite fictional character?

Edward Cullen. But he doesn't count because he's not fictional, right?

RIGHT!?

What are you most afraid of?

The dark. It's freaky scary! And I tend to trip a lot. So me and the dark? Not a good mix.

If you were stranded on a desert island, who would you want for company?

See above (under favorite fictional character).

If you could travel in time, where would you go?

Yes! Time travel question. I *love* these. I would go back to eighteenth-century France to hang with Marie Antoinette. That girl seriously knew how to party! But I would probably try to split before the whole beheading thing started.

What's the best advice you have ever received about writing?

"You can't fix a blank page."—Nora Roberts. That is brilliant, brilliant advice. Of course, she didn't give it to me personally; I read it somewhere. But that doesn't lessen its brilliance. When you're a writer you have to write every day. No matter if it's good or not. Just keep writing. You can always fix (or delete) stuff later. I like to say, "Sometimes you have to write through the crap to get to the good stuff." I know that's not as eloquent as Nora Roberts, but it's true.

What do you want readers to remember about your books?

If a reader closes one of my books and says, "Now, *that* was funny," then I will consider my mission accomplished. I only seek to entertain. Nothing more. If one of my stories makes you think or inspires you to do something to better the world or yourself, that's just icing on the cake. Laughter is my first and foremost goal in writing.

What would you do if you ever stopped writing?

I'm not sure I *could* ever stop. Even if I was no longer publishing novels, I'd have to keep writing. In some form or another. It's what I do. I once heard someone say, "Dancers dance because they have to." I think it's the same for writers.

What do you like best about yourself?

I question everything. My parents instilled that in me. Even when I was a kid, I never accepted anything anyone told me without scrutinizing it myself and deciding if I agreed. It used to drive my teachers nuts. Sometimes it can be a curse, but most of the time, I'm glad I have that quality. It keeps me alert. And I think it makes me a better writer.

What is your worst habit?

I have a terrible oral fixation. I'm always chewing on something. Pens, gum, my fingernails. It's a nervous habit. Like the energy has to come out somewhere and it comes out through my teeth. My dentist is making a fortune off of me.

What do you consider to be your greatest accomplishment?

Every novel I finish is my greatest accomplishment. Because at some point during *every* single novel I write, there's a period of time when I don't believe it will happen. When I swear this is the worst thing I've ever written, I'll never finish it, and my career will be over. And since I'm convinced that each "meltdown" is worse than the last, when I finally get to the end, I consider that an even bigger accomplishment than the last one I finished.

Where in the world do you feel most at home?
Probably at my parents' house. Surrounded by their four dogs. No matter how bad my day is, how much trouble my current novel is giving me, those dogs always put a smile on my face. They should be therapists. Seriously.

What do you wish you could do better?
I wish I had a bigger vocabulary. I've always thought that was one of my weaknesses. (Particularly in high school when I was taking the SATs.) And even more so now that I'm a writer. I wish I was one of those people who walked around spouting off impressive-sounding words, causing everyone around me to say, "Ooh . . . what does *that* mean?" But alas, I am not one of those people. When I talk, everyone seems to understand everything I say. Bummer.

What would your readers be most surprised to learn about you?
Everyone is always surprised to learn that I was *not* a reader when I was a kid. Actually, I hated to read. Because it always felt like work to me. It wasn't until college that I realized there were actually books you could read for "fun." Books that made you laugh. And from that moment on, I became determined to write those kinds of books. The ones that make you laugh. That don't feel like work. I hope I've succeeded.

When a sixteen-year-old girl is discovered floating amongst the wreckage of Freedom Airlines Flight 909—*alive*—the miraculous story spans headlines across the globe. And although physically unharmed, the girl has no memories of boarding the plane, no memories of her life before the crash, no memories . . . *period.*

A mind wiped clean. A love unchanged.

UNREMEMBERED

JESSICA BRODY

Find out the truth of her past, in

UNREMEMBERED.

0
AWOKEN

The water is cold and ruthless, lapping against my cheek. Slapping me awake. Filling my mouth with the taste of salty solitude.

I cough violently and open my eyes, taking in the world around me. Seeing it for the first time. It's not a world I recognize. I gaze upon miles and miles of dark blue ocean. Peppered with large floating objects. Metal. Like the one I'm lying on.

And then there are the bodies.

I count twenty in my vicinity. Two within reach. Although I don't dare try.

Their lifeless faces are frozen in terror. Their eyes are empty. Staring into nothing.

I press a palm to my throbbing temple. My head feels like it's made out of stone. Everything is drab and heavy and seen through a filthy lens. I close my eyes tight.

The voices come an hour later. After night has fallen. I hear them cutting through the darkness. It takes them forever to reach me. A light breaks through the dense fog and blinds me.

No one speaks as they pull me from the water. No one has to. It's clear from the looks on their faces they did not expect to find me.

They did not expect to find anyone.

Alive, that is.

I'm wrapped in a thick blue blanket and laid on a hard wooden surface. That's when the questions start. Questions that make my brain hurt.

"What is your name?"

I wish I knew.

"Do you know where you are?"

I glance upward and find nothing but a sea of unhelpful stars.

"Do you remember boarding the plane?"

My brain twists in agony, causing my forehead to throb again.

Plane. Plane. What is a plane?

And then comes the question that awakens something deep within me. That ignites a tiny, faraway spark somewhere in the back corners of my mind.

"Do you know what *year* it is?"

I blink, feeling a small glimmer of hope surge from the pit of my stomach.

"1609," I whisper with unfounded conviction. And then I pass out.

1

ANEW

Today is the only day I remember. Waking up in that ocean is all I have. The rest is empty space. Although I don't know how far back that space goes—how many years it spans. That's the thing about voids: they can be as short as the blink of an eye, or they can be infinite. Consuming your entire existence in a flash of meaningless white. Leaving you with nothing.

No memories.

No names.

No faces.

Every second that ticks by is new. Every feeling that pulses through me is foreign. Every thought in my brain is like nothing I've ever thought before. And all I can hope for is one moment that mirrors an absent one. One fleeting glimpse of familiarity.

Something that makes me . . . *me*.

Otherwise, I could be anyone.

Forgetting who you are is so much more complicated than simply forgetting your name. It's also forgetting your dreams.

Your aspirations. What makes you happy. What you pray you'll never have to live without. It's meeting yourself for the first time, and not being sure of your first impression.

After the rescue boat docked, I was brought here. To this room. Men and women in white coats flutter in and out. They stick sharp things in my arm. They study charts and scratch their heads. They poke and prod and watch me for a reaction. They want something to be wrong with me. But I assure them that I'm fine. That I feel no pain.

The fog around me has finally lifted. Objects are crisp and detailed. My head no longer feels as though it weighs a hundred pounds. In fact, I feel strong. Capable. Anxious to get out of this bed. Out of this room with its unfamiliar chemical smells. But they won't let me. They insist I need more time.

From the confusion I see etched into their faces, I'm pretty sure it's *they* who need the time.

They won't allow me to eat any real food. Instead they deliver nutrients through a tube in my arm. It's inserted directly into my vein. Inches above a thick white plastic bracelet with the words *Jane Doe* printed on it in crisp black letters.

I ask them why I need to be here when I'm clearly not injured. I have no visible wounds. No broken bones. I wave my arms and turn my wrists and ankles in wide circles to prove my claim. But they don't respond. And this infuriates me.

After a few hours, they determine that I'm sixteen years old. I'm not sure how I'm supposed to react to this information. I don't *feel* sixteen. But then again, how do I know what sixteen feels like? How do I know what *any* age feels like?

And how can I be sure that they're right? For all I know, they could have just made up that number. But they assure me that they have qualified tests. Specialists. Experts. And they all say the same thing.

That I'm sixteen.

The tests can't tell me my name, though. They can't tell me where I'm from. Where I live. Who my family is. Or even my favorite color.

And no matter how many "experts" they shuttle in and out of this room, no one can seem to explain why I'm the only survivor of the kind of plane crash no one survives.

They talk about something called a passenger manifest. I've deduced that it's a kind of master list. A register of everyone who boarded the plane.

I've also deduced that I'm not on it.

And that doesn't seem to be going over very well with anyone.

A man in a gray suit, who identifies himself as Mr. Rayunas from Social Services, says he's trying to locate my next of kin. He carries around a strange-looking metal device that he calls a cell phone. He holds it up to his ear and talks. He also likes to stare at it and stab at tiny buttons on its surface. I don't know what my "next of kin" is, but by the look on his face, he's having trouble locating it.

He whispers things to the others. Things I'm assuming he doesn't want me to hear. But I hear them anyway. Foreign, unfamiliar words like "foster care" and "the press" and "minor." Every so often they all pause and glance over at me. They shake their heads. Then they continue whispering.

There's a woman named Kiyana who comes in every hour. She has dark skin and speaks with an accent that makes it sound like she's singing. She wears pink. She smiles and fluffs my pillow. Presses two fingers against my wrist. Writes stuff down on a clipboard. I've come to look forward to her visits. She's kinder than the others. She takes the time to talk to me. Ask me questions. Real ones. Even though she knows I don't have any of the answers.

"You're jus' so beautiful," she says to me, tapping her finger tenderly against my cheek. "Like one of those pictures they airbrush for the fashion magazines, you know?"

I don't know. But I offer her a weak smile regardless. For some reason, it feels like an appropriate response.

"Not a blemish," she goes on. "Not one flaw. When you get your memory back, you're gonna have to tell me your secret, love." Then she winks at me.

I like that she says *when* and not *if*.

Even though I don't remember learning those words, I understand the difference.

"And those eyes," she croons, moving in closer. "I've never seen sucha color. Lavender, almos'." She pauses, thinking, and leans closer still. "No. *Violet*." She smiles like she's stumbled upon a long-lost secret. "I bet that's your name. Violet. Ring any bells?"

I shake my head. Of course it doesn't.

"Well," she says, straightening the sheets around my bed, "I'm gonna call you that anyway. Jus' until you remember the real one. Much nicer soundin' than Jane Doe."

She takes a step back, tilts her head to the side. "Sucha pretty girl. Do you even remember whatcha look like, love?"

I shake my head again.

She smiles softly. Her eyes crinkle at the corners. "Hang on then. I'll show you."

She leaves the room. Returns a moment later with an oval-shaped mirror. Light bounces off it as she walks to my bedside. She holds it up.

A face appears in the light pink frame.

One with long and sleek honey-brown hair. Smooth golden skin. A small, straight nose. Heart-shaped mouth. High cheekbones. Large, almond-shaped purple eyes.

They blink.

"Yes, that's you," she says. And then, "You musta been a model. Such perfection."

But I don't see what she sees. I only see a stranger. A person I don't recognize. A face I don't know. And behind those eyes are sixteen years of experiences I fear I'll never be able to remember. A life held prisoner behind a locked door. And the only key has been lost at sea.

I watch purple tears form in the reflecting glass.

you'll find laughter, love, and wit in these great reads!

Get Well Soon
Julie Halpern
ISBN: 978-0-312-58148-0

**The Sweetheart of
Prosper County**
Jill S. Alexander
ISBN: 978-0-312-54857-5

The Espressologist
Kristina Springer
ISBN: 978-0-312-65923-3

Paradise
Jill S. Alexander
ISBN: 978-1-250-00484-0

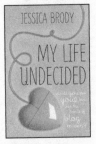

My Life Undecided
Jessica Brody
ISBN: 978-1-250-00483-3

**Into the Wild Nerd
Yonder**
Julie Halpern
ISBN: 978-0-312-65307-1

Flirt Club
Cathleen Daly
ISBN: 978-0-312-65026-1

The Poison Apples
Lily Archer
ISBN: 978-0-312-53596-4

The Karma Club
Jessica Brody
ISBN: 978-0-312-67473-1

SQUARE
FISH

MACKIDS.COM